ULRICH

Barbarians of Rome: Book One

James Walker

DEDICATION

Dedicated to Jenny, and my family, and everybody who believed in me. And to Joan Kelley, my editor, who helped to make my dream possible. Thank you.

CHAPTER ONE

A red, gibbous moon hung low over the mist-shrouded castle-town of Hamburg. In the deep shadows of a dark, thatch-roofed stone barn, Ulrich hid. He hid from the unearthly light of the waning moon, he hid from the shouts and panic in the streets, and he hid from the lurid glow of the flames that cast themselves up into the smoky air from the burning stables. A patch of dry thatch ignited and exploded upward in a red flare, casting back the shadows, and the young boy slid deeper into the darkness.

Ulrich was twelve years old. His father's men were fighting against the lackeys of his jealous uncle. He knew they still fought because he could hear the distant thump of steel on wood. It was the sound of shield walls meeting, and he could imagine the sweating, cursing men pushing against each other, screaming at the enemy that was only inches away, flailing with sword and axe at the wooden boards and driving great splinters high into the air—air that stank of blood and sweat and fear and death.

A horse screamed, and Ulrich resisted the urge to run to the burning stables. He wanted to dash barefoot across the damp yard and pull his horse Whisper from the inferno. She was a gentle, bay mare with large brown eyes and a long silky black mane. He resisted the temptation because he could see figures moving in the shadows of the dancing flames. They were his uncle's men, and they laughed as they watched the flames and threw logs and debris into the fire. A horse screamed again, and Ulrich hoped it was not Whisper trapped in her stall. He hoped she died quickly. He hoped a heavy beam from the roof of the stables fell and crushed her, that she was not burning and panicking from the pain as the flames engulfed her.

The far-away sounds of battle from the great hall continued, and Ulrich moved off into the darkness. There was nothing else to do here. The dark shapes of his uncle's men still moved around the flaming stables, and he knew that Cenric was already dead. The stable boy lived in the loft above, and when his uncle's men had started the blaze, Ulrich had seen a small form rush out only to be forced back into the flames by the brutal swords that waited in the night.

Cenric had been Ulrich's closest friend. Together, they would sneak out of the fortress to play in the green lands beyond. They would fish with string and maggots at the small pond that lay in a grove of cedar trees just outside the wooden town walls. Ulrich would often let Cenric take Whisper's reins, and the two of them would canter, two to the saddle, in long loops that would take them almost to the borders of his father's kingdom. Ulrich felt a surge of hatred at his traitorous uncle as he thought of the wine-breathed men forcing Cenric back into the burning stables.

Ulrich moved through the outskirts of the town in the shadow of the tall wooden palisade that stretched high into the darkness. His feet moved softly over the muddy, rounded, paving stones of the silent streets. The houses lay dark and quiet, but Ulrich doubted that any slept this night. The houses contained the old and the women and the children who huddled and waited to discover their fate. They knew well that their men were engaged in a death struggle. Neighbor fought neighbor, and friend killed friend in blood and sweat and struggle that night. Wives and daughters hugged each other and prayed to their god or gods that their men would win. They knew too what awaited the families of the defeated as the grasping, raping victors flooded the town, drunk on wine and blood and death.

A body lay face down in the empty street. Ulrich slid from house to house, growing more confident as he approached the still form. In his right hand, Ulrich grasped a knife, the knife his father had given him for when they went on hunts of boar and pheasant. It was a small knife, no more than six inches of double-bladed steel with a leather-wrapped handle, but it was sturdy and well made, and it kept a keen edge. It was as useful for filleting fish as it was for skinning deer.

Ulrich was not more than five paces from the still form when it

6

suddenly stirred. He gripped the knife tighter and jumped back into the shadows. The man on the ground groaned and struggled slowly to his knees. As the man bent forward, Ulrich could see drops of blood, jet black in the moonlight, fall from the man's face onto the worn stone cobbles of the street. It was then that Ulrich saw that the man wore a red headband. Ulrich had seen this before on the figures running and reeling around the stables and on the heads of the first men that clashed with his father's bodyguards in the streets. The headband marked his uncle's men. It identified them so they would not accidentally kill each other in tonight's bloody coup.

The headband-wearing man was having trouble keeping upright, though whether this was from injury or from drink Ulrich could not tell. The man walked a few unsteady paces away and then stopped to lean heavily on his sword. It was a long, heavy blade, and the man held no shield. Casting off his hesitation, Ulrich slid out from the darkness and stalked toward the staggering figure. He was a big man; Ulrich hardly came to his chest, but the man did not hear the boy approach until Ulrich was almost upon him. At the last minute the man turned, but it was too late. Ulrich stabbed the small knife up, plunging it deep into the soft skin under the man's chin. The man grabbed at the knife, but Ulrich put both hands on the handle and pushed, forcing the cold blade deep into the man's neck. Ulrich rammed his shoulder into the man's chest, knocking him backward onto the street where he wheezed and died, the knife protruding from his throat.

Ulrich had no time to savor his small victory. He reached down and retrieved his knife, cleaning the blood from the blade on the dead man's clothes. He sheathed the knife and took the man's sword and helmet. The sword was much too big for his young frame; it would have been a cumbersome weapon even for a large man, but Ulrich did not care. His blood pounded hard in his veins. He raced openly down the street toward his father's hall, sword in one hand, visored helmet in the other.

The fighting around the king's hall was drawing to a close. Bodies lay piled in front of the meager shield wall that blocked the open, double doors. The red-banded men had abandoned their own shield wall and stood jeering in the street, hurling rocks and insults at the few heavily-outnumbered defenders that remained. They did not notice Ulrich step cautiously into their midst in the darkness. All eyes were on the hall as a man stepped out into the night.

The man had close-cropped dark hair over piercing blue eyes. His face was proud, and he stood before his enemies clad in a cuirass of ancient scale armor. Its rows of rounded bronze medallions gleamed across his broad chest. It was armor that heralded of older days, of heroes of myth and legend, and the epics of faraway lands. Splashes of red blood, fresh and bright, dulled some of the beauty of the shining bronze. Blood ran in rivulets down the man's heavy double-bladed axe. His square shield was scarred and tattered, but still the white sigil of the dancing horse—the seal of Ulrich's family—could be seen on its dark surface. He stood tall and proud, without weakness or fear, and he wore no helmet. Ulrich gazed at his father with wonder, and his heart soared for he believed that all was not yet lost.

"Come, brother," King Ædwin called into the dark mass of men before him. "Come and let us end this."

A dark man stepped from the crowd and crossed into the empty space in front of the king. The family resemblance was apparent, but while Ædwin's eyes were clear and proud, uncle Edwald's eyes were shifty and mean. Edwald's hair was long and matted, and he carried a battered longsword that he hefted in one hand. He wore a coat of dull steel mail, and he carried an oval shield with the same symbol of the dancing horse.

"This day has been too long coming," said Edwald. "Today I take what is rightfully mine." He sneered at the bronze king and spat derisively; he slapped down the slitted visor on his dark conical helmet and advanced. The king went forward to meet him.

The usurpers in the courtyard cheered as the champions closed in the torchlight, but the king's men slumped exhausted on their weapons. The defenders were watching the impending fight with fatalistic resignation.

The two men approached each other in a shuffle, shields held low, each peering over the painted wood. Edwald attacked with a horizontal swing of his sword that Ædwin blocked easily, not bothering to reply. With an oath, the dark man charged, and shining Ædwin let him come. He deflected Edwald's sword point with the steel boss of his shield and then stepped forward. The king spun as he moved and hit Edwald's helmet with the blade of his axe. The axe head glanced away, and Ulrich's uncle staggered. Ædwin followed up the blow with a shield bash, knocking Edwald flat on his back. Ædwin stepped forward to bring the axe down in the killing blow, but Edwald jabbed his sword forward, digging into the flesh of Ædwin's leg, releasing a trickle of blood and forcing him away so that Edwald could regain his feet.

Edwald seemed stunned from this first encounter, and he stepped back. With a furtive glance toward his own men, he conspicuously raised his visor with his sword hand. Ædwin, thinking his brother might call a truce, hesitated. He was wrong. Edwald raising the visor was a signal. An arrow flew from out of the crowd and struck the king in the leg. He fell to one knee, and Edwald ran forward and kicked him onto his back. Edwald raised his sword and stabbed down once. Blood ran onto the street as Edwald lifted the reddened sword high in triumph. Ulrich's mother, a blonde woman in a long white dress, ran from the citadel and threw herself over her hero. Edwald, his mouth open in a roar, flaunted his victory. With another slashing stroke the sword came down again, and the queen was dead. Edwald's men surged toward the keep doors, and the king's defenders threw down their arms and surrendered.

Ulrich, shaking with rage, gripped his stolen sword tight and began to push his way through the press of men toward where his uncle stood. A hand shot out of the crowd and grabbed his arm. Ulrich pulled against it, but the hand was immensely strong, and it pulled him back. He turned to see the town blacksmith, Wiglaf, standing over him with concern on his face. The blacksmith wore no armor and carried no weapons, but Ulrich would not have expected him to. Wiglaf had put away the sword years ago. His right leg had been crippled fighting against the savage invaders from the north. Ulrich pulled against Wiglaf's iron grip with a snarl.

"He will kill you, young lord," Wiglaf warned over the roar of the surging crowd.

"Let me go," Ulrich ordered.

Wiglaf shook his head. "No, boy. You won't find vengeance here, only death."

Ulrich cursed at him and twisted away. Wiglaf sighed. Ignoring the pain from his stiff leg, he stepped quickly after the boy, snatched the sword from his grasp, and brought its heavy steel hilt down on Ulrich's helmeted head.

"I am sorry, son," Wiglaf murmured as he gathered up the

stunned child. He spirited him away through the surging crowd.

The town of Hamburg burned, seethed, and wept as Wiglaf rode a loaded wagon. It was heavy with a blacksmith and his family plus one unconscious young boy as it trundled off into the darkness.

The year was 346 A.D., and the German people of the green forests beyond the Roman border lived as they had for centuries. Each fiercely independent tribe claimed ancestral lands with a fierce savagery. They were clans of warriors, ready to howl into battle for gold, for women, to defend their lands, or to conquer. They fought, too, for the warrior's greatest prize: reputation, and they fought with pride because fighting was in their blood. West of the Rhine, the Roman Empire brought civilization and Christianity, but the rule of law ended at that river boundary. The Romans had ruled Europe for four centuries, but that conquest had its limits. The Rhine was a fortress, separating civilized Gaul from wild frontier lands where barbarians squabbled.

CHAPTER TWO

Wiglaf retreated with his family far across the land. They moved to a farm near a small town called Brunswick, toward the southern edge of the Saxon kingdoms. There, he rebuilt his shop, and rather than fashion the weapons of a king's guard, Wiglaf crafted horseshoes and mended plows and harnesses. The open country and dense woodland were plentiful with deer and boar, fish and fowl. It was here in the Saxon countryside of Germania that Ulrich grew. Wiglaf knew that the scrawny youth would quickly grow into a barrel-chested bull of a man, and he was proved right. Ulrich grew tall and strong and healthy.

Before taking the role of king's blacksmith, Wiglaf had been a warrior, and so he taught Ulrich the ways of war. Daily training with a sword and swinging a hammer at the blacksmith's forge gave Ulrich powerful shoulders and massive strength.

In the early seasons of that new life, Wiglaf worried that Ulrich would allow his anger to turn him dark and bitter. Ulrich was naturally reticent, but his initial anger gave way to a natural resilience, and the youth's melancholy faded into the background of a quiet stoicism.

Ulrich delighted in his life and he delighted in the training. He loved the smell of the leather armor and the power of the sword as he grasped its leather-wrapped hilt. Wiglaf was a demanding teacher, but Ulrich learned quickly. The cool hours of the morning were inevitably spent at practice. Afterward they would remove the cumbersome armor and return together to the forge or go afield to hunt or tend their few acres of cabbage and wheat.

Wiglaf's wife Johanne was a Frisian. She had been a slave of a rival kingdom before one of King Ædwin's raids had captured and freed her. Ædwin had detested slavery and promised that no man or woman of his kingdom would suffer from its practice. This proved to be a shrewd maneuver, as it had ensured that Ædwin's personal guard was never at a loss for volunteers among freed slaves. Other kingdoms had been able to boast larger armies, but none could rival the loyalty of King Ædwin's personal guard of devoted warriors. But times had changed. Now that Ulrich's father was dead, slave ships traded openly on the rivers and ports. Wiglaf and Johanne stayed away on those occasions when the defeated of Edwald's battles were sold like cattle in the town square.

Johanne was a small, gentle woman who had admired King Ædwin dearly. When she had been brought before him in his throne room before all the court more than ten years ago, she had expected to be scorned and to be assigned a new master from the King's retinue. This had happened to her many times before, traded from kingdom to kingdom since she was a child. She had been a slave for so long she did not remember her parents, who she was told, had been killed defending her from the Saxon raiders. She had been surprised, then, when Ædwin smiled down at all of the prisoners brought before him. His twinkling blue eyes crinkled at the corners, and Johanne had wept when the King granted her freedom. She had been given a small pension, a pair of cloth sandals, and had been set loose to find a new life in this realm, free from rapine and servitude.

On the surface it was not that different being a free woman or being a slave. She still performed the same daily tasks: cooking and cleaning and tailoring for a household while indebted to a man as her protector, but she was happy with her new life. What mattered was that she had been free to choose her man, and she loved Wiglaf dearly. At first, she feared Ulrich, the dark brooding youth whom Wiglaf had brought into their household, but soon she saw the strong resemblance that he bore to his kind father. It was not long after that Johanne and Wiglaf had two healthy children of their own, and Johanne noticed how fondly Ulrich took to them, playing gently with them as they learned to walk, and picking them up carefully when they would fall.

Johanne was as talkative as Ulrich was reticent and filled the silence with stories of Hamburg and of his father and mother. Ulrich remembered his father as a stern but fair man, quick to rebuke and sparing in his compliments, but always just and even tempered. He would make Ulrich sit with him in his throne room for tedious unending council sessions while Ulrich would squirm to be down in the town, running through the streets with Cenric or exploring the nooks and crannies of the high town walls. At the end of each session, Ædwin would remind Ulrich that he would take his place one day, and that the running of a kingdom was an important lesson for a young prince to learn. Ulrich's mother was a powerful woman, who was as close an advisor to her husband as any of his court. She was a forbidding woman to the King's opponents, savvy in political maneuvers with a skill for shaming even the most reluctant warlord to join the King on the field of battle. She was, however, always gentle to her only son, and Ulrich remembered her chastising his father for trying to force Ulrich to grow up too quickly.

But that life was gone now, and Ulrich soon thought of Wiglaf and Johanne as his father and mother. As the seasons turned to years, memories of his childhood faded, and he was happy. Once Ulrich was nearly fully grown, Wiglaf guided him in making his own weapons and armor. Wiglaf supervised their construction closely. Together, they began by crafting a shirt of chainmail. Creating mail was an inherently simple, but incredibly tedious process. Hundreds of small iron rings were carefully woven together one by one, each tiny link forged and trimmed of steel, then bent together to create a fluid sheet of metal chain. Wiglaf knew how tall the boy might grow, and so the links dangled long. Wiglaf then folded the cuffs, hem, and shoulders of the mail upon itself to fit snugly. For most warriors, a chainmail shirt of this quality would be all the armor they would ever wear, or could ever afford, but Wiglaf was a master armorsmith, and he had one final trick up his sleeve.

Wiglaf had journeyed far in his younger years and had even learned from the armorers of the far-marching Roman Legions. There existed a stronger armor than chainmail. Better even than the ancient bronze scale armor of Ulrich's late father. This was a heavy armor, one that none but kings could afford, and Wiglaf knew how to make it. He even knew what the Romans called it: *lorica segmentata*. It was the greatest armor of the Imperial Legion, and Wiglaf saved iron, copper, bronze, and charcoal for years waiting for the right moment.

Together, Wiglaf and Ulrich forged iron into strips, each a handsbreadth wide. He used Ulrich's frame as a guide and modeled the bands to wrap either side of his chest and abdomen, arching up and over his shoulders, and looping around his upper arms. Each of the iron pieces, once crafted, was soft and pliant, so Wiglaf case-hardened them to make steel. He did this by coating them in a mixture of charcoal, ground bone, and powdered hooves, sealing each thus-treated piece in a solid iron case and driving the case deep into the smoldering furnace. The box remained in the heat for two days and two nights, and when it was removed, the steel inside was as hard as rock crystal. The once-bright metal came out darkened and deeply colored with organic whorls of browns and blues dancing across every piece. The patterns of each segment were unique and hauntingly beautiful.

The armor was fastened together with rivets and brass joints. Hinged in the rear and fastening across his front, when the armor was complete, Ulrich was clothed in overlapping segments of steel from clavicle to waist. Arched loops of steel went over his shoulders and upper arms. A heavy leather skirt hung from the hem down toward his knees, reinforced with thick metal medallions to protect his groin. A plain steel helm covered his head with hinged steel cheek pieces that strapped tightly beneath his jaw.

When Ulrich first donned his new armor, he moved awkwardly. His shoulders chafed, and the weight made his movements cumbersome and ungainly. Together, they padded the inside of the armor with extra layers of leather so that the sturdy young man could more comfortably wear the slightly oversized cuirass. As Ulrich grew, he removed each extra layer of leather to grow into his armor.

Next, Wiglaf and Ulrich fashioned what would be Ulrich's shield. The shield was a simple thing in the German style, an inch-thick rectangular board of oak planks riveted together and nearly the height of a grown man. Massive iron handles on the back were affixed through the wood to a sturdy round iron boss on the front and would deflect a determined blow or bash an enemy off balance. The shield, even more than the sword, was the mark of a warrior.

The Romans had brought the modern way of war to the Germanic tribes, and that warfare revolved around the massive shields of the shield wall. It took a strong man to carry a full-length shield, and dropping the shield on the battlefield was the first mark of the fleeing coward.

Finally, they fashioned Ulrich's weapon. Wiglaf had been a swordsman, but even as Ulrich had grown, he had never grown to understand the finesse of the parry and repartee, the utility of the short jab to throw an opponent off balance before the swift killing thrust. Despite all Wiglaf's teaching, Ulrich was destined to be a brawler. Ulrich could not resist the temptation to throw himself bodily at an enemy and swing and swing with his remarkable strength. Wiglaf could tell that the sturdy youth was bound to grow into a massively strong man, and after much deliberation, decided that the best weapon for Ulrich was the war-axe. While Ulrich worked on his shield or tethered the oxen and plowed their small fields, Wiglaf poured all his skill into the making of a brutal weapon.

The head of the axe was a long, heavy, convex blade of blackened, dagger-sharp steel mounted on the end of an iron-sheathed, oak shaft. The axe blade had a hooked base to disarm an opponent, pull a rider off his horse, or hook over the top of a shield and expose an enemy to the thrust that would open the way into the enemy's shield wall. The end of the shaft was sharpened to a deadly point, and the massive blade was counterbalanced with an equally intimidating spike as long as a man's forearm.

"Your father used an axe," Wiglaf said simply when he surprised Ulrich with the unexpected present, and Ulrich's eyes were wet with gratitude as he embraced his friend.

Ulrich trained daily in the new armor, sweating profusely as he hacked and slashed at Wiglaf's staunch guard. He took quickly to his new weapon and was soon so proficient with the heavy single-bladed axe that Wiglaf would tire long before Ulrich, and Ulrich would train alone, hacking and slashing at imaginary opponents into the dark hours of the night, building endurance and agility in the heavy armor with the cumbersome weapon.

For years the family continued to live peacefully. Ulrich grew into his armor, and as he gained strength and stature, the family prospered. He ranged far into the countryside to hunt deer. He would stalk silently through the woods before felling the wary creatures with a long hunting bow crafted from the heart of a sapling yew. He expanded the fields that they cultivated to feed the two young children that grew energetic and healthy. He learned more and more of the blacksmith's art, and while he never forgot his uncle's treachery, he was content to live free with his happy family.

The nearby town of Brunswick was little more than a collection of houses clustered around a convenient bend on the river Wesser. The town was not rich; neither was it large. It was, however, fortuitously located. It lay deep enough within the kingdom to avoid the typical border raids from the Frisians to the north or neighboring German Kingdoms to the east and south. It was also far enough from the coast to provide some safety from the Northmen that sometimes rose from the stormy waves. In the complacency of a town enjoying the soporific of peace, the people of Brunswick slept unprepared.

CHAPTER THREE

The spring of the year 356 A.D. was a good season. The wheat and barley grew green and fast in the fields, and Ulrich was now a fully grown man, who had filled well into the empty spaces of his suit of segmented armor. Word had come that there was a trade ship in town, and so on a warm spring morning, Wiglaf hitched his pony to a small two-wheeled cart and headed to the docks to trade. He carried well-made horseshoes, framing nails, iron loops for harnesses and other such wares of the blacksmith's trade. Ulrich waved as Wiglaf rode off and then turned back to the homestead to begin the chores for the day.

The family owned only one other draft animal: an old mare Ulrich affectionately nicknamed Mule. Mule was an ornery, old beast, but she liked Ulrich well enough, and soon Ulrich had her hitched up to the plow. Mule had always refused to be ridden. If Ulrich tried to saddle and sit her, Mule would not buck or start, but would simply stand obstinately, and no amount of begging or pleading would move her. So instead, Ulrich held the reins and walked slowly alongside Mule as they plowed the rows. A warm breeze ruffled his thin wool shirt, and he wore cow's leather breeches over sackcloth sandals.

Ulrich absently petted Mule's mane and let his mind drift as they plodded along. The land they plowed bordered a small stream and consisted of soft, loamy soil that crumbled gently in the hand and gave off the heady smell of rich earth. He and Wiglaf had recently cleared this acre into the deep woods with axe and fire, and their expanded holdings into this unclaimed forest gave them the freedom to allow the nearer fields to lie fallow and recover as they rotated their crops year by year.

Ulrich brushed some flies away from Mule's eyes and enjoyed the warmth of the day, the soft loam under his feet, and Mule's easy company. By late afternoon, he led Mule back into the stables, brushed her down, hauled well water for her trough, and released her to graze in the fenced pasture by the house. He noted curiously that Wiglaf's pony was still not back. He removed his wool shirt, rinsed the sweat off his face and shoulders with water from the trough, put his shirt back on and walked into the house.

Johanne prayed to the new God. Most Saxons of the countryside still believed in the old ways, but Johanne had faith in the light of Christianity. Wiglaf did not mind. Although he preferred the old gods, years ago he had bought her a finely crafted silver crucifix to wear around her neck. He figured there was no harm in appeasing one more god; there were so many already. Johanne clutched that totem because she was worried. Wiglaf had been gone for too long.

When he entered the house, Ulrich saw the fear on her face. The children sat on a bench at the small wooden table. Johanne was laying out the evening meal, and both kids seemed unnaturally subdued.

"Sit down, sit down," Johanne said. "We will go ahead and eat. We won't wait for Wiglaf. I will just leave the rest of the stew on the fire for him. I'm sure he will be home soon."

Ulrich sat across from Johanne's four-year old son, Gebhard, and began eating; he dipped his wooden spoon in the thick barley stew and found that he was voraciously hungry. Gebhard was dipping his fingers in the stew and then licking them off, but little Ælfwine, a perceptive five-year-old girl, was not eating at all.

"Papa said I'd get to ride Hod when I am a little bigger," little Gebhard informed Ulrich. Hod was the tractable pony that Wiglaf was raising to replace Mule and that he used to make his occasional trading rides into town.

"But you have already ridden Hod," Ulrich replied with a smile. Which, in fact, was true. Yesterday, when Ulrich was down by the river mending one of the fish traps, Ulrich had heard a yell and had run back to the house to see Gebhard riding bareback around the little pasture with Wiglaf limping after him yelling. Ulrich had run across the field and calmly stepped in front of the cantering horse, carefully pulling the grinning Gebhard from the pony's back before handing him over to Wiglaf for a spanking.

"I mean ride him when I'm allowed to," Gebhard said with a

mischievous grin.

Ulrich could not hide a small chuckle as he drained his stew, holding his bowl with both hands.

"Where is Papa?" Ælfwine asked, speaking for the first time. Her face was serious. Ulrich noticed that she still was not eating. Johanne stood by the hearth.

"He's just down in the town honey. He will be back soon," Johanne responded. "Now eat your supper."

Ulrich pivoted in his seat to look at Johanne. He took in how worried she looked and how she fingered the silver cross at her bosom. Ulrich did not like waiting. He made his decision without hesitation.

"I will go down to town and look for him," he said. Johanne's eyes, which had been absently staring into the distance, focused on him with a questioning look. Ulrich tried to sound reassuring, "I'm sure he is fine. Perhaps he just bartered for more iron than he can carry at once. I will go help him out."

Ulrich turned back to Ælfwine. "You should eat, little one. I will be back soon." Ulrich stood and walked out the door, across the yard, and into the stables. Once there, he stepped into the adjoining pasture and whistled. Mule came plodding over, expecting a treat.

"I'm sorry girl, but we are not yet done today," he said to the gentle mare. He led Mule into the stable and began hitching her up to the big four-wheeled farm cart they used to haul hay and crops in from the fields. Mule was cranky; she was tired and not used to doing more than one chore in a day, but she complied sullenly. Once she was hitched, Ulrich fed her a handful of grain and climbed onto the high bench of the cart. Ulrich grasped the reins and stopped. A strange sense of dread gripped him. The hairs on the back of his neck stood on end. After a moment's hesitation, he climbed back down and walked back into the stables, leaving Mule tethered in the yard with the cart.

It was here that Ulrich kept his armor, his shield, and his axe. He removed his comfortable clothes, the simple woolen shirt and frayed, worn, hide pants, and put on instead a close-fitting leather tunic and thick leather breeches. Fitted leather gloves covered his hands, and sturdy leather boots replaced his lightweight sandals. He strapped the metal cuirass about his chest. It was then that he noticed Johanne standing in the doorway watching him. She walked silently over and helped him finish fastening his armor. Once he was fully armored, she turned him around and looked him in the eye.

"I see." She paused, considering, then continued, "I see that you have a bad feeling about this as well," Johanne said. "Bring him back. Be careful, but bring my Wiglaf home. Promise me that you will."

Her small voice held deep emotion and Ulrich smiled. "I promise I will bring Wiglaf back," he said.

Ulrich tucked his helmet under his arm, hefted his axe, and walked across the yard. He tossed his burdens into the back of the cart and climbed deftly into the seat. By now his heavy armor felt as natural as a second skin. He grasped the reins in both hands, and the cart rumbled off toward the road and the town beyond. Johanne watched him go. She clasped the crucifix with both hands and prayed.

CHAPTER FOUR

The evening sun was nearing the horizon as the wagon trundled down the road toward town. The flat, paved causeway wound its way through peaceful fields and over low stone bridges. The bridges and road were remnants of when the Roman empire had once extended deeply into Germania. They were beautiful, but Ulrich's heart was heavy. There were occasional travelers on the wide road, but they moved out of the way of the big cart with its forbidding rider. Ulrich was in a black cloud, filled with dark premonitions and paying no heed to his surroundings until he came upon something very strange.

Just off the road, there was a man plowing a field. This by itself would not have been strange, but the man had no horse, no ox, no draft animal at all. Instead, the massive man had both hands on the heavy plow and was pushing it bodily through the hard ground. Ulrich was amazed at the sight. It was an impossible task requiring superhuman strength. The man pushing the plow was huge. He was bigger even than Ulrich, and when he got to the end of the row, he simply lifted the heavy wooden plow into the air, turned it around, and started down the next row.

Ulrich stopped the cart. "Hey!" he called. "Hey, you!"

The huge man stopped, let go of the plow and walked ponderously over to the road where Ulrich sat on the cart. As he came closer, Ulrich saw that, even though the man was massive, he was gaunt, and his clothes were ragged. He looked as though he had not eaten in days, and his toes poked through the front of worn cloth shoes.

"You were pushing that plow by hand," Ulrich commented,

dumbfounded.

"Yes, sir. I was," the gaunt giant responded.

"Why?"

"Why, because that is what they tell me to do."

"Who tells you?" Ulrich asked.

The man turned and pointed. On the top of a low hill, Ulrich saw a rich hall. The place was ornamented with stone facings and stood next to a newly built stable of dark oak, itself large enough for a dozen horses. Ulrich had seen the place before but had not paid much attention to it in his rare trips to town. It was clearly the manor of a very wealthy landlord, one whom Ulrich guessed could afford to treat his servants better, if he so chose.

Ulrich looked down at the man who stood next to the road. The man had a kind, wide face with brown eyes and a gentle disposition. When he spoke, the big man's voice was a soft tenor, a surprisingly gentle noise coming from such an imposing figure. Ulrich immediately decided he liked this man.

"What's your name?" Ulrich asked.

"Sigmund."

"They pay you, Sigmund?"

"They feed me."

"But not very well, I see," Ulrich observed.

"Well, it's been a couple of days." Sigmund admitted.

Ulrich frowned. "Come with me, Sigmund. I will feed you."

Sigmund did not move; he looked curious but unconvinced. "And to where exactly would we go?"

There was a shrewd look in Sigmund's eyes, and Ulrich realized that the big man might not be as simple as he looked. Ulrich sighed. He thought before answering. "My friend—my father—has not come back from town today, and that worries me. I do not know if something bad happened, but I could use another strong hand if something went wrong. If it's nothing, you can come right back, and there is no harm done. If there is trouble, you can use your own judgement as to whether you wish to become involved. In the meantime, I have extra food, and you look hungry. It is your choice."

The big man considered for a moment then shrugged. He dusted his hands off on the rags that passed for pants and clambered up onto the bench next to Ulrich. When he sat, he hunched, but even bent over, Sigmund was at least a head taller than Ulrich as they sat side by side. Sigmund looked sideways at Ulrich as the cart began moving down the road.

"In truth, you had me convinced when you mentioned food. I will admit I'm a bit peckish," said Sigmund.

Ulrich had noticed earlier, that in the back of the cart, next to his helmet and axe, was a burlap sack. Ulrich reached back, grabbed it, and put it on the bench next to him. Opening it with his free hand he saw that Johanne had packed generously for the trip. There was a thick slice of salted beef, three apples, and even a small wedge of yellow cheese.

"Here, you can have this," Ulrich said, and pushed the bundle toward the big man.

Sigmund began to eat very delicately. He ate a small bite of the meat, a bite of apple, and a very small nibble of the cheese before repeating the whole process. He ate slowly, savoring each morsel as it went down, but Ulrich noticed, that by the time he was done, he had even eaten the cores of the apples.

The sun was setting by the time Ulrich and Sigmund reached Brunswick. The air felt heavy, like a storm brewed in the distance, although the sky was clear. The houses on the outskirts of town were lit, and Ulrich could smell the mixed odors of wood burning and meat cooking. From the occasional house, he could hear soft singing, and naught looked amiss, but for some reason, something felt off, though he could not quite put his finger on what it was.

It was only when they got deeper into the town, to the crossroads near the town center, that Ulrich found something to feed his suspicions. No candlelight showed from the shuttered house windows, and from the nearest dwelling, he could hear muffled sobbing. He parked the cart and climbed down.

"Wait here and watch the cart," he told Sigmund. The big man nodded, grasped the reins, and shifted nervously in his seat.

Ulrich reached into the back of the cart and pulled out his big axe. He held it low and stepped cautiously toward the house from which the sobbing emanated. He noticed that the door was ajar and leaned lopsidedly from its hinges. Splintered wood littered the floor; the door had clearly been forced from the outside. He pushed it open gingerly and walked into the small room. He gave his eyes a moment to adjust to the darkness within. The furniture in the room was recklessly thrown about, and in the corner, he found the source of the sobbing. An old woman sat miserably on the floor by an upended table. At his approach she drew back into the corner.

"No, no!" she yelled. "Go away! Go away!" She threw something which Ulrich could not identify in the darkness. Whatever it was, it clanged harmlessly off his breastplate.

"Calm down," Ulrich said, "I am not here to hurt you. What happened?"

He saw her blink and gasp in the darkness. "Oh, thank God! I thought they were back," she said.

"You thought who were back?" Ulrich insisted.

"Frisians. Frisians raiders were here. They took my Inga, my poor daughter and her baby. I tried to stop them, but they hit me!" the woman wailed. "They took the baby! Why did they take the baby?"

Ulrich swore. "Where did they take them?" he asked.

"They were in the boat. They came by the river," the woman told him.

"Oh, gods!" he swore. Without another word he turned and dashed back into the street. He threw his axe into the back of the cart and jumped lithely into the seat.

"Alright, Mule, let's go! We're in a hurry now." Surprisingly, Mule seemed to sense his urgency and trotted faster down the road.

"What is going on?" asked Sigmund.

"Raiders. Frisians, it seems," Ulrich growled.

"Oh," Sigmund said then lapsed back into silence.

Ulrich gritted his teeth and gave the reins a little whip. He could only hope he wasn't too late.

CHAPTER FIVE

Ulrich headed for the docks by the river. He saw what he was looking for. He could just make out the tall mast of a single ship moored at the quay, but he stopped short because he saw Hod.

Hod, the pony, stood tethered, still harnessed to Wiglaf's small two-wheeled cart, on the side of the road in the heart of the town. Ulrich drove the big wagon over to the other side of the road and jumped down, axe in hand. He left his helmet behind.

"Wait here and watch the cart," Ulrich ordered once again.

"Again? I'm beginning to notice a pattern here." Sigmund chuckled, but a grave look from Ulrich silenced him.

The marketplace seemed to be the only part of the town that was awake. Two strangely dressed men stood outside a large torch-lit double-doorway beyond which Ulrich could hear the murmur of many voices. Ulrich headed first to Wiglaf's cart and peered inside. He swore. The cart was empty. There were none of the horseshoes bearing Wiglaf's mark, none of the small iron fasteners for harnesses, and none of the precision tools which were worth their weight in gold. Also, there were none of the heavy, dull bars of smelted iron for which Wiglaf had come to trade. Ulrich swore again softly and began walking toward the torch-lit building.

The two men guarding the doorway were dressed in a fashion Ulrich had never seen. They wore gaudily decorated tunics of blue, white, and yellow over long chainmail shirts with fur collars. They carried long pattern-steel swords and painted round shields. They watched him approach, and the nearest greeted him in German that had a stiff northerner's accent.

"Stop there," the guard said. "If you have come for the auction you may not bring your weapon."

Ulrich spat on the ground derisively. "I come for no auction, and you are welcome try to stop me." He did not break his stride.

Ulrich had never seen Frisians at war. He had heard stories often enough to fear the opportunistic Frisian raiders in their long fast ships. They would appear suddenly to pillage and murder, and then they would be gone like the morning mist. Sometimes entire villages would disappear; the men would be killed, the women and children would be dragged off into slavery, and the town would be burned. Only ash would remain. An unreasonable terror endowed these men with superhuman malice, and a small part of that fear welled up in Ulrich's throat. Just as quickly as the fear took him, it left. The two men before him were simply men. He could see their own uncertainty as an unknown armed man walked so confidently toward them. Their hesitation made him bold, and he quickened his pace.

The Frisian guards did not know what to do. This man who approached wore strange steel armor and carried a massive axe with its head held low to the ground. They closed on the doorway with their hands on their sword hilts. They were expecting him to stop or to swing his weapon, but instead he dropped his armored shoulder and bowled into them. The man on Ulrich's left attempted to grab his arm to stop him, but Ulrich shook him off. The man on his right grabbed the handle of his axe and tried to pull it away from him. Ulrich didn't bother to fight him; he simply tightened his stone grip and made the Frisian guard's efforts to disarm him futile. He pushed his way through the doors.

Beyond the low archway was an open-air corral thronged with people and ringed by torchlight. Ulrich recognized the place. It was where he and Wiglaf had bought Hod. This corral was used for auctions of livestock, and tonight, it was being used for that purpose again.

Immediately in front of Ulrich was a large stage upon which a gaudily dressed man lounged in a chair. From his bearing, he was clearly the leader of this war band. He was toying with the tip of a long slim sword. Before him, on her knees, was a woman who was weeping and holding a girl of perhaps twelve years of age. There was blood on the front of the girl's torn white dress. The blood began at the crotch and ran down to her feet where it dribbled slowly onto the wooden floor of the stage. Mother and daughter were bound by ropes which wound around their necks. Both ropes were held by an ugly squat brute of a man who stood near the leader's throne. This man leered at the crowd with small eyes that were almost lost in his fat face. Like the young girl's, the crotch of his brown tunic showed bright red underneath rough leather armor.

Behind knelt half a dozen more prisoners who were bound with ropes around their wrists and necks. Wiglaf was among them. He was crouched on the stage, bent forward over his knees, and Ulrich could see bruises on his face. These prisoners were being guarded by two more Frisians. To Ulrich's left and right stood the Saxon townspeople. They were unarmed, disheveled, and seemed cowed by the presence of the heavily armed Frisian warriors. Ulrich stood among them, while in an empty space to the fore, a dozen Frisian warriors guarded the stage. Their drawn swords held the crowd at bay.

The commotion of Ulrich's entry had not gone unnoticed, and the place fell silent. The townspeople were surprised to see such a heavily armored man erupt in their midst, and the fearsome snarl on Ulrich's face was enough to make the crowd draw back. The enthroned leader straightened and spoke.

"Who is this man?" he asked.

"I do not know," answered the Frisian to Ulrich's left. He grasped Ulrich's armored arm again, but this time, Ulrich could not shake him off. "He just walked in off the street."

"Well, perhaps he has money. Maybe we will let him barter. " The seated man stood. He wore a red cape that draped almost to the floor. His long blonde hair was bound neatly with silver chain and his sharp eyes were green. His movements betrayed supple power. A sea monster swam on the front of his white tunic, itself fitted over fine, polished chainmail that glittered in the torchlight. He gestured at Ulrich with the long, gleaming sword.

"Who are you?" The man addressed Ulrich. "And why are you here?"

"Who I am is not important," Ulrich responded. "But what is important is that you have my friend there, and you should let him go." With his axe, Ulrich gestured at Wiglaf who looked up, eyes clearing with recognition.

The gaudily-dressed man turned to look at Wiglaf and chuckled.

"Oh, I see. Well, what are you willing to pay for him?"

"Pay?" Ulrich asked.

"You seem confused." The leader smiled condescendingly. "You cannot simply get something for nothing. If you want something, you must pay for it."

Ulrich glared, and the tall man began to pace the stage, ignoring Ulrich as he addressed the crowd. "Your name may not be important, but mine is. My name is Ejnar, Serpent of the Waves. I am a pirate and I merely ask you to pay." He stalked before the crowd, sword point held low.

"See this one?" Ejnar returned to the center of the stage and poked the young girl with the point of his sword. She seemed not to notice; she stood dazed, dead to the world, though her mother shrieked and tried to pull her away. Ejnar paused for a moment, amused at the reaction. He indicated the ugly, bloody man who held the rope. "Thudolf here may have tainted her a bit, but that does not matter. She is ours. We won her in a fair fight, and now she is our property. If you want her back, you can buy her, but if you do not buy her, she stays property of my men." Ejnar spoke in a honeyed voice, as though he were explaining the ways of the world to children. He smiled at the crowd and flashed white teeth. There was a muted grumbling among the townspeople, but nobody challenged him.

Ejnar addressed Ulrich. "You, there. Would you like to buy this girl?" He had long fingers with which he gestured as he spoke, moving in deliberate, graceful movements.

Ulrich remained silent. Ejnar stared unblinking at him for a long moment, then sighed. "I thought you might be willing to barter, but if you do not, I am no longer amused by you. Finn, Holguf. Disarm him and bring him here. I want his armor."

With a quick movement, the Frisian to Ulrich's left slipped his arm around Ulrich's bare neck and held him fast. At the same time, the Frisian on his right renewed his efforts to wrench the axe from his hand. Ulrich managed to keep control of his weapon, but struggle as he might, he could not break loose from his captors.

CHAPTER SIX

A fter Ulrich had bulled his way past the guards at the door, Sigmund, overcome by curiosity, had left the cart. He had tied Mule to a convenient signpost and followed Ulrich inside. Once he entered through the double doors into the outdoor corral, nobody seemed to notice the ragged giant with the mild face and downcast eyes. The first thing Sigmund saw, though, was the pain in the young girl's eyes as she stood on the stage, and rage began to build within him. Sigmund hated pain. He was a gentle man, but he could read cruelty in the face of the ugly brute in the brown tunic who held the rope so casually. Sigmund stared at the man uncomprehendingly until he noticed the blood on the man's pants.

As Sigmund stood in the crowd, tears began to well out of the corners of his eyes. The tears clouded his vision and began to roll down his face. He barely saw the captive woman scream and twist her daughter away from Ejnar's sword point. The man with the blood on his pants was sneering in triumph, and Sigmund began to push his way through the crowd. How could a man take pleasure when causing pain? A Frisian warrior stood on the hard-packed dirt floor between him and the stage and blocked his way with an outstretched sword. Sigmund kept walking. He slapped the sword out of the way, reached out with his other hand, and grabbed the top of the man's painted shield. In one fluid motion Sigmund ripped the shield out of the Frisian warrior's grasp. He lifted it straight up then brought it down hard on the man's helmeted head. The man slumped to the ground, and Sigmund stepped over him toward the stage.

As Ulrich struggled with the two Frisian guards at the door, a huge roar erupted from Ulrich's right, and he saw Sigmund leap up onto the stage. The big Saxon grabbed the man who held the girl and her mother prisoner, wrapped one of his huge hands around his neck, and lifted him bodily into the air. Ulrich could see tears streaming down Sigmund's face as he held the man high and shook him like a doll. Roaring incoherently, weeping, he used his free hand to twist the man's head around until, with an audible crack, Ulrich heard the ugly man's neck break.

Ejnar stood frozen, momentarily stunned at this sudden turn of events. The crowd was shocked to silence, and quite fortunately for Ulrich, his two captors momentarily loosened their grip. Ulrich used this moment to wrench his axe with his right hand and twist away from the guard who pinioned him. As he pulled, the sharp hook on the lower end of the axe blade tore into the man's groin. Ulrich continued pulling, and the warrior screamed as he was disemboweled. The pungent smell of entrails and offal wafted into Ulrich's nose as he freed his blade from the Frisian warrior's flesh, and in the same movement, he whirled on the other warrior who had attempted to restrain him. This man was unprepared for the attack and had not so much as drawn his sword before the heavy axe thumped deep into his shoulder. The honed blade slid through the chainmail like so much cloth, and the man went down in a spray of blood.

Ulrich freed his blade and spun toward the stage. The crowd had surged. Shouts of anger and pain filled the night as unarmed Saxons, suddenly unleashed from their fear by Sigmund's attack, mobbed and overwhelmed their Frisian tormentors. Several less courageous townspeople jostled past Ulrich in their haste to escape through the door. Ulrich could not see past the panicked crowd. He pushed through the throng and made it to the open space before the stage. Two Frisian warriors blocked his way. He could hear the unseen clang of steel on steel ahead and knew that Sigmund would need his help. He had to get through these two quickly.

These men were ready for him. They had drawn swords and were carrying shields. Ulrich had no shield but instead hefted his heavy axe in both hands. His opponents seemed hesitant, as though neither wished to be the first to assault this steel-clad stranger with the massive, blood-drenched axe.

Ulrich did not wait for them to come to him. He charged into them and swung his axe in a wide horizontal arc at the rightmost warrior. The Frisian lifted his shield to block the swing, but Ulrich had expected him to. It had been a glancing blow that was meant to throw the man off balance and force him on the defensive. As Ulrich launched his attack, he felt time slow. He immediately felt all the anxiety and uncertainty wash away. Ulrich had plenty of time to parry the blow that the man on his left launched at his unprotected side. As his axe glanced off the first warrior's shield, Ulrich turned the long handle of his weapon to intercept the blade that came whistling high at his head. The blade glanced up; his attacker stumbled, and Ulrich had the momentary advantage.

Sliding his left hand off the axe handle, Ulrich grabbed the nearest attacker's wrist before the man could recover and brought his axe up fast. The big blade slid easily through mail and flesh and bone, slicing the immobilized arm clean off at the elbow. The Frisian warrior slumped to his knees, and Ulrich dropped the severed arm, which was still clutching its sword, before turning back to his other attacker. This man had recovered from the heavy blow on his shield and was now holding his sword low toward Ulrich. The warrior stepped in fast and thrust at Ulrich's groin. Ulrich parried by quickly lifting the axe, knocking the sword up and away with the reverse of the axe before he stepped forward and smashed down with the heavy blade. The Frisian just managed to get his shield up in time to block the blow which thumped heavily into the wood, breaking the warrior's arm on impact. Ulrich took advantage of the Frisian's sudden pain to plant a steel-clad boot in the man's torso, throwing him onto his back. Ulrich then stepped quickly forward, put one boot on the man's sword arm and chopped the heavy blade of the axe down into his enemy's chest.

Ulrich pulled his, now thoroughly blood-soaked weapon from the dead Frisian's torso and looked up at the stage. Sigmund was there, and he was attacking Ejnar. Sigmund looked pathetically vulnerable in loose shirt and ragged trousers, while his opponent was equipped with chainmail armor. Sigmund swung a sword clumsily at the gaudy Frisian leader. His strokes were wild and undisciplined. Every attack threw him off balance and left him desperately imperiled. Ejnar, Serpent of the Waves, seemed be enjoying himself and was toying with the big, wild Saxon. Sigmund was bleeding already from a dozen wounds, and as Ulrich watched, the pirate easily parried another of Sigmund's wild strokes and deftly planted the tip of his blade in the big Saxon's unprotected shoulder.

"Ejnar!" Ulrich called. The pirate leader looked down. "If you want a challenge come and fight me."

Ejnar stepped back from Sigmund who hunched forward, winded and bleeding. Ejnar cast a disparaging look at Sigmund and then hopped lightly from the stage. He threw up a cloud of dust from the earthen floor as his blood red cape swept down behind him. There was no fear in the pirate's clear green eyes as he strode forward. He looked at the blood on Ulrich's weapon and the fallen warriors at his feet and smiled.

"That is quite an axe you have there," Ejnar commented. "But it looks a bit slow." He flourished his slim blade. "Shall we see just how slow it is?"

Ejnar's voice was smooth and calm, and he stepped forward. Ulrich raised his axe, but in the blink of an eye, Ejnar's long sword came whistling in toward his face. Ulrich had no time to parry but instead had to leap back to get away from the threat. Ejnar's blade flew in again, low this time, and Ulrich just managed to knock it aside with the iron-sheathed handle of his axe. The pirate retracted his sword and stabbed forward again. Ulrich had not yet recovered from the last parry, and the tip of the blade rang hard against the steel over his chest. It did not pierce the sturdy metal.

"Well, now, that is something." Ejnar stepped calmly back, deliberately inspecting the tip of his sword. "Very impressive armor, I must say. For a moment, I was worried that I had blunted my sword. I simply must have that armor. With some tailoring it could fit me quite nicely." Ejnar grinned at Ulrich, who, enraged, attacked.

Ulrich's charge was accompanied by a wild overhead swing of his axe which Ejnar sidestepped easily. The axe blade whistled harmlessly down to thump into the soft earthen floor. Ejnar danced away to Ulrich's left as Ulrich swung again, this time in a horizontal swing that Ejnar stepped back from before dancing forward to deliver a quick stab which glanced off of Ulrich's armored shoulder. He stabbed again, and Ulrich hopped back to avoid the blow. He stabbed a third time, this time low, and when Ulrich tried to parry the feint, Ejnar's sword was already jabbing at his neck. The long sword caught on Ulrich's tall armored collar, and Ejnar pressed it forward, using the leverage to throw Ulrich backward. As Ulrich stumbled his feet became tangled on one of the Frisian warrior's bodies lying on the earthen floor, and he fell.

Ulrich landed heavily on his back and felt the wind go out of his lungs. Ejnar wasted no time; he stepped over Ulrich, and sneering in triumph, stabbed the sword down at his face. Ulrich twisted away just in time and rolled to his knees. Still kneeling, he swung his axe in a flat arc at Ejnar's ankles. Ejnar hopped back to avoid the blade, and Ulrich climbed to his feet.

Ulrich was sweating and gasping for breath. He felt himself tiring. Ejnar seemed to be just as quick as when the fight began, while Ulrich was moving slower and slower. His only chance at victory was to end this fight quickly else Ejnar would outlast him.

But Ulrich was learning too. He noted how dramatically Ejnar evaded his attacks. He seemed to be avoiding allowing his slim sword to meet Ulrich's heavy blade. Ulrich wagered that Ejnar's slender weapon would not be able to sustain a blow from his study axe. Being unable to parry was a grave weakness, one which Ulrich could use to his advantage. With this in mind, Ulrich aimed his next wide horizontal swing not at where the pirate stood, but slightly beyond him, wagering that Ejnar would again attempt to leap out of the way and get caught by the unexpected blade.

Instead, Ejnar surprised him. As Ulrich swung his axe, Ejnar stepped in toward Ulrich and thus under the blade. He grabbed Ulrich's swinging arm with his free hand, ducked beneath the blow and stabbed up into Ulrich's armpit, where no steel plate protected. Ulrich howled from the pain and stepped back. Ejnar brandished a triumphant smirk.

"It seems that armor has a weakness or two," Ejnar explained mockingly, wiping the bloody tip of his blade on his red cape. "Did you know that?"

Ulrich ignored the shooting pain of the wound and stalked toward Ejnar.

Meanwhile, Sigmund untied Wiglaf. There were no other enemy nearby, as the remaining guards had either fled or been torn apart by the angry crowd.

"Who are you?" Wiglaf asked.

"Oh, I am nobody important. After my own farm failed, I have been working as a farmhand of Lord Gilbert up the road, but I have been thinking of finding new employment. I came with him." Sigmund gestured toward Ulrich. "My name is Sigmund. Are you

Ulrich's father?" Sigmund asked. The big man's voice was friendly, and he extended a hand amiably.

"Adoptive father perhaps. Thank you, Sigmund," Wiglaf said, taking the hand gratefully. Freed from his bonds, he stood to look around the corral. Inspired by Ulrich and Sigmund, the angry townspeople had rushed their tormentors, and the Frisian raiders had died. It was a victory, but the casualty rate was high. The armed raiders had taken many of the townspeople to death with them. Bodies lay scattered on the floor. At least twenty Saxons were hurt or dead, but among these were the corpses of a dozen Frisian warriors. The enemy bodies were being stripped and looted where they lay.

Sigmund carefully removed the ropes from around the necks of the young girl and her mother. The mother looked up at him gratefully, but the girl merely flinched at his touch. Her eyes remained fixed on the floor of the stage. There were four other prisoners on the stage, and Wiglaf forced his bruised and battered body to walk over and untie them. They were all women. Wiglaf had been captured because, when he had seen the Frisian raiders knocking down house doors in the town, he had tried to stop them. He wondered why he had not simply been killed; he was too old and crippled to be worth anything as a slave. He decided that the Frisians must have been enjoying humiliating him.

Wiglaf turned back to watch Ulrich and the pirate leader circle each other on the dirt floor. He saw the blood running down Ulrich's armor and dripping from Ejnar's sword, and he sighed. Sigmund decided that Ulrich needed help and he moved to rejoin the fight. A massively heavy wooden podium stood on the edge of the stage. It was held in place by thick iron bolts, but with a great tearing of wood, Sigmund pulled it up, ripping a large chunk of the stage along with it. He began to walk toward Ejnar, bearing this huge improvised bludgeon like a club when Wiglaf stopped him.

"He needs to do this on his own," Wiglaf said. Sigmund was quizzical, but Wiglaf was insistent.

"My son needs to learn to fight," Wiglaf said.

Sigmund sighed and dropped his burden with a crash. "Will he win?" Sigmund asked.

Wiglaf nodded. "He has to."

Sigmund was bleeding from a dozen shallow wounds. He shrugged. "I was tired anyway," he said and sat heavily on the overturned podium.

CHAPTER SEVEN

Ulrich glared at Ejnar. He was sure that this fight would not end in any way other than a bloody death. Either the pirate would die, or Ulrich would, bleeding slowly into the hard, dry earth. At this rate, the latter seemed more likely. The trouble was that the man was too quick. Ulrich had not managed to land a single blow, and Ejnar would surely bleed all the strength out of him, stab by stab, until he could no longer stand. Then the killing blow would come.

Suddenly Ulrich realized that there was another weakness he had not considered. He grinned when he realized that Ejnar's own vanity would be his undoing. Ulrich charged. As he rushed forward he swung his axe one-handed, and Ejnar, anticipating the attack, danced lightly away, but the charge was a feint. As Ejnar dodged, Ulrich reached with his free hand to grab the Frisian's brightly colored cape and managed to close on a full fistful of the rich fabric. Ulrich yanked hard, expecting to leash his foe and pull him off balance. He was disappointed to find that the clasp released easily at Ejnar's neck, leaving Ulrich with a useless heap of fabric. There was a jab of pain as Ejnar, stepping to Ulrich's unprotected left, slid his sword beneath Ulrich's armored cuirass, sinking the blade into the hip until it scraped on bone. He leapt lightly away from Ulrich's enraged counter swing.

Ejnar laughed. "I won that drapery in a land far to the south. There are men there who fight Iberian bulls—great black beasts with sharpened horns as long as a man's arm." He grinned as he spoke, relishing the story. "I have never fought a bull myself, but I have seen it done. The bullfighter, you see, waves around the red cloth to distract the beast. Then, the bullfighter bleeds the beast to death. He stabs it again and again as it charges, and once the animal is so weak that it can barely stand, the bullfighter puts it out of its misery." Ejnar flashed white teeth in a grimace of triumph and pride. "So, come at me again, beast, and I… " He flourished his sword, spraying blood in a high arc. "will put you down."

Ulrich's cold rage boiled over. His mind recalled the look of triumph on uncle Edwald's face when he drove his sword into his father's chest amid the lurid flames of Hamburg. Ulrich's vision narrowed and turned a livid red. With renewed energy he charged Ejnar and swung his axe. Ejnar leapt away, surprised at the Saxon's sudden change in speed, and Ulrich swung again and again. Ejnar twisted and dodged, but he was on the defensive now as Ulrich poured all his rage and frustration into swing after swing.

Ejnar could not respond, only retreat as Ulrich's ferocity drove him back. One forceful, half-parried swing knocked Ejnar against the stage. The next, narrowly dodged by the agile pirate, drove great splinters of wood into the air. Ejnar dove forward and stabbed, slicing into Ulrich's cheek near the ear and drawing a small spray of blood, but Ulrich took no notice of the small wound. Ulrich turned in fury and swung hard. Ejnar brought his sword up to protect his face, and their blades clashed together. With a sound like shattering crystal, Ejnar's slim sword burst into fragments. Ejnar dropped the useless hilt and snatched a discarded shield off the ground. He spun in a half crouch to see Ulrich already standing over him, axe held high. Ejnar raised the shield just in time, and the axe came down, smashing into the shield and knocking Ejnar flat. The shield broke into two useless pieces and fell from his arm.

Ejnar saw death coming. He was dazed by how quickly the fight had turned against him. To his horror, he realized that his sword hand was empty. Ejnar was from a land by the sea, far to the north. There, they believed in their own old gods, and he knew that he must die with sword in hand to be admitted to the afterlife, to battle and feast for eternity. He felt no fear, only regret at having failed his ancestors, as the axe was lifted high for the final blow.

But in Ulrich's moment of victory, his rage ebbed. Concern for Wiglaf's safety distracted him from his prey, and he looked away. Ejnar was watching his foe for the slightest chance, and when he saw Ulrich's eyes, for the briefest of moments, flick to the stage, he seized the opportunity. Quick as a striking snake, he slammed the edge of the broken shield into Ulrich's shins, unbalancing him. The axe came down wide, and Ejnar leapt to his feet. He dashed to the edge of the paddock, climbed the fence, and disappeared into the night.

Ulrich rubbed his bruised shins. He grunted in frustration then shook his head. He walked to Wiglaf.

Wiglaf knelt on the stage to come level with Ulrich. "You should not leave an enemy alive," he warned, indicating where Ejnar had vanished into the darkness.

"I am glad to see you are okay." Ulrich replied. His relief showed plainly on his face.

Sigmund came over and squatted on the stage too. Blood dripped from several wounds, but the big man seemed unfazed. The fight was over. People were helping wounded townsfolk to their feet. A tearful father fiercely hugged the white-clad woman and their stunned child.

Sigmund's eyes followed the family, and they were wet with the hint of tears. "I am glad that I came with you." He said. "These people needed our help." Sigmund's realized his daughter would have been six years old this year, had the sickness not taken her away.

"I am glad you did too, friend." Ulrich responded.

Sigmund gave a wan smile, then frowned.

"So where do you think that pirate is going?" Sigmund asked.

"The Serpent of the Waves. Came by ship, so he's returning to his ship," Ulrich guessed. "I saw the top of a mast at the quay, it must be docked there."

Sigmund attempted to stand, struggled, and sat heavily.

"Sigmund, stay here for now and catch your breath. Wiglaf, see what you can do about his wounds. When you are ready, meet me down at the pier. I am going after the pirate." Ulrich rose and hefted his axe. He stretched, winced slightly at the gash at his hip, and followed Ejnar over the low paddock fence and into the darkness.

CHAPTER EIGHT

Hunter stalked prey down the dusty, moonlit streets. Ejnar was making no effort to hide from his pursuer but instead walked briskly down the middle of the road. Occasionally he turned to look back at Ulrich, visibly unsettled to be shadowed by the big axe-wielding Saxon.

The town was dark and quiet. The walk was short. Already the cool breeze off the river could be felt. It rustled among the thatch roofs and bent the long stalks of grain that rose in the fields, gently cooling the night from the heat of the day's sun. Ulrich felt a curious sense of detachment. He could feel the pain of his wounds, but they seemed distant and unimportant. Lightheaded, he paused.

"What am I doing?" he asked himself softly. He looked down at the red blood slowly crusting over the blade of his axe and frowned. He was tired. He knew Johanne was worried, and he looked forward to the relief on her face when Wiglaf arrived home safely. He wanted to go home and see the children sleeping peacefully in their beds. Further bloodshed and fear seemed too high a price to pay to avenge the attack on the town or retrieve Wiglaf's missing tools. Still, pulled by curiosity and pushed by fate, he kept walking.

Ahead, Ejnar disappeared around a corner. The road turned sharply beyond a large warehouse. Curiosity growing, Ulrich hurried. He rounded the bend to see a great red ship filling the harbor.

Ulrich had never seen a ship like this. The Frisians along the northern sea built their vessels long and high-sided with tall prows and tall sterns and a great mast which stretched far into the heavens. Next to this elegant ship, the shorter, shallower, German merchant boats looked crude and ungainly. Two fat-bellied trading boats burned in the harbor. The burning hulks had been cast loose, and they twisted in the river as they drifted away downstream, smoke billowing upward into the night sky.

Fifty paces in front of Ulrich a low, wooden pier jutted from the shoreline into the deeper water. It was at the end of this walkway that the red ship was tied. Ulrich watched as Ejnar ran down the wooden planks and up a short ramp into the ship. All was quiet as Ulrich approached the dock. He half expected the wooden gangplank to be withdrawn and for the boat to sail off into the night, oars rising and falling as they carried away the gaudy pirate and whatever treasure he had stolen from this pillaged town, but the boat lay silent and unmoving.

Ulrich had made it half the way down the long pier when three armored heads appeared over the red ship's high railing. Two warriors leapt from the boat. These men were big, fully armed, and ready for him. They carried round shields and long swords. They wore long chainmail shirts, thick leather trousers, iron-banded leather boots, and conical metal helmets with long nose guards. They locked shields and waited for Ulrich but did not advance. Standing abreast, they took up the entire width of the long pier. Ulrich paused to consider them.

Just then Ulrich heard a distinctive creaking sound and looked up. The third Frisian warrior stood on the railing of the ship and aimed a longbow at him, arrow nocked, and string drawn. Panic surged like liquid fire through Ulrich's veins. He swore, for he had fallen into a trap. He glanced back up the pier and saw that the shore was much too far. The archer would have a leisurely time loosing arrows into an easy target if Ulrich retreated now.

Instead Ulrich dove forward. The bowstring twanged, and the arrow slammed into the wood where he had been standing. Feeling desperately vulnerable, he scrambled to his feet. Ulrich charged toward the warriors in front of him. With no shield and no helmet, he knew his only chance for survival was to catch these men off guard with the ferocity of his assault, push them out of the way, scale the boat, and kill the bowman before an arrow found its way into his unprotected head. The two Frisian warriors, anticipating the rush, braced themselves on the wooden planks. At full tilt, Ulrich smashed into the men, protecting his vulnerable head with the haft of his axe held high in both hands.

Ulrich drove his shoulder into the shield of the man on his left. The warrior's boots slid on the smooth wood of the pier, and the man stumbled, dropping both shield and sword to scrabble on all fours to avoid being pushed into the water. The man to Ulrich's right thrust his sword at Ulrich's chest, but the point glanced harmlessly off the hard steel cuirass. Ulrich, not wanting to lose momentum, lifted his leg high and kicked his attacker bodily off the pier to splash backward into the water. Ulrich quickly stooped to take the dropped shield from the warrior he had knocked down, kicked the man as he struggled to his feet, and then held the Frisian shield above his head. He sprinted the last few paces to the ship.

An arrow plunged into the shield, its sharpened steel point protruding through the wood just inches from Ulrich's gloved hand. A man attempted to lift the gangplank into the ship, so Ulrich threw his shield at the man. Spinning like a discus, the iron-rimmed wood struck the man's arm. With a howl of pain the man released the gangplank, and Ulrich launched himself up it. He swung his axe at the stunned warrior, and the blade sliced into the man's face, launching him backward with a spray of blood. Ulrich vaulted the boat's high rail and froze, shocked at what he saw.

The moon shone brightly on dozens of men chained to the benches, oars in their laps. They were galley slaves. The eldest had gray hair and a thin, emaciated body. The youngest slave was a blonde boy with a round innocent face; he could not have been more than eleven or twelve years old. All the slaves wore formless shirts of sackcloth, and their chains clanked with the rhythmic rocking of the ship. Most looked up at Ulrich, their faces white ovals of surprise in the moonlight, but some gazed dully down, too browbeaten or too exhausted to even recognize the presence of a stranger in their midst.

Ulrich was disgusted by the sight of the chains. There were chains everywhere. Chains ran across the deck and across benches. Chains led to each man's wrists. Ulrich stretched his arms self-consciously, imagining chains restricting him, binding him, taking away his freedom. The archer's bow twanged again, and an arrow shaft slid across the night to glance harmlessly against Ulrich's armored shoulder, spinning crazily off into the darkness.

Ulrich snapped out of his reverie and turned toward the man who had fired. Ulrich was in the waist of the ship, and Ejnar stood alongside the archer at the stern. Between Ulrich and the pirate leader were four men, two loading a crate down into the bowels of the vessel and two standing guard with drawn weapons. Toward the ship's bow on the opposite side were three Frisian warriors who advanced with swords raised.

Enraged at the sight of the enslaved humanity around him, heedless of the danger of the archer, and seeing only his foe, Ulrich stalked down the narrow gangway between rowers' benches toward Ejnar. The two men who had been loading the crate stopped to draw swords and block his path. The archer's bow twanged again, and Ulrich swore and ducked. The arrow flew mere inches from his head to clatter harmlessly on the deck. Meanwhile, the three Frisians from the ship's bow closed in with weapons held high.

Ulrich was trapped. He swung at the men blocking his path, but his axe was parried by one of the Frisian warriors. Sensing danger to his rear, Ulrich turned and swung at the enemy coming up from behind. His weapon swished through empty air as the closest danced away. Raised swords advanced from both sides. Anger and frustration rose to lump in Ulrich's throat. Suddenly the nearest enemy warrior staggered and fell, tripped by an oar. More oars thrust toward the Frisian warriors, jabbing them in the sides, the bellies, and the legs. They did no serious damage, but they slowed Ulrich's attackers, who turned to hack in retribution at the sea of bound slaves around them.

Ulrich grinned with savage triumph. Raising his axe high, he brought it down on the nearest chain. For each bench, a single heavy chain led from an iron ring set in the deck amidships, through rings set in the slaves' shackles, and out to a final fixture near each oar port. He cut down again and again, and each of Ulrich's swings shattered links, freeing an entire bench of rowers. A cheer rose from the slaves as shackled hands reached for their slavers, dragging them down into a sea of gaunt faces and terrible starved wrath. The nearest Frisian warriors, kicking, screaming, and flailing wildly with their weapons, were pulled to the deck by grasping hands. Ulrich ignored them and dashed along the gangway, pushing his way through the nearly naked bodies of the rioting slaves to bring his axe down again and again until the deck swarmed with newly freed men. Most rose to their feet, fire in their eyes, to leap into the fray, brandishing oars, lengths of chain, or just wielding unbridled fury at their captors. Some just stood and stretched, rubbing their still-shackled wrists or atrophied legs, so long unused. A few, the eldest, sat blankly, broken shells of men, blinking with confusion at the violence that swirled around them.

Slaves rushed down into the lower deck of the ship, and screams issued from the hatches. In the bows, the slaves quickly overwhelmed the few slavers who stood their ground. In the stern, three Frisians still stood, swords red to the hilt with blood as they thrust and slashed at the slaves penning them in. The archer stood behind them, firing wildly into the mass of humanity. Ejnar was beside the archer. Safe behind his men, he watched the chaos. He caught Ulrich's eye and gave a wry smile. He made an elaborate shrug and lifted his hands, spreading his fingers as if to concede some minor argument, then he turned away. The pirate loosened his collar and started disrobing, tugging his chainmail shirt over his head.

Ulrich was having difficulty pushing through the crowd. The gangway was packed with freed slaves. Some were crowding in to join the battle at the stern. Others were looting the dead Frisians, pulling off their armor and using teeth and fingernails to tear apart the seams of their clothes, looking for hidden jewels or silver. Seeing that the aisle down the center of the ship was impassable, Ulrich leapt to the rowers' benches and began to vault toward the stern, jumping the gaps between benches and over discarded oars. As he was making his way back, he saw an oar flash out of the crowd and come crashing down on the head of the leftmost Frisian swordsman defending the stern. The warrior fell to his knees, stunned. As he attempted to rise, two slaves, barehanded and clad only in loose, dirty sackcloth shifts, wrestled the sword out of his grasp. They turned the slaver's own sword on him, cheering as they stabbed him through the ribs. The remaining two Frisian swordsmen edged backward. They were joined by the archer who, out of arrows but not lacking in courage, threw down his bow and drew his sword. Meanwhile, Ejnar, behind them, crouched to pull off his leather boots.

An ill-judged leap brought Ulrich down on a loose oar, lying discarded on a bench. The smooth wood rolled under his boot, and he stumbled, his momentum carrying him forward to thump, chest first into the next bench. Unhurt but grunting in frustration, Ulrich scrambled back to his feet to see Ejnar, barefoot now and clad only in a thin wool shirt and brown leather pants, walk to the rail at the stern of the craft. As the pirate climbed the wooden railing, Ulrich hefted his axe, judged the distance, and threw with all his strength. The flying axe was wide by inches, and the heavy blade thudded deep into the wood of the rail as Ejnar, without a backward glance, threw himself headfirst from the doomed ship. He arced into the water in a graceful swan dive.

Ulrich could not hear the splash over the commotion, but he rushed to the side to see Ejnar, long pale hair streaming out behind him, swim swiftly off into the darkness.

CHAPTER NINE

Wiglaf arrived at the dock to find an astonishing scene. In the river, the great red ship burned, and the former slaves looked on from the safety of the bank. All emotion spent, they stood or sat as they could on wooden crates piled on the shore or simply squatted on the ground, watching the ship slowly revolve as it was pulled deeper into the current. Ulrich sat a short way apart from the crowd, his great axe driven blade-deep into the soil. His eyes followed Wiglaf as he approached, but he did not attempt to rise. He felt exhausted.

"What happened?" Wiglaf asked.

Ulrich did not know what to say at first; he merely waved a hand at the scene in front of him. Then, after a moment's thought, he did his best to explain. By the time Ejnar had escaped into the river the fighting was drawing to a close. The few remaining Frisian slavers, even seeing their leader flee, never attempted to surrender. One died where he stood—pulled down into the surging mass of enraged slaves. The final two turned to leap over the side. The first did not make it; he was grabbed from behind as he attempted to clamber over the ship's railing. The final warrior made it into the water, dropping over the stern to fall heavily into the river below, but encumbered as he was with heavy iron chainmail, he sank immediately, never to resurface.

Female slaves, their value not to be wasted in pulling an oar, had been stored in the cargo hold below decks, penned together like cattle. Amid that carnage, as the screams of the slavers rang through the ship, sweet reunions were made. Father and daughter, husband and wife, mother and son, they clung to each other as they scrambled

45

out of the dank, fetid hold, up into the light and away from the horror of enslavement.

Some grabbed what loot they could carry. The first slave to the captain's cabin was a slight, young Saxon who found a small chest filled to the brim with gleaming silver coins. Anxious over the danger that greed can engender even in his companions, he ripped the shirt from his body and wrapped it around the wooden crate, disguising the plunder beneath the cheap sackcloth. Naked and bearing his hidden treasure, he turned and ran out the door, slipping unmolested through the chaos and straight out into the night. Other slaves grabbed sacks of grain, reams of fabric, even loose chunks of iron ore. The bodies of the slavers were stripped where they lay.

It had been mayhem, a mad scramble driven by men who had been forced to sit and row for months and months. Given the opportunity to stand and walk, they leapt, and they ran. Ulrich had retrieved his axe then stood befuddled amidst the confusion, unsure of what to do next. The old and weak were already being helped off the ship by those only marginally less so. Ulrich saw the young boy with blond hair stoop to gently lift an old man to his feet. He helped the old man to the side of the boat where helpful hands carried him down the wooden plank to the dock. As soon as he had discharged the old man, the boy turned around to help others. The weight of oppression gone, freed slaves worked together, tending to the wounded and counting their blessings. Even the bodies of the fallen slaves, killed in the fighting, were respectfully carried to shore. Several of the braver townspeople, having witnessed the overthrow, had come down from the town to help.

"Then we torched the boat," Ulrich said to Wiglaf. "There was nothing left."

As the crowd thinned, a dark hand had reached up, wielding a ball of shimmering fire. At first Ulrich had thought that the man had somehow become covered in charcoal dust. He was as dark as night from head to toe; even his thick hair was the color of pitch. This strange man had stood in the waist of the ship with a lit torch held high. His teeth were bared in a grimace and gleamed startlingly white from a dark face. His deep brown eyes were fixed on Ulrich, as though waiting for an order. Ulrich had quickly realized what the man was asking and held his arms forward, palms up, for the man to wait. The deck was clear, but Ulrich climbed down the companionway into the hold to do a final check. He needed to ensure the ship was evacuated before they burned it. It had taken his eyes a few seconds to adjust to the uncommon gloom of the hold. There were, indeed, still two people down here. At the far end of the passage the blond youth was struggling to lift an elderly woman to her feet. The woman was conscious, but weak and emaciated, and Ulrich strode to them quickly. He lifted the woman easily and placed her gently over one shoulder, carrying her up the ladder. He passed her to a strong Saxon townsman on the pier and bellowed for all to stand clear from the ship. Once he was satisfied that none remained save him and the black man, he turned and nodded his assent. The dark-skinned man smashed a whale-oil lamp on the deck and tossed the lit torch onto the flammable spill. The fire spread quickly. Ulrich and the black man returned to the quay, slashed through the mooring ropes, and allowed the hated boat to drift away.

As Ulrich told the story, Wiglaf gazed at the conflagration. The rushing tide of the hectic day was beginning to ebb. A weariness descended upon Wiglaf, and he rubbed his bruised wrists where the Frisians had bound him. He wondered at the boundless cruelty of this world and at what amusement the gods must have at the pain of man. He looked sideways at Ulrich and saw a man who was proud and strong, who sat as inscrutable, blooded, and unconquered as the great lords of his bloodline. Yes, Wiglaf thought to himself, this must be how the world was meant to be: Through victory in battle we bring honor to our forefathers and earn our right to sit at the feast hall in the afterlife. The new religion of the Christian priests claimed that glory was earned through humility, through peace and weakness, but their feeble God had no place on the field of battle. In this world, strength of arms was the only commandment.

With a fresh, wry smile Ulrich turned to Wiglaf. "I cannot believe that skinny bastard got away," he said, shaking his head.

Wiglaf laughed aloud. "That 'skinny bastard' nearly killed you," he exclaimed, and the somber mood was broken.

"And I, him," Ulrich grinned back.

Wiglaf snorted at that. "You got lucky," he retorted. "Next time be better. Next time be so skillful that you don't have to rely on luck."

They turned as two men and a boy approached, climbing the gentle slope to where Wiglaf and Ulrich sat. With a cheerful expression the giant Sigmund led, followed by two former slaves clothed in sackcloth. First came the blond youth, who plopped down in the grass with an expectant look. After him was the mysterious ebony man, who knelt before Ulrich, knees and palms pressed into the dirt, head downturned.

"What is this?" Ulrich asked.

"No idea. Maybe he dropped something?" Sigmund joked.

"Stand man. You don't need to kneel to me," Ulrich said. He was embarrassed by this deference. The dark man responded with several quick words in a language Ulrich could not comprehend. "Stand up, friend. Tell us your name. Do you speak German?" Ulrich asked.

The man stood. He was tall and gaunt, thin from his time as a slave, but his eyes were bright with genuine humor. "I am Tau, and I thank you for freeing me. I am impressed to meet such a formidable warrior." With a smile, he stepped forward and grasped Ulrich's right hand with his own, palm to palm. "I owe you a great debt, warrior. While I am without home or gifts, my spear and my shield are yours."

He spoke German fluently, and his voice was rich and deep as though it came from a much larger man. After clasping palms, Tau pulled his hand away with a foreign gesture, snapping his fingers to his palm as he did so.

Ulrich frowned, "I appreciate the offer of your spear and shield, but I am no lord, and I have nothing to give in return." He turned to Wiglaf with eyebrows raised. Tau stepped to Wiglaf with hand outstretched, repeating the snapping handshake.

"If you are willing to plow a field and to seed and harvest grain, you are welcome in our home." Wiglaf said to Tau. "We have more land to till then we have men to work it." He turned to Ulrich. "You would be wise to accept the help you are offered. This will not be your last battle."

Ulrich nodded in respectful acquiescence. He turned to the blond youth. "What about you? Where are you from?"

The boy's face fell. "I have no home. My parents died, and my village was burned," he said. "They call me Rag." His eyes fixed on the patch of grass before his feet.

Wiglaf kneeled in front of the boy. "You are welcome in our home as well, son. Can you hunt or fish?" He asked.

Rag shook his head miserably. He looked as though he might cry. Wiglaf tousled the boy's lanky hair. "That's okay, boy. We will teach you." He smiled, and Rag grinned back through tears that welled in his blue eyes.

Sigmund coughed politely. "Pardon me," he said, "I don't mean to be the one asking the awkward questions here, but is this man the actual devil?" His eyes considered Tau with a playful humor.

Tau laughed, a rich melodic sound. He started to express denial, but Sigmund gave a broad grin to show that he was joking. Ulrich examined Tau's ebony visage. Indeed, he had never seen any person with skin as dark before; even in the height of summer, no German skin ever got as tanned as this. The man looked as if he had been spawned from a shadow itself; he would positively disappear in the settling dusk.

"He will terrify our enemies," Ulrich said cheerfully.

"Wonderful to meet you, Tau. I am named Sigmund," the big man said. Tau, smiling, approached and repeated his rapid, snapping handshake.

"Hey, that was neat," Sigmund exclaimed. "Wait, wait! Come back. Let's try that again." Tau showed him the gesture again, and Sigmund copied it clumsily, snapping his own fingers against Tau's as they pulled away. "Okay, all right, I think we can be friends," Sigmund said jovially.

Ulrich noticed Wiglaf inexplicably grinning at him. "What?" Ulrich asked, feeling suddenly self-conscious.

"Your father," Wiglaf explained. "He too had a penchant for making friends in the strangest places."

Ulrich smiled. He glanced at the rising moon, hoping nobody noticed him brush away an unexpected tear. "Come on," he said. "Let's go home."

CHAPTER TEN

That summer was mild and productive. Between Ulrich, Sigmund, and Tau, acres of dense woods were cleared and put to the plow. Wiglaf oversaw the extension of their home with additional rooms, and Ulrich honed his woodworking skills with beds and chests for the new members of the family. Green barley shoots sprouted from the soft loam, and the wheat grew thick and tall.

One warm day Sigmund, out playing with Ælfwine and Gebhard, discovered a rabbit den on the edge of the field. Johanne gathered green onions in anticipation of rabbit stew, but her appetite was disappointed when the gentle-hearted giant intervened. The curious mother rabbit, trailed by her four tiny brown kits, had nuzzled the big Saxon's foot, and Sigmund fell in love with the tiny beasts. He and the children brought them dandelions from the fields, and Ulrich built them a sturdy wooden cage by the house where they would be safe from foxes and hawks.

The resilience of youth was strong in Rag and the energetic boy took quickly to his new family. Ulrich taught young Rag how to bend hooks and make bait, but to his chagrin the boy soon out-fished him. Whether it was just luck or something in the way he flicked his line, Rag could somehow always manage to bring in twice his catch. The larder was continually stocked with freshly smoked trout and river perch. The boy had not known when his birthday was, so Wiglaf decreed it to be the summer solstice, and on that day they threw him a feast. For a treat Johanne cooked a sweet porridge flavored with cream, almond, and roasted apple. That night he found a delicately carved wooden fish on his pillow, left by Ulrich, and he held it when he slept, holding it carefully away from his face so the tears of happiness would not spoil the yellow ochre with which it was painted.

Rag idolized Ulrich, which was obvious to everybody except Ulrich himself. The boy followed the reticent Ulrich wherever he went. He mimicked his axe practice with a stick that he swung against a tree. He pretended to be the big brother to Ælfwine and Gebhard, watching over them with mock sternness as they played in the yard just like he saw Ulrich do. He even copied the way Ulrich hunched over his bowl, slurping down his supper stew with only nominal use of his spoon. Johanne thought that this was adorable, and she encouraged it, even calling him Little Ulrich when Ulrich was not in earshot. Ulrich, meanwhile, would likely not have noticed even if she had, and tolerated the boy's company with the same pragmatic stoicism with which he approached all things in his life.

Meanwhile, Tau's favorite days were spent bow hunting far afield, camping with his companions under the stars, and bringing home deer and boar for the family. It was an idyllic summer, and the family prospered. But even in the midst of this peaceful existence, Wiglaf was canny. He did not know from whence the next threat would come, but he knew that battle was a part of life, and the next fight was never far away. He believed too that Ulrich's eventual fate would be to reclaim his father's lost kingdom, and he insisted that Sigmund and Tau learn the rudiments of battle. He worked diligently to provide them with weapons and mail, and he drilled them daily. Even young Rag would soon have to learn to fight.

As the town of Brunswick recovered from the brutal Frisian raid, life went back to normal.

CHAPTER ELEVEN

Ulrich froze as a scream pierced the morning sky, interrupting a pleasantly warm fall dawn. He and Wiglaf were sharpening reaping scythes in preparation for the year's harvest, a tedious job of which even Rag grew bored and would wander off, but the cry broke loud over the strident squeal of the grindstone. Ulrich dropped the scythe, threw open the wooden door of the blacksmith's shack, and rushed out into the yard. Perhaps a dozen strangers on horseback were visible in the far distance, riding hard to the south. One seemed to be carrying a large bundle thrown across his saddle. Without a backward glance, they crested a low hill and were lost to sight. Johanne was running toward the shop.

"They took Rag," she shouted as she ran.

"Who?" Ulrich asked.

"I don't know. I don't know, but they were speaking German," Johanne responded in a rush.

Ulrich's thoughts raced, but his hesitation lasted only an instant. The family owned only two horses, Hod and Mule, and neither would be able to run down the fast-galloping war mounts that he had glimpsed. "Find Tau and Sigmund." He told Johanne. "Tell them what happened. Tell them to bring their weapons and armor and to follow the road. They can take Mule and the big cart."

His heavy war axe was propped against the wall just inside the shop. Ulrich stepped back inside and snatched it up. Wiglaf still sat at the sharpening wheel, although he had stopped his work to look up with an expression of concern.

Wiglaf took stock of the situation quickly. "Never go to a fight without armor," he warned, reading Ulrich's thoughts.

"There's no time," Ulrich said brusquely, stepping out of the doorway. "Stay with the family. I'm going after them." Unknown men had taken Rag. He did not know who they were or why they had done this, but he was not about to let them escape. He ran, leather cowhide boots pounding on the cobbles of the old Roman road. Two hundred paces later he cut left, climbing the grassy hill where he had last sighted the kidnappers. The hoof prints of their horses were dug deep into the turf where they had ascended before him. He paused to catch his breath as he crested the hill. The horsemen were nowhere in sight, but he could see where they had gone, as the trampled undergrowth gave clear sign of their passage. He continued to jog along their trail, noting that the hoof prints had become shallower and closer together as they descended from the top of the hill. This meant that the horsemen had slowed to a trot once they were out of sight. As he had suspected, the trail led back down to the Roman road, where he followed it south.

The road ran, as all Roman roads did, along the high ground, avoiding dense woods and other places prone to ambuscade. It curved along farmsteads and over a series of small creeks by way of small, elegantly crafted stone bridges. Ulrich fell into a comfortable running stride, moving as quickly as he could maintain. The day was warming as the sun rose from the horizon. He trotted along the road, heavy axe clutched in his sweating palm. He had run for a long time and was breathing hard by the time he smelled the blood.

The smell was harsh, metallic in his nostrils, and he stopped. His eyes searched until he found a smear of red in the grass beside the causeway. Dense shadows from the easterly woodland lay across the road, and the fresh bloody trail was dark. He hopped off the road to follow it. The road ran over a small stone bridge, and under it, Ulrich found the crumpled body of an old man. There was a raw gash across the old man's scalp from where a blow had caved in his skull. Ulrich knelt to check if any life remained. There was none, but the body was still warm and the wound was fresh. Suddenly, from a thick copse of trees, he heard the whinny and stamp of a horse. He spun, raising his axe and fearing that a sudden rush of mounted men would burst upon him from the trees.

After a long, tense, moment, nothing happened. He approached the copse to find a slight depression in the ground that hid three riderless horses tied to low branches alongside a narrow path. These were all large, fast beasts, well laden with sacks and pouches for a long journey. No local farmer would have use of such expensive animals; these horses were bred for war. He recognized the trappings, sure that these three belonged to members of the same raiding party that had taken Rag. To his right was the muddy bank of the same small river that ran under the stone bridge. In the river shallows, there were several empty fish traps just paces away from a well-used, stone fire pit. To his left was a narrow path, and he followed it. It led to a clearing that contained a small barn and a modest wooden cottage. He walked toward the small cottage, axe held low, taking care to tread on the soft turf beside the path, avoiding the telltale crunch of dry leaves beneath his boots.

He paused at the door. He could hear sounds from inside, there was muffled sobbing. A man laughed. Ulrich took a deep breath and slammed his shoulder into the unbarred door, it crashed open, thumping heavily into the wooden wall, and Ulrich burst into the room. He discovered three men attempting to rape a naked woman. She was struggling against them, her mouth bound with a wad of fabric. Two men held her spread-eagled on the floor while a third had dropped his pants. The men stared at the newcomer wide eyed, frozen with surprise.

A hot rage overtook Ulrich. He moved quickly, axe coming up fast in a powerful backhand swing. The sharpened blade struck the nearest man in the midriff, cutting deeply into his unprotected belly and lifting him bodily off the earthen floor. He flew backward screaming, striking the wall high before crashing to the ground. The two other men had let go of the woman and were reaching for the swords at their waists. The nearest stood to Ulrich's left, right arm crooked to grasp his sword hilt, and Ulrich's fierce return swing caught the man in that arm, ripping it clean off at the elbow. The man spun, falling to the floor as his severed forearm, still grasping his sword, was flung to the far corner of the room. The third man made a desperate attempt to lunge his sword into Ulrich's face, but was hampered by the woman, who had grasped his ankles, binding him in place. The man stumbled, and before he could recover Ulrich stepped forward. With contemptuous ease, Ulrich brought his axe down on the man's skull, splitting it open in a spray of blood and gray matter.

Just as quickly as it had started, the fight was over. It could not have lasted more than a few seconds, but three bodies littered the room as the woman climbed to her feet, spitting out the wad of fabric that had been used to gag her. She looked furious. Two of the men lay still; but the man with the severed arm was moving. He sat up and stared in disbelief at his severed stump, which was dripping blood.

The woman was named Ima, and she was livid. These laughing thieving bastards had attacked her grandfather and then thought to try and rape her. No reason could penetrate the red fog of her fury. She stooped and snatched up the amputated arm from the dirt floor. With a powerful wrenching tug, she ripped the sword from its dead grasp. Cursing, shaking with rage, she stalked toward the last wounded man, who with his remaining hand, backed feebly into the corner, whimpering. His breeches turned dark and wet as he pissed himself.

Ulrich stepped between her and the wounded man. "Wait," he said placatingly. He held his arms wide and dropped his axe. It thumped heavily onto the rushes. "His companions kidnapped my friend. I need to know where they are going." His voice was reasonable and pleading, and she paused, eyes flicking from Ulrich to the man on the floor. He took advantage of her hesitation to turn to the wounded man, looming over him.

"Quickly! Speak to me before you die. Where are your friends going?" Ulrich demanded. "And what do they want with the boy?"

The man whimpered in response. "Please don't kill me." He spoke in German but with a strange accent that Ulrich could not place. "Please! I'll tell you whatever you want to know. Just let me live." There were tears in the man's eyes.

Ima, still naked, was fidgeting impatiently with the sword, and Ulrich squatted low, coming level with the man, leaning in toward his face. The man's eyes looked like those of a wounded animal, confused, afraid, and in pain. Ulrich felt sorry for him.

"I will make no promises. Just tell me what you know," Ulrich said. He felt shame at harboring pity for the bandit. The man did not deserve it.

"South! We're going south," the man stammered.

Ulrich growled.

"Toward Kassel. That is where Chnodomar is," the man continued.

"Kassel?" Ulrich asked. "What is that?"

"The King of the Alemanni gathers his forces there. Kassel is his headquarters. He has claimed the lands of Germany." He spoke in a rush.

Ulrich frowned. Kassel. Chnodomar. Alemanni. The names meant nothing to him, but he had what he needed. The men who had taken Rag were continuing south, so that is the direction he would go.

"One last question," Ulrich continued. "What do you want with the boy?"

The man's face twisted from fear to an expression of scorn. "He is a Frisian. An inferior race. He will be strung up before our people as a demonstration of our superiority over that weak tribe."

Ulrich stood, and the fear returned to the bandit's eyes. Ulrich turned away. "He is yours," he told the woman.

"Wait... no!" the man screamed; his scream was cut short as the sword in Ima's hand came forward. Ulrich stepped out the door of the cottage. He stood and let his mind go empty. Sunlight washed the eastern horizon with brilliant orange. A gentle breeze rustled the treetops and carried the fresh smell of heather and hay. He rested his axe, the blade still wet with blood, against the side of the cottage. A sudden chirping drew his eyes upward to a pair of robins flitting among the trees. The red-breasted male alighted on a branch and looked down at him cautiously. The smaller, dull female perched on the rim of a small nest, her beak partially open as she fed three tiny, chirping chicks. Ulrich gazed up at them, and stood perfectly still, struck by the fragility of the scene as though it could be shattered by the slightest movement. He held that moment for as long as he could.

The pad of footsteps sounded behind him, and Ulrich turned. The woman stepped out of the cottage. She was clothed now, wearing a blue tunic that hung to her calves. In her hands she held the bloody sword, which she wiped with a cloth rag. She looked to be close to Ulrich in age, perhaps in her early twenties. She was tall and slender with a fair complexion and long blonde hair that she had bound loosely with a leather cord. Her hands were strong and calloused from years of farm work. Her muscular, bare arms were tanned by the sun. She was beautiful, and Ulrich, feeling uncomfortable under the gaze of her intensely blue eyes, looked away.

"My grandfather..." she began, then stopped, unable to complete her thought. There was the edge of hope in her voice. Ulrich realized immediately who he had found under the bridge.

Ulrich shook his head. "I am sorry. He is dead." He gestured toward the road where the broken body of the old man lay. His heart felt heavy. Ima gazed in that direction and said nothing.

"Does anybody else live here?" Ulrich asked, changing the subject.

Ima shook her head. "No, it was just me and him."

The woman stood in silence for a minute. The fiercely proud look had not left her face, but there were tears on her cheeks. "Who are you?" she demanded.

"My name is Ulrich. I live with my family to the north." He picked up his axe and pointed up the Roman road. He frowned, trying to estimate the distance he had run that morning. "Probably five miles that way." He turned back to her. "Those bandits. I don't know who they are or what they want, but they took my friend. They went south from here, and I am going to get him back."

"I am Ima." She responded simply. Ulrich waited for her to offer more, but she did not. She paused. "My grandfather deserves a funeral. Will you help me bury his body?" she asked, her eyes meeting his.

Ulrich fidgeted impatiently. "I need to go south." His answer made him feel ashamed. He shook his head and looked back into her blue eyes. "I have to go after them. I cannot wait."

Her chin jutted out in defiance, and for a moment she looked furious, then she had an idea.

"Give me just a moment," she insisted as she turned back to the cottage. "Go get my grandfather's body. Bring him here," she commanded as she vanished inside.

By the time Ulrich had retrieved the small shattered body of the old man, Ima was back in front of the cottage. She looked ready to travel. A satchel rode on a leather strap across her body, she had a long dark woolen cloak draped over her shoulders, and she was wearing tough, serviceable leather boots.

"This way," she ordered. Ulrich followed her around the cottage to a small shed which sheltered dry stacks of freshly cut firewood.

"Put him there," she said, pointing. He carefully placed the body atop the pile. Mercifully, the old man's eyes were closed.

Ima moved quickly. First, she cleared the ground around the shed of any flammable debris; she did not want the fire to spread. Then, she set about scattering hay and scraps of tinder on the body and between cracks in the wood. When she was satisfied, she produced flint and steel from her satchel and set the hay ablaze. Once the fire was well caught, she stepped back, dropped to her knees, and produced a small wooden hammer on a simple leather cord. For a short minute she held the totem and prayed quietly. Ulrich could not hear the words, but he sat beside her until she was finished.

"What was his name?" he asked, his voice quiet against the crackling flames.

"Hugbert," she said. "The name means bright heart, and that is what he always was to me." Tears flowed down her cheeks. "He was a good man." She choked off a sudden sob then took a deep breath and stood, composing herself. She hung the totem around her neck, hiding it beneath her tunic.

"If you are going after those bastards, I'm coming with you. There were six others, and they will pay for what they have done here," she said. Her voice was firm.

Before Ulrich could respond, a sound made him turn. On the road Mule, the docile horse, stood patiently, hitched to the big hay wagon. Sigmund sat on the driver's bench, and Tau jumped down, running across the pastureland toward them. Ulrich raised a hand in greeting.

"Friends of yours?" Ima asked.

"More like brothers." Ulrich smiled.

Tau stopped a respectful pace away. "What is going on? Is Rag here?" he asked.

"No. He was taken farther south," Ulrich replied. "Ima, this is my friend, Tau."

Few in the German countryside had seen a man with black skin before, and Tau was accustomed to drawing curious stares wherever he went, but to Ima's credit, she did not flinch. She clasped his outstretched hand to receive his customary snapping greeting and warm smile.

"You don't have to come with us—" Ulrich began, addressing Ima.

"The men who killed Hugbert are not here," she interrupted. "I am coming with you until I find them."

Ulrich could tell from her determined expression that further argument would be pointless. They made preparations to leave. Ima and Tau untied the bandits' three horses and led them to the road.

They were still saddled, and heavy with plunder and supplies. Ulrich recovered a small number of assorted coins from the corpses of the three dead men and dragged their bodies into the woods to be left for the wild animals. The bandits' extra weapons and equipment went in the bed of the cart, which already held Ulrich's armor and Tau and Sigmund's chainmail and weapons. Ima kept the sword she had ripped from the bandit's severed arm. It was a big weapon, with a blade somewhat longer than a typical longsword and with a rare two-handed grip. She strapped it diagonally across her back. She mounted the first warhorse. Ulrich and Tau mounted the other horses, and Sigmund drove the cart.

Together they rode south, the smoke of the burning pyre fading behind them.

CHAPTER TWELVE

They rode all day without pause and continued riding as night fell. Some hours after the sun had set, they began to see light on the southern horizon, but it was not the light of dawn. It was the orange light of torches, bouncing off the scattered nighttime clouds. It seemed that they were coming up on a large settlement.

Ima frowned. "I know what is down this road," she said. "I recognize this place."

"What is it?" Ulrich asked.

"There is an old fort here, but it has been abandoned for generations." She paused. "I think the Romans built it." She pointed off the road to the right. "The Roman lands lie to the west across the Rhine. The people who live yet further to the south do much trade with them. They are great silver workers called the Chatti, and I have seen their trading caravans before. But that fortress. It's empty. I don't know why anybody would be there."

"Well, I'm sure this fine gentleman will tell us," Sigmund said lightly. Seated on the tall driving bench of the cart, he could see farther over the gentle rise of the road than his mounted companions.

Ulrich kicked his horse ahead of the slow cart. Sure enough, just up the road was a small guard post at the road's side. It was little more than a few pieces of lumber holding up a slanted thatch roof, but it was enough to shelter two bored-looking men who sat on milking stools. They were illuminated in the light of two torches burning nearby. Beyond them Ulrich could see that the road led to a large earthen fortress, its banked ramparts topped with a freshly-build defensive wall. The newness of the palisade was evident in the greenness of the wood. The gates of the fortress were open, and the light of many torches streamed up from within, reaching up into the night sky like a beacon.

"Stop there," the nearest sentry ordered as Ulrich approached. He stood and spoke in that same strangely accented German as the bandits from earlier. He wore a white tunic over chainmail and had a long sword strapped at his waist. "The toll to enter is two pieces of silver." He glanced at Tau and Ima coming along on horseback, and Sigmund driving the cart behind. "Two pieces for men or horses and four pieces for carts," he corrected. He looked up at Ulrich expectantly.

Ulrich ignored the demand. "What is this place?" he asked brusquely.

The man sighed. "You stand before Kassel, headquarters of the great and powerful Chnodomar and his Alemannic allies." He sounded bored, and mildly annoyed.

Tau rode up alongside Ulrich. The second guard started in surprise, falling off of his stool when he saw Tau's black skin. "What in hell is that?" he exclaimed from the ground. Tau grinned back in answer.

The first man was unfazed. He blinked at Tau passively. "Is there anything else I can help you with?" he asked.

"Did a band of men come through before us? A group of warriors on horseback, carrying a young blonde boy with them," Ulrich demanded. He touched the war axe strapped across his back threateningly.

The man saw the gesture but was unruffled. He kept his arms folded passively on his chest. "Yes, yes," he said. "I do not want any trouble. There were eight men, Chnodomar's men, and a boy trussed up on the saddle. They came through just before sundown and went right into the town." He smiled. "Now are you going to pay the toll or are you going to slice us up with that big scary axe?"

Ulrich, disarmed by the man's calm demeanor, sheepishly reached into his saddlebag and paid with some of the dead bandits' coins. The four companions continued on into the city.

Once through the gates, they could make out the layout of the place. Kassel was shaped like a fat rectangle, and they had entered through the northern gate. The southern rampart bordered a fast-flowing river. There was a second gate there, leading a to Roman, stone bridge stretching over the water and connecting to the paved causeway where it continued south. To the east and west, the wooden palisade stood on earthen ramps, protecting the space within which the town sprawled. Several tall Roman houses of stone marked the center of the fortress town, but the rest of the buildings were timber and thatch in German fashion. It was a busy place; fires burned in hearths and dogs barked. A double row of torches lit the main road through the town. Three children ran into the street in front of Ulrich, and he checked his horse. They laughed as they chased a cat down one of the town's many alleyways.

"Much of this construction looks new," Sigmund remarked, pointing out several houses made of fresh green wood.

"About five years ago my grandfather and I tracked a deer to this place, but all that was here was the ruins of those old Roman buildings in the center." Ima offered.

To the left of the road was a fenced pasture where dozens of horses were picketed. Ulrich led his companions into the field, and they dismounted.

"What now?" Sigmund asked. As if in response, a roar of laughter carried down the street. It came from the largest of the Roman houses and betrayed the presence of a sizable crowd.

Ulrich shrugged. "Let's go see what they are celebrating." They tied off the horses and returned to the road. The Roman causeway was brightly lit by torches, and they followed it deeper into Kassel.

They reached the largest Roman building. No door barred the brilliantly lit open archway of smooth stone. As Ulrich stepped through the entryway, he found himself amazed. This was a feast hall, and it was the most beautiful hall he had ever seen. The broad room of polished marble was lit by countless candles. The floor itself was a decorative mosaic, made of a thousand tiny painted tiles. A massive fire burned in a hearth along one wall, but somehow the room was astonishingly clear of smoke. Indeed, the air was kept fresh and clear by a constant breeze that wafted gently into the room from the open doorway. Colorfully decorated marble columns held up a high vaulted ceiling of intricate plasterwork. Inside was a celebration. Nearly a hundred men drank and sang from the benches of a dozen tables.

The men seated at the tables were astonishing to Ulrich as well. The standard garb of all within was a strikingly clean, white, sleeveless tunic. It was worn belted about the waist and hung to the knees. He could see that many were whitened in spots with chalk that rubbed off on their fellows as they drank and sang. Some men wore sashes of various colors, and a few even wore loose togas of flowing cloth that draped to the floor and were clasped at the shoulder with gaudy bronze rings.

"Are these Romans?" Ulrich asked Sigmund. Neither had ever seen a Roman. Sigmund just shook his head in confusion. Tau and Ima seemed equally baffled. A man at the table nearest them rose suddenly and pushed past Ulrich and his companions to vomit violently in the street. From the way he retched and staggered off, the man seemed unlikely to return. Ulrich, seizing the opportunity, sat in the man's vacated space. The man who sat across the table frowned at Ulrich for a moment then smiled and drunkenly lifted his ale in mock salute. Ulrich scooted sideways on the bench to make space for his friends. It seemed that nobody at the drunken revel had taken much notice of the interlopers.

Ulrich looked around and felt shabby. His rough leather shirt and trousers seemed primitive alongside the bright clean tunics of these men. He stared in amazement at the fireplace. Most German buildings were built in the same way. Stout timbers were fitted closely together beneath roofs of thatch and wattle. Fire-pits, when indoors, meant that the room filled with the dense black smoke that did not all find its way out of the simple hole in the roof. This fireplace, however, was an offset construction of stone beneath a tall chimney into which the smoke seemed to be magically wafted up and away from the room, thus generating light and heat for the occupants but without the choking smoke.

Tau broke into Ulrich's reverie. "While this is all quite fascinating, I am going out to have a look around." Ulrich nodded, and Tau stood, quickly exiting the hall through the front archway. He pushed past another group of drunken revelers that stumbled in. Ima followed him out.

Sigmund, on Ulrich's right, was using both hands while he scarfed down a leg of roast mutton that his oblivious neighbor had left unguarded on a wooden plate. A servant hurriedly placed a large tankard of ale on the table before rushing off again. The genial man across from Ulrich grasped the tankard and offered him a cup. "So where are you from stranger?" the man asked in heavily accented

German.

"Are you Roman?" Ulrich blurted out in response. Despite being just across the frontier from Rome, Ulrich had never visited a Roman town, though he had heard much about them. He knew they had fancy clothes made of linen and lived in stone houses. These men seemed to fit that description.

"Roman?" the man retorted, sounding offended. "Roman?" he repeated louder, and heads at nearby tables turned to look. "Death to Rome!" he shouted suddenly, and the chant was taken up by the men around them. The call grew and was repeated until the whole hall was chanting in unison. "Death to Rome! Death to Rome!" they yelled in their loudest voices.

At the frenzied climax of this commotion, a massive man seated at the head of the largest table rose to his feet. He was an imposing figure, tall and burly with a barrel of a chest and broad shoulders. His long red hair and beard were bright in the candlelight. He raised his hands, and the hall fell silent as King Chnodomar began to speak.

CHAPTER THIRTEEN

Meanwhile, Tau and Ima proceeded cautiously down the road into the darkened town.

"We have to find the boy," Tau said quietly.

Tau was determined to help his friends. Ten years he had pulled an oar as a slave, sold again and again by brutal masters, and his debt of freedom was something that he did not take lightly. Had Ulrich not rescued him he would have died on that oar, worn to nothing like so many others had been.

Tau spoke little of his past, but in truth he was born a prince. He had been raised in the great palace of Koumbi Saleh, capital of the Empire of Awkar, called Ghana by outsiders, and known to all as the land of gold. He remembered elegant towers of stone and orange brick, stretching their brilliant spires far into the heavens. The tall grasses of the savannah waved beneath the African sky. The great desert lay to the north, through which the long camel caravans carried their heavy golden loads.

As a child, golden rings adorned Tau's arms and golden buckles fastened his fine linen robes. His father had been the proud Emperor of a warrior nation. His mother was a gentle woman who had died of a hacking, bloody cough by Tau's tenth birthday. It was his father new wife, Kansoleh, who upon the birth of the son of her own blood, had betrayed him. One night she had paid cruel men to kidnap young Tau and sell him to the harsh slavers of the western coast. The memory of those terrible years was hard, but he resolved to draw from it strength and do his best to help others in need.

Ima, meanwhile, had been acutely uncomfortable in the feast hall. Other than a few servants scurrying about, she had been the only woman in the building. She had been self-conscious of the curious glances that so many of the strangely dressed men threw her way. She was hurt and angry. She hated that these men were celebrating on the night of her grandfather's death. While in the hall she had taken a careful scan of each of the tables, but none of the men who had been present at that murder were seated within. The image of the murderer himself was burned into her mind—a tall, ugly man with a scarred, pinched face. He had sneered as he struck down Hugbert.

Ima had much experience with thoughtless, violent men. A dozen such raiders had killed her parents and burned her farmstead when she was just a child. She had been in training to be a warmaiden. She was learning navigation to flesh out her natural abilities. She was learning sword play and how to handle a shield. But she was still just a child with a wooden sword the first time the bandits attacked. She had survived only because her grandfather had spirited her deep into the woods until the men had gone. Together they had buried the pitifully charred corpses of her family and started again. A small cache of coins, buried deep in the muddy marshland nearby, had been missed by the raiders. They had purchased a few acres far, far away and were promised protection by a local lord in a territory that had been mercifully peaceful for generations.

It was a barbaric and violent age, and Ima had survived thus far by learning to judge men quickly and to judge them well. She saw something that she trusted in Ulrich and his companions. Ulrich himself she judged to be honest, though simple, and perhaps a bit naïve. He was quick to anger, but with a good sense of right and wrong. His clear-headed and straightforward manner made him an easy leader. Sigmund was clever. He spoke much, full of a dry wit and frequent sarcasm. But Ima suspected that his loquacity covered a buried pain, a hurt that he hid beneath a smiling humor. She wondered what it was. Tau was harder to read. He was polite and formal, seeming to have a proper eloquent response and gesture to every circumstance. In him she sensed deep loneliness, one which might be only partly accounted for by being a conspicuous outsider wherever he went.

A noise made her turn. The sound came from beyond a darkened alleyway to her left. The alley ran between two low, wooden dwellings. The alley was empty, but she could see it opened into a dimly lit space beyond the houses. She started cautiously down it,

Tau trailing silently behind her. As they rounded the corner a tragic sight met their eyes.

Three wooden cages stood on three large, unhitched wagons parked on the beaten turf. The cages were filled with people crammed together so tightly that they were forced to stand upright. There seemed to be no rhyme or reason to who was imprisoned here. In the cages were women and men, both young and old. Some were dark haired and others light. They seemed to be drawn from a great number of different tribes and communities. They looked miserable in the confining cages.

A man stepped out of one of the houses on the other side of the yard, candlelight spilling from the suddenly opened door behind. Tau grasped Ima's hand and pulled her into the shadow of some ale barrels stacked against the nearby wall. They were hidden now, and just in time too, for a dozen more men left the house and walked toward the cages.

The first man said something, a joke that Ima could not hear across the yard, and the closest of his comrades laughed. The jest was repeated, and the rest of the men joined in the mirth. The man climbed onto the nearest cart, loosened his tunic, and began urinating into the cage. A small boy was being doused by the stream and tried to pull away, but the cargo of prisoners was so tightly packed that he could not squirm more than a few inches in any direction. The poor child's hair and sackcloth shirt were dripping wet by the time the man was finished. The boy sobbed loudly.

The man buckled his tunic and turned, climbing to the high driving bench of the big cart. He had a deep scar ascending the left side of his pinched, ugly face. Ima growled softly.

"That is him," she told Tau in a whisper. "That is the man who killed Hugbert." She fingered the hilt of the big sword still strapped across her back, but she did not move. Thirteen men were too many for the two of them to take alone.

"And there is Rag, our friend," Tau responded, pointing to where the boy stood, his back to them, crammed into the nearest cage.

The scarred man spoke, this time loudly enough for Ima to hear. "Weaklings!" he addressed the captives. "You know why you are here. You are here because you were unable to defend yourselves. Your men," he spat indiscriminately into the nearest cage. "are weak. You women, you children and those of you who are pathetically old,

67

your warriors have failed you. You are Chatti, you are Frisian, you are Saxon, and you are Cheruski." He thumped his chest. "But we are the Alemanni. Our tribe is stronger than your tribe, and for that reason, you will die tomorrow." He pointed at a pile of rough-cut logs piled haphazardly in the corner of the yard. "You will be strung up on these posts as a demonstration of the weakness of your people for all to see. Our blades will cut into your bellies, and the ravens will pick the dead eyes out of your skulls." He could see that his words were having a terrifying effect on the captives. He was enjoying himself. He laughed.

At the same time across the town another speech was taking place. Chnodomar was addressing his men. "Companions!" King Chnodomar roared to the feast hall, "Suebi, Alemanni, who are we?"

"Alemanni!" the hall shouted back in unison.

"We are the heirs to all Germania and the conquerors of the Roman legions." He continued bombastically. "Feast and drink my champions. You have earned it."

The hall cheered, and men raised their cups and tankards toward their chieftain.

Red-haired Chnodomar continued. "Together we conquered the weak Chatti. Their women are now our playthings, and their men are now our slaves. Soon, all the weak tribes of Germania shall fall. Our allies, the Marcomanni and the Buri, shall bear witness to our triumph. They will be impressed when they see the captives taken by our brave warriors."

This drew another cheer from the crowd. Chnodomar waited for it to die down before continuing. "When they see our fallen foes strung high, all will know the weakness of our enemies and the strength of the Alemanni. None shall defy us. And once we own Germania," he reached to the table and grasped a greasy beef bone. He held it over his head like a club. "We shall destroy Rome. They shall pay dearly for the lies of the treacherous Caracalla. They shall pay for the subjugation of our people. At the points of our spears, they shall bathe in their own blood." He took the thick beef bone in both hands and effortlessly snapped it in half to the roaring of the crowd.

Ulrich and Sigmund decided it was time to leave. Amid the uproar they inconspicuously left the hall to find Ima and Tau waiting for them in the street. All four ducked into a nearby alley, and Ima explained what she and Tau had seen. Ulrich grunted. He unslung his axe, but Ima grabbed his arm.

"We cannot just charge in there." She said, sounding exasperated. "There are thirteen guards, and even if we could fight them all, the sound of fighting would raise the alarm. We need a plan," her eyes narrowed. "And we are going to save them all. Not just Rag but all of the men, women, and children held captive in those cages."

CHAPTER FOURTEEN

Ima explained what they had to do. She pointed out that the Alemanni had scores of men patrolling the high-timber palisade about Kassel, but those men were looking outwards, not in. The doors of the fortress city were thrown wide open, because in truth, the Alemanni had little to fear. They had struck hard and fast into this land, and few of the local kingdoms were even aware of the growing threat. It was now some time after midnight, and the revelers would soon stumble drunkenly back to their beds. Ima had read the arrogance on the Alemanni faces and knew that, as the night wore on, the guards' vigilance would be tempered by drink and hubris. Thus, part one of the plan was to wait a while until the majority of the town fell asleep.

The second part of the plan would address a danger foreseen by Ulrich. No matter how they wanted to escape, they could be ridden down if the Alemanni had use of their horses. They briefly discussed loosing the beasts from the paddock and driving them toward the open countryside, but that plan could be easily countered by any quick-minded guard simply closing the town gates, and besides, the commotion would awaken the Alemanni to their plan as quickly as a noisy attack on the guards. Sigmund had a solution to this problem. They could pen the horses in right where they stood, and he offered his massive strength to that task.

Finally, there was the logistics of the actual escape of the prisoners. Tau, sympathetic to the sight of men and women in chains, suggested cutting them from their bonds in the yard, but Ima wisely pointed out that dozens of men and women fleeing Kassel would be conspicuous. To do this right, they needed subtlety, and though a handful of wagons leaving before first light would be suspicious, it was certainly less obvious than a ragtag huddle of nervous prisoners rushing the gates. The captives would have to stay in the carts until they were safely out of town.

Thus, after the noise of the great celebration had died down, as the torches guttered in their sconces, and as the overconfident defenders of the fortress dozed, Ulrich and Sigmund worked. The stable pasture was surrounded by a great semicircle of new wooden fence. There were only two gates through which the pasture could be accessed, and they blocked both of them. In the wake of so much new construction, extra lumber, mostly in the form of rough-cut logs, was piled in the space between the palisade and the pasture. Mercifully, it seemed that not a single man was tasked to patrol the pasture itself, so the two men went undisturbed. They painstakingly dragged the heavy logs to bar the two gates, and at least temporarily, trap the Alemanni horses where they were. Ulrich and Sigmund wedged the logs together as they piled them, knowing that even a few minutes gained on their pursuers might be just the time they would need to escape.

After he finished, Ulrich untied Mule from Wiglaf's old farm cart. The old, slow mare had no place in a potentially violent cross-country chase, and so with a heavy heart, he left her behind. The old horse looked confused, sadness in her big brown eyes as she followed her master to the fence. Ulrich patted her fondly on the nose.

"No, girl, you have to stay here," he said. She had been a patient and gentle beast, and Ulrich knew he would likely never see her again. "I am sorry," he said, scratching her behind the ears. He gathered their equipment from the cart and turned to go, unable to meet Mule's hurt, questioning gaze.

While Sigmund and Ulrich worked on their task, Ima and Tau led four spare warhorses through the back alleys. Three were the same mounts they had taken from the raiders before, still saddled and packed with gear and plunder, the fourth was a strong stallion taken from the yard, replete with a wide saddle and capacious, though empty, forage nets. Together they returned to where the prisoners were waiting in their cruel cages. Leaving the mounts tied in the street nearby, Ima and Tau crept toward the yard to reconnoiter. From the ale barrels, no guards were visible, so the two of them gingerly circled the yard, eyes searching the shadows for any armed men. Many of the prisoners in the cages appeared to be sleeping while standing, leaning propped against each other in the tight cages. In the nearest cage, a man and a woman, holding each other as they stood, shifted uncomfortably. The woman opened her eyes and saw Ima creeping around the edge of the yard. The woman's mouth opened as if to speak, but Ima put her finger to her mouth, gesturing for silence. The woman complied, but she gently shook awake her dozing partner. One by one all the prisoners opened their eyes, silently watching Ima and Tau with curiosity. Rag, in the nearest cage, smiled and gave a small wave when he recognized Tau.

When Ima circled to the other end of the yard she saw her enemy. There were only six men now, and they lay on cloaks spread on the dry ground under the shelter of a low thatch overhang. The scene was lit only by the dying embers of a red cooking fire and by the pale sheen of the half-moon, breaking through the clouds. There was no evidence of the rest of the men she had seen mocking the prisoners. All six men looked comfortable, peaceful; the nearest was snoring gently. For a moment she hesitated; then she found the scarred ruthless man who had killed her grandfather, and her resolve hardened. She slowly drew her long sword from its cloth-lined scabbard. She pointed to the scarred man.

"That one is mine," she whispered to Tau.

Tau had hesitated too. He had never considered himself to be a violent man. Although he had often prayed for the violent deaths of many slavers through the years, his first true fight had been that spring when Ulrich had burst onto the deck of the red ship. Ulrich had been a raving berserker, carving a bloody path through his captors to free Tau from slavery. During that frantic melee, Tau had fought two men with a broken oar, beating down one who had attacked him directly and killing another who had threatened a fellow slave with a blood-soaked sword. That summer, Wiglaf had insisted that he train, teaching him to wield the sword and carry the shield in the Saxon way. Tau, however, had discovered that he was fast. What he lacked in Ulrich's brute strength, he made up for in lightning-quick reflexes.

As he had trained, Tau had quickly come to hate the heavy encumbering shield. He had experimented instead with carrying two swords, one in each hand. These swords were long, slim, and light, recovered from the heap of weapons taken from the Frisian slavers.

Wiglaf, acting as their trainer, had at first been unconvinced. Wiglaf had fought in the traditional shield wall the Saxons had learned from the Romans, a brutal, confining battlefield where speed meant little, and the fragile-looking longswords had little place there. It was only when Tau had demonstrated his skill that Wiglaf gave his begrudging acceptance. Tau had sparred against both Ulrich and Sigmund at once. They had started by advancing toward him with shields raised, but he danced into them, dodging their wooden cudgels with ease as he tapped Ulrich on the helm with a mock wooden sword. He circled around Sigmund before the bigger man could turn, and Tau pushed him firmly from behind until the big man stumbled.

Wiglaf had nodded then. "You are fast. You're a natural fighter. But never forget your shield. When the time comes for war, nobody fights alone."

Today, Tau was carrying his two longswords. He had them sheathed at his belt, and he touched them lightly as he looked down at the men he would have to kill. Like Ima, he too had hesitated, but he could feel the eyes of the imprisoned men and women rest on him as they waited in their misery. Failure to act now would doom them all. He unsheathed his swords deliberately and stepped amidst the sleeping enemy.

Ima was standing over the scarred man who had killed her grandfather. She dropped one knee onto his chest. She wrapped her free hand over his mouth to silence him and slapped his face with the flat of her sword blade. His eyes snapped open in surprise.

"You remember me, don't you?" she asked him. She watched the recognition dawn on his face as her sword slid into his throat. She shoved down hard until she could feel the blade grate on bone. He died quickly and silently. Most importantly, he knew why he died. Ima felt a surge of relief. Her grandfather's death was avenged.

Tau was not so clean with his kill. The first man he stabbed squealed in surprise and suddenly all the guards were waking. They sat up and scrabbled at sword hilts, pushing away blankets as they rose. Tau, silently cursing himself for his mistake, moved fast. His blades darted like lightning into the rising men. He aimed for mouths and throats, ambidextrous hands stabbing with both swords. His pulse raced as he danced among the men. Ima wielded her big sword in both hands, swinging like the warmaiden she had trained so long to be. In a matter of seconds, it was over. He and Ima stood with bloodied swords, and six men lay twitching and dying on the turf. Tau and Ima were trembling, blood pumping in their ears as they strained to hear. Had the noise of the scuffle betrayed their plans? Surely the town guard would soon come running. After an anxious, silent moment, they whirled to face the sound of boots thumping on turf, only to sigh with relief as Ulrich and Sigmund jogged breathlessly into the yard.

Sigmund stopped, momentarily stunned at the sight of the bloody bodies. Tau glanced at Ima as he cleaned and sheathed his blades.

"This death was necessary," Tau said. He knew he spoke the truth, but he still felt numb. There was little honor in this fight; the guards had stood no chance. He turned to the packed prisoners, who stared with wide eyes. Rag stood quietly, gripping the bars in the farthest cage. He looked miserable but appeared to be unhurt.

"You did well," Ulrich commended soberly.

Sigmund led the horses into the yard as Ima spoke to the prisoners in a low voice.

"We are going to get you out of here," she said. "We have to keep you in the cages until we leave the town, but, with luck, you will all be able to go home soon. It is vital that you stay silent until we are past the gates."

Fortunately, the big wagons were still hung with traces and harnesses. Tau and Ulrich helped Sigmund hitch the horses as Ima introduced her companions to the huddled prisoners. Tau's dark skin drew many curious glances, but the prisoners were grateful, and they stayed quiet and compliant.

Once the wagons were hitched up, Ima decorated the three cages with the cloaks and bedrolls of the dead guards in an attempt to hide their true nature. The convoy looked odd, a blocky mass of furs and fabric atop three tall carts, but Ulrich hoped that nobody would inspect them too closely this dark night. Tau and Sigmund donned their chainmail and checked their weapons. Ima found the dead guard closest in size to her own and took his mail coat. She pulled it over her head as Ulrich donned his heavy armored cuirass and strapped his axe across his back. Ulrich went to the street and mounted the last warhorse. Ima, Sigmund, and Tau each climbed to a driving bench of the prison carts and followed.

When they reached the main street, Ulrich was about to turn north and retrace their path out of the town when he changed his mind. He held up a hand.

"We go south," he called back softly.

They had intended to go north, but Ulrich was struck with the sudden realization that, if they went back the way they came, they would be leading any potential pursuers directly toward Wiglaf and Johanne's home. The plan would have to change. He decided to go south and lead the enemy away. They would cross the bridge over the wide river beyond the town and enter into unknown territory. To return home they would have to circle back and find another way to re-cross the river. He knew it was a big risk, but, when he thought of Johanne, and Ælfwine, and Gebhard, he paled at the thought of leading the ruthless Alemanni straight to their doorstep.

Ulrich led the three wagons southward. He was anxious. Their progress was painfully slow. It was only a matter of time before the bodies of the guards were discovered, but to hurry would be suspicious too. The ungreased wooden axles of the heavy carts squealed as they lumbered along the road. To Ulrich it seemed the noise of his heart pounding in his ears must be loud enough to wake the whole town on its own, yet as they neared the southern gate, the houses remained dark. The peace was undisturbed.

A man sat slumped on a milking stool, apparently the only sentry to the wide-open southern gate. He was wearing a white tunic with a red sash, and Ulrich hoped that he had been one of the revelers in the hall that evening, made comatose with drink. Ulrich could hear the man snoring loudly. The sentry did not stir from his sleep as Ulrich's horse plodded by.

Ulrich passed through the gateway and into the countryside beyond, riding at the head of his small cavalcade. Ima, Tau and Sigmund followed, driving the wagons to which each of their horses were hitched.

The Roman causeway sloped down gently from the fortress before meeting a stout stone bridge that stretched across a dark, swiftly flowing, river. Beyond the bridge, the road continued south through deep, marshy land. On either side of the marsh, dry turf ran to high ground that stood above the swamp. What Ulrich saw on those hills checked his breath in his lungs. He had made a terrible mistake.

CHAPTER FIFTEEN

Thousands of tents dotted the land. They stretched off to east and west, continuing in their orderly lines until the hills fell away from his gaze. Camped there was an army the size of which Ulrich could never have imagined. Entire herds of horses were picketed in many scattered pastures. Above the multitude of tents stood banners and pendants of a dozen shapes and patterns. The camps were mostly dark and quiet, but between the pale moonlight and a loose scattering of still-lit fires, the whole host seemed to be cast in an ominous, almost unearthly, glow within the shadow of the night.

A gruff shout behind him made him turn. He saw Tau lean from his wagon to slash his sword down at the, now-awake, guard, who stood mouth open and sword drawn. Tau's sword point ripped the man's throat out, but the damage was already done. As the guard's howl of pain echoed off into the night, new lights glowed fresh in the nearby guardhouse. Ulrich swore.

"Come on," he shouted back to his companions. He encouraged his horse into a brisk trot. Ulrich felt angry at himself. He should have scouted out their escape route, and now he was leading his friends and all those poor captives into a trap as grave as the one they had just escaped. He had grossly underestimated the strength of the Alemanni. The men billeted in the town were only a handful of the force, and the banquet they had witnessed must have been just the tribal leaders and favored men. He stared anxiously at the tents to either side as the wagons hurried down the road. How many men were here? Hundreds? Thousands? He could not even begin to count them all.

The wagons had begun crossing the bridge when he heard the first mustering horn blare from the town. The noise was mournful and poignant. Somebody must have either spotted the bodies they had left or had noticed that the hostages had escaped. Either way, the chase was on. By the time they reached the end of the bridge, the first enemies were beginning to spill from the town gates. They must have had trouble freeing their horses from the blocked pasture, because the leading pursuers were jogging after them on foot. Ulrich was not overly concerned about those men. Even slowed with the burden of the three big carts, their horses could still outpace men on foot. He was far more worried about the owners of the herds of horses picketed free on the pastures outside. When those men were alerted, he, Ima, Tau, and Sigmund would be ridden down and butchered. The prisoners they had tried to free would be hanged as examples of the weakness of the free tribes of Germany. The Alemanni would have won, and Ulrich and his friends would be dead.

Ulrich needed a new plan, and he needed it quickly. They crossed the bridge. The road in front of them was a raised causeway, stretching over soft swampy land. Tall reeds, muddy earth, and patches of freestanding water stood on either side of the road. The river curved in a wide arc astride this low-lying plain, and it must flood deep when the river spilt its banks, for the Romans, consummate engineers that they were, had built the road very high, standing tall and dry to be out of reach of the worst springtime floods. Ulrich suddenly had an idea. The marshiness of the land itself could be used to their advantage. He urged his horse on for another minute, then pulled sharply to a stop. He leapt down from the saddle.

Tau, Ima, and Sigmund had followed close, their carts single file on the road. Behind them, a half mile distant, dozens of men were streaming across the bridge. Beyond this, enemy fires were lighting in the faraway camps of the great army. Ulrich could see activity among the tents. Horses were being saddled, and men were mounting to begin the chase.

Ima drove the foremost wagon. She sat on the bench and looked down at him expectantly. Ulrich was impressed that there was no fear in her eyes, only a quiet determination. Her confidence gave him courage. Sigmund and Tau climbed down to meet him.

"Cut the traces from the carts and take the horses forward," he told them. He ran to the first cage and unlimbered his axe.

The doors to the small prisons were bolted shut by heavy wooden locking bars that were reinforced with iron strips. Securing the bars were bronze padlocks that accepted a key. Ulrich had no key, so he simply smashed the delicate workings of the padlocks with the steel blade of his axe. They shattered one after another, and the prisoners flooded out. The advancing enemy imbued them with panic, and the fugitives fled southward. Ulrich made no move to stop them. He had brought them this far and given them a glimmer of hope, but he could take them no farther. They were on their own from here.

Rag leapt from the last cage, and with tears in his eyes, flung his arms around Ulrich. Ulrich embraced the boy briefly then pointed to where Ima waited with the unharnessed horses.

"Get on a horse quickly," he said. "We are not staying for long."

Ulrich shouted to Sigmund, and together they ponderously overturned the first cart. It crashed onto its side on the roadway, wheels spinning into empty air. Tau ran to help as they dragged over the second cart and tipped it over beside the first. The carts would create a makeshift roadblock, forcing their pursuers to wade through the cloying mud. By the time they were pushing the final cart over, the first breathless Alemanni were almost upon them. In seconds they would be overwhelmed and the final cart was still some feet short of its goal. Without a word, Tau drew both of his long swords and threw himself into the space beyond the carts, slashing out at the attacking men. Spears thudded into the wood as the final cart toppled over to fill the gap. Ulrich realized with horror that Tau had trapped himself on the other side.

The three big carts completely blocked the high causeway over the swamp. Swords rang on the other side of the obstacle, and Ulrich, fearing for Tau, leapt for the lip of the nearest cart. He drew himself up to see the scuffle beyond.

Tau was holding his own. He had launched his attack on these men with the sure knowledge that he would win. His enemy were tired and breathless from running from the town, but Tau was fresh and ready. In their eagerness, these men had left behind their shields and mail coats to dash ahead of their fellows. Tau, with his two swords drawn, was a fox among rabbits. He spun and danced, swords flashing. In a matter of moments, three men were wounded and bleeding at his feet. The next group of enemy, seven Alemanni warriors brandishing spears and swords, checked their advance at the sight of flashing steel and spraying blood. They breathed heavily, palms sweaty on their weapons as they judged their foe. Another man arrived, this one holding a javelin that he leveled. He began judging the distance for a throw. Tau had slowed the enemy, but he was running out of time as more men flooded down the road. He backed toward the carts.

"Tau!" Ulrich shouted. He grunted and leaned out over the high barricade. His weight was on his chest as he balanced on the cart's lifted edge. He reached a hand down for his friend. Tau, seeing his salvation, tossed his swords over the barricade. He jumped for safety, grasping Ulrich's wrist tight. Ulrich heaved, pulling his friend over the carts as a javelin thumped into the wood, skewering the spot where Tau had been standing only a moment before.

They landed together heavily on the dusty road. Ima was ready for them, sitting on one of their horses nearby. With Rag behind her in the saddle, she held the reins for the other horses as the men climbed to their feet.

"Come on," she urged them, but Ulrich waited. Further down the road, the panicked mass of freed humanity had not yet vanished into the darkness. Forty or fifty innocent men, women, and children were desperately trying to escape. Every moment Ulrich could give them might mean the difference between freedom and certain death. He hefted his axe.

Tau and Sigmund stood with him. Tau snatched up his swords and Sigmund produced a large spiked mace. Sigmund had been an indifferent pupil to combat. In their innumerable sparring sessions that summer, Sigmund never took to the sword. Despite his great size and strength, he was a gentle man, especially with his friends. Further, he seemed entirely incapable of taking their training seriously, regardless of how often Wiglaf scowled at him. After he discovered the litter of rabbits near the house, he was hopeless. Sneaking from the practice field, Sigmund would be found dozing in the shade, brown mother rabbit resting protectively on his chest as the four kits bounced joyfully about. Wiglaf despaired of his student.

Still, Wiglaf knew that one day Sigmund may have to fight. He had figured that the big man would never develop the finesse to properly use a sword. Even when he used an axe, the blade would often twist sideways in his indifferent grip, so the blacksmith crafted a simpler weapon for him. A heavy iron ball adorned with sharp iron spikes was mounted on a short wooden shaft. Sigmund hated fighting, but his friends needed him, so Sigmund reluctantly hefted Wiglaf's mace.

Ulrich saw two men flanking the wagons to his right. They were coming slowly, pushing through thick mud that came up to their knees. These men were wearing mail and bearing drawn swords but had no shields. Ulrich stood on the edge of the road and slashed down at the nearest man, who raised his sword to parry the over-hand axe stroke. Their blades rang together, and the axe was deflected, but the enemy was also thrown off balance by the force of the blow. He stumbled forward and ended up on hands and knees with a mouthful of mud. The second man stabbed with his own sword, but the point of the blade scraped harmlessly against Ulrich's hardened breastplate. Ulrich swung at the second man. His axe caught the man's sword at the cross guard and flung it out of his grasp, flipping it end over end to vanish into the murk. The disarmed man's eyes widened in terror, and he held his hands out in front of him placatingly, backing away slowly and losing a boot in the sucking mud. Ulrich sensed Sigmund standing behind him. "Check the other side. I can hold here," Ulrich growled, glaring at the two men who faced him nervously.

On the left-hand side of the barricade, Tau was having trouble. His nearest opponent was carrying a wide rectangular shield that he ducked behind as he came through the mud. With the tall barrier of the overturned wagon on his right and the deep mud to his left, Tau was unable to use his speed against the man's stout defense. Tau hacked and pushed at the shield, but he was being forced backward step by step.

More enemies were piling behind the first. Reinforcements were working their way around the overturned wagons, moving to flank the three men. Sigmund saw Tau struggling against the shielded man, and he charged this enemy, putting his momentum into a powerful tackle as he slammed his shoulder into the Alemanni shield. The man behind the shield was thrown backward, but did not fall, as he was bolstered by the weight of the men who followed. Sigmund dropped his mace and grabbed the enemy shield with both hands. He used his massive strength to lift it up, and the helpless man came with it, still clinging to the handles. It was a ludicrous sight with Sigmund shaking the shieldman like a terrier shaking a rat until finally the man let go and dropped to the ground. Reversing the shield, Sigmund held it sideways and pushed it forward. Two more men had stepped over the first, swords outstretched, and Sigmund slammed the wooden board into them, forcing them back.

Tau saw more enemies coming around to their side. A dozen sword-bearing men had foregone their shields to wade through the deeper mud farther out, angling around the fugitives to cut them off. Their progress was slow, but Tau stood to Sigmund's left, threatening the enemy with his long swords and protecting his friend's flank.

Meanwhile, Ulrich was now holding off a half-dozen men alone. His pulse was racing, and he was sweating with the effort. He had killed one man who had struck at him with a long spear, and he had slashed and injured two others. The dead body of the first man lay at his feet, slowing his attackers, but Ulrich knew time was running out. Men on horseback were beginning to push through the crowd. He watched one horseman swing wide through the swamp, feeling his way for drier turf. The horse stepped into a soft patch of mud and sank to its chest. The animal panicked, flailing its head about and trying to pull free of the muck while its rider toppled forward into the morass. But, dozens of horsemen were leaving the road now, and some were having better success picking their way through the swamp.

Ulrich heard a man scream just behind him and turned. Ima, still on horseback, had stabbed a man who was attempting to climb over the carts. Her sword blade had caught him in the neck, and blood bubbled at his bearded mouth as he fell backward. Rag, wide-eyed, was clutching her tightly about the waist as he sat behind her in the saddle. More hands appeared on top of the wooden barricade, and Ulrich knew they would soon be overwhelmed.

"We are out of time," Ulrich bellowed. "Get to the horses."

He turned and ran toward the waiting mounts, and his opponents, seeing him retreat, followed, pulling themselves out of the muck and climbing over the dead body on the berm. Ulrich scrambled into a saddle and held his axe at the ready. Tau, after leaping quickly up his beast's flank, rode to defend the slower Sigmund who had paused to snatch up his mace before clambering onto his own horse. Tau had scabbarded one blade and was holding the reins in one hand; with the other hand, he slashed his sword down into a pursuer's face, spraying blood. Ima kicked her horse past Ulrich and into the fray to slam her mount bodily into the approaching men. One man was shoved roughly aside by the beast's weight, and another went down under flailing hooves.

Once all four companions were finally mounted, they turned and galloped away down the road.

CHAPTER SIXTEEN

They had a small but significant lead on their pursuers, and the gap widened as the leading enemy footmen were quickly left behind by the companions' swift horses. It would be a few minutes until the Alemanni horsemen had cleared the obstacle to gallop along the causeway's dry surface. As Ulrich led his companions south, he noticed the panicked mass of fugitives was no longer in sight. He hoped those men and women had the sense to leave the road and scatter into the countryside. They rounded a dense patch of willows and ash trees, and Ulrich let his horse drop out of the gallop and into a fast trot. Their mounts were still fresh and energetic, but he wanted to shepherd their strength. This could turn into a long chase.

"Well, that was a mess," Sigmund said drily.

Tau laughed. The noise surprised Ulrich who was still edgy with the thrill of battle. Tau leaned from the saddle and clapped Sigmund on the back. "That was a good fight, my friend. You saved me from that man with the shield." Tau chuckled. "You shook him like a leaf in the wind."

Sigmund was embarrassed. "Well, I guess I could have let him kill you, but then I would have to find a new black fellow to be friends with."

Ima shook her head. "If I didn't know any better, I'd think you idiots were enjoying yourselves," she said.

Sigmund's face was flushed with exertion, but he looked warmly at his companions. "I'm just glad we are all okay," he said. He trotted his horse alongside Ima's and reached over to muss Rag's blonde hair. The boy, still clutching Ima's waist, grinned back at him.

They were now riding along a straight highway that stood tall out of the swampy land. These Roman roads were wonders of construction, levelled and graded and topped with wide flat paving stones skillfully fitted together to make a smooth hard surface. The road had curbs on both sides—lengths of stone a few inches high designed to keep cart wheels from sliding off the road and down into the steep stone drainage ditches. The face of the road was curved slightly into a gentle crown, peaking in the center and sloping down on both sides to allow water to run off in even the hardest downpour. Ulrich took in the road with a sense of wonder, realizing that the investment of time and skill for each section of this road must be on par with the expense of building a castle wall, and yet the road went on, tall and unbroken, for miles and miles.

Ulrich realized he had been holding his breath. He let out a long sigh, letting some of the tension drain away. He was suddenly tired. Until now, he had been running on adrenaline, but the exertion of the long chase after Rag's captors, followed by the sleepless night, was beginning to take its toll. He knew his companions must be feeling the same. Worse yet, the danger was nowhere near over. He cleared his throat.

"The way I see it, we have three problems," Ulrich began. "First, we are about to have a whole army on our heels."

"And I think they might be a bit peeved at us," Sigmund interjected.

Ulrich continued, "Second, I do not know where all those people we rescued went off to." He peered at the road ahead. The earliest hint of light was growing in the east, and a morning fog was thickening in the lowland ahead. It was an empty swamp, and there was not a soul in sight.

"If they have any sense, they will scatter into the marshlands or hunker down in a dense patch of woods," Ima said.

Ulrich nodded. "I agree. I hope they make it home. I'm afraid there is not much more we can do for them now." Ulrich shook his head before continuing. "But our third and final problem…" He twisted in his saddle to look behind him. "is that home is that way." He pointed north. "On the other side of that Alemanni hornet's nest."

"Hornet's nest?" Sigmund mused rhetorically, "It was more like an anthill, really. I mean, they can't fly, can they?"

Just then a band of Alemanni horsemen rounded the bend behind them. There were twenty of them. They were still about a mile away, but they were coming fast, swords out, horses at full gallop. A cloud of dust followed them, wafting gently into the still, pre-dawn air.

"Perhaps they can," Ulrich responded with a grunt. He kicked his own horse to the gallop, and his companions followed. A short distance ahead, a narrow footpath led from the high surface of the road and across into some deep woods. Ulrich angled for it until Tau stopped him, putting his horse out front of the racing pack.

"We need to draw this chase out for as long as possible," Tau shouted over the din of the pounding hooves.

"He is right," Ima agreed. "The more of them chasing us, the fewer will be going after the fugitives. Besides…" She looked back. Even at this distance she could see the pursuers' mounts tossing their heads and shortening their stride. Ima knew horses, and she was judging the enemy. "They'll never catch us," she said. She was confident in that. The impetuous Alemanni must have been driving their horses at a sprint since they cleared the roadblock, and their mounts were already tiring. Meanwhile, the companions' horses had spent the preceding minutes saving their strength and were still fresh. The chase continued down the road.

A few miles later, their pursuers' horses were blown, and the enemy was forced to drop to a trot. When Ima saw this, she also allowed their mounts to slow. She guided the pace, shepherding the horses' strength while keeping the distance comfortably open.

The first light of dawn was creeping over the eastern horizon. On one of the far hills to the east, Ulrich thought he caught a glimpse of the fugitives. There were dozens of figures that moved along the ridgetop before disappearing over the crest. He prayed they would stay unseen. He prayed that they would find their way home.

The chase went on. The pursuing horsemen occasionally put on bursts of speed, but with Ima's guidance, Ulrich and his companions continued to outpace them, and the distance steadily grew. The sun rose into a reddened sky, and dark storm clouds threatened from the south, riding high on a stiff southerly wind. By late morning, the sun was lost behind dense clouds, and a thin drizzle of warm rain was falling on the road. From the north two more bands of horsemen followed the first, but none were able to close the distance.

The swamp had fallen away, and they were riding into a dense woodland. Thick oaks and tall beech trees bordered the highway. In most areas, the woods were cleared back from the road for several feet, but in others overgrowth had begun to invade the verges. The road began to weave around thick bogs and occasionally cut through low hills. Their pursuers became lost to sight behind the bends and curves. Ulrich, anticipating that the unseen enemy could be gaining on them, wanted to push the horses harder but Ima, with a firm confidence, kept them close in hand. The clouds grew darker, and the rain picked up. The wind blew the warm, heavy droplets hard into their faces.

Eventually, the woods gave way to a small clearing, and a crossroads appeared. A stone marker stood by the road bearing a Roman inscription. Ulrich had some basic schooling in reading and writing in his youth, but that knowledge was distant and rusty. Still, the meaning of the marker was simple. It was a milestone. The inscription facing the road continuing south read: Augusta Vindelicum, 240 miles and below it Roma, 800 miles. The road marker facing west read Mogantiacum, 120 miles. To the east, the road bore no inscription, and they went that way.

Ulrich did not know if the Alemanni would follow. He doubted that their tracks could be easily traced in this blowing rain, but they dared not slow. After a few more miles, a trail branched off to the left. This track paled in comparison to the great Roman road. It was a simple dirt path, grooved by cart tracks and muddy with rain. They left the causeway to follow the narrow path north, and Ulrich hoped it would bring them home. If the wide river through the Alemanni encampment still ran east, they should eventually meet it again.

Soon they came upon a town. Or, at least, they found what had once been a town. This village had been burned to the ground. The destruction was recent. Charred timbers stuck crazily into the air from a half dozen blackened foundations. They stopped. Ulrich dismounted.

"Let us take a quick break," he said, stretching. His muscles were sore from the long ride. It was afternoon, and they had been riding hard since before dawn. They had taken enough forks that it was possible that the Alemanni could have lost their trail. Ulrich hoped they had. His horse, grateful for the rest, began cropping the long grass around the burned cottages.

The rain had never stopped falling, and they were all wet and miserable. Ulrich knew that stopping was a gamble but hunger and fatigue were powerful motivation. He stepped into the bushes to relieve himself. Sigmund found a small sack of grain in his own horse's saddlebags, and he shared it among their mounts. Ima found an open trough nearby and led the horses there. It was half full of rainwater from which they drank thirstily.

Tau found a large, half-burned length of timber and dragged it to a patch of turf by the roadside. He and Ima were sitting and talking when Ulrich joined them. Sigmund found himself a dry spot on a stump, and Rag perched on a boulder nearby. They guessed rightly that the bandits would have stored some food in their packs. Together they shared what little they found. There was some wine and cheese, a couple of pounds of smoked beef, a half-dozen bruised apples, and a flask of fresh goat's milk.

Sigmund broke the silence. "I think this place was burned down on purpose," he said.

"How can you tell?" Rag asked.

Sigmund pointed toward the nearest burned-out house. "See the bones?" He indicated a pile of whitened skeletons, outlined against the black soot of the ruined foundation. The bones were clustered together, lying on top of each other, as if they had embraced as they burned. Two human skulls stared at the midday sky. Their empty eye sockets were fixed on the heavens. "If my house were on fire, I would run out the door. Something was keeping those poor people in there, and what could do that? My guess is, it was the points of enemy spears."

Ulrich tried to imagine it: his home burning around him, trying to flee only to be pushed back by sharp steel, holding tight to your loved ones as you choked and coughed on the thick smoke. He shivered. That was how Cenric had died.

Sigmund munched on the core of an apple, spitting out the seeds one by one as he chewed. He plucked the stem off and finished the apple before standing. He walked off the path and kicked at a loose mound of earth.

"Somebody was searching in the ground for something. Gold probably," Sigmund said, indicating small holes dug at the corners of the foundations. And that made sense. Ulrich knew that it was clever practice to hide wealth in case of bandit attack.

Sigmund continued. "Locals would have remembered where they

buried their own wealth. They would not have had to dig so many holes. This is the work of raiders."

"Do you think it was the Alemanni?" Ima asked.

Sigmund shrugged, "I don't know, but I also don't know anybody else who has been going around bragging about killing and enslaving the local populace, and there certainly were enough of the bastards."

"That big guy with the red beard, Chnodomar; he said they just conquered the Chatti," Ulrich interjected.

"I wonder what they were like," Rag's small voice piped up.

"Probably a lot like Saxons. Probably a lot like us," Sigmund responded, and his voice was sad.

Ulrich stood and stretched. He felt somewhat refreshed after this small break, but they had gone from dawn to dawn without rest, and he wanted nothing more than to just throw himself on the wet ground and let sleep overtake him. Instead, he walked to his horse and released the reins from where they were looped about the feeding trough.

"Come on," he said to his companions. "We still have a long way to go."

CHAPTER SEVENTEEN

From the ruined town the trail continued north, and they followed it onward. They rode into the gloom of a dense wood and ducked under low-hanging branches that dripped heavy droplets of rainwater onto the muddy path. The going was slow here as the path grew narrow. Eventually they came across their goal. The woods opened into a clearing that sloped gently downwards to the bank of a wide, fast-rushing river.

"I know this river," Ima said, "this is the Fulda again. The bridge at Kassel crossed over it. Now we just have to get back across." She frowned, considering the challenge. It was an intimidating proposition, for the current was strong, and the river was close to two hundred feet wide.

"Down there," she said finally, pointing. Downstream lay an island. It was low and sandy, and the river split in two as it flowed about it. "By using that island we split our crossing into two parts. It will be difficult, but we can make it." She sounded confident.

The companions doffed their chainmail and boots and stored them in their saddlebags. Ulrich's heavy armor was fastened securely to his horse's saddle. Ima led them onward and stopped at a point on the bank some way upstream of the sandy island. She had readjusted and now held Rag in the saddle in front of her. He was supported by her arms as she held the reins lightly. Without hesitation she drove her horse into the deep water.

Ima had grown up training horses, and she was the best rider among them. She made the crossing look easy. Leaning forward in the saddle she gently held the sides of her horse's head, keeping him swimming for the opposite shore as the current pushed them downstream. They landed easily on the island, horse pawing the sand as it climbed onto the beach. She turned her mount lithely and waved back at them from across the river.

Sigmund swore in astonishment, and Tau was grinning. Not to be outdone, Tau plunged in next, quickly crossing the gap and cheering when his horse mounted the island.

Sigmund looked at Ulrich with big eyes. "I have never been much of a fan of water," he admitted nervously.

"Do you know how to swim?" Ulrich asked.

Sigmund shrugged, "Mostly," he admitted. "I had a dog once, and he taught me to paddle." He grimaced. "Well, I guess there is no sense in wasting time. I will see you on the other side." He gingerly led his horse to the water.

Sigmund's crossing was not as smooth as Ima or Tau's. His horse hit an eddy halfway and was twisted with the current. Ulrich could hear the big man's terrified yell as he struggled to keep his horse on course. Eventually he made it across, although he landed quite a bit downstream from where Tau and Ima had landed. Visibly shaken but safe, Sigmund rode onto the island.

Ulrich was the last to cross. He was nervous too. While he had no fear of water, he was not a skilled horseman. He loved horses, but not having ridden since his youth, he lacked Ima's confidence. Mule was a lovely beast, but she was nothing like the proud warhorse he now rode. He had a sudden flash, remembering poor Whisper, who died so tragically in his father's castle. He shook his head to clear the memory and rode into the water.

For the first few moments everything went well. He bent low like he had seen Ima do, and placed his hands on either side of the horse's head to keep it pointed toward the island. The water rose to his waist as the horse's hooves left the ground and the beast began swimming, working its long powerful legs against the current. Then, a gout of water smashed into Ulrich's face, and suddenly the world was spinning. They had hit turbulence where the river's flow spun about unseen rocks deep below the surface. All momentum lost, they turned chaotically in the current, horse and man swept downstream together.

The horse tossed its head in fear, and Ulrich lost his grip on the wet mane. He slid from the saddle. He treaded water for a moment, regaining his senses. The horse was close by, and he grasped the reins. The beast was panicking, eyes wide and head tossing as its hooves thrashed at the surface. His companions were standing on the shore, shouting and waving as they watched his plight. He looped the reins over his arm and began swimming for the island, pulling the horse behind him. With his guidance the horse began to calm, and it followed him toward safety.

He finally reached the shore and climbed up the sand. The horse was shaken and shivering, but Ulrich calmed it, stroking its nose and talking to it in a soft voice. "Shh, good boy. Well done, boy," he said to the spooked animal.

His companions reached him, hurrying along the beach, and Sigmund offered a handful of barley. The grain was damp from the river crossing, but the horse accepted it eagerly, calming as it munched the grains.

Sigmund, Ima, Tau, and even Rag were staring at Ulrich with concern. He looked into their anxious faces and felt ridiculous. He laughed. The tension evaporated, and they laughed too, relief showing on their faces. He wrung water from the front of his wet shirt, and they moved on.

There was one remaining section to the river crossing but that was much easier. To get from the island to the opposite bank of the Fulda, a narrow channel blocked their path. The water flowed slower and shallower here than on the other side. Still, Ulrich decided to take no chances; he led his horse to the water by the reins and swam with the animal in tow. Once north of the Fulda they struck out across country. There was no visible road, but the woods had given way to wide, grassy fields and low, sloping hills, and the going was easy.

In the late afternoon, the rain finally stopped. The sun came out, and in its light Ulrich felt fear grip his heart. Tragedy had struck the countryside. As the dark clouds retreated northward and the sunlight broke through, patches of black smoke could be seen dotting the land. In every direction, dirty plumes rose into the cool air. The Alemanni were on the move. The enemy had struck north, making good on their promise to conquer all of Germania. The smoke Ulrich saw was evidence of the homesteads and villages that burned in their wake. Ima had her bearings, and she led them quickly on as they hurried for home.

They saw no other travelers, but they stayed well away from the main road for fear of running into an Alemanni raiding party. They skirted around the numerous places from which smoke rose, sullen and black. The sun was sinking into toward the horizon by the time they approached Wiglaf and Johanne's farm.

Ulrich's heart sank. Over the trees he could see a dense column of dirty black smoke. It was rising from his home. They had been keeping to the forest, approaching cautiously from the east, but Ulrich could wait no longer, and he broke from the cover of the leaves onto the open fields. He could hear Tau shouting at him from behind, urging him to wait, but he put the horse to the gallop and raced full tilt the last quarter mile.

He rode toward ruin. The damp wood of the house had burned poorly, and the wet thatch had caved in as the eaves disintegrated. Ulrich felt numb as he dismounted. The walls of the smithy still stood, and the door hung open, but nothing was visible inside beyond the pile of thatch where the roof had collapsed. Smoke rose from where embers burnt feebly at the wet structure.

There was a body in front of the house. Ulrich approached slowly. He did not want to believe what he saw. An old man lay face down in the mud. A broken sword was clenched tight in a deathly-white hand. The man was Wiglaf. He had been pierced through many times by blades, and blood stained his clothes, seeping into the wet turf about him. Ulrich reached a hand out and touched Wiglaf's back. It was cold.

Ulrich cried then. Silent tears flowed down his face. Wiglaf had raised him, taught him to fight, taught him to hunt, and had been as close to him as a father to a son. Ulrich had been away, and the man had died. Ulrich had not been there to protect him. Gradually, the sadness was replaced by anger. He clenched his fists. This was Chnodomar's doing—Chnodomar and the Alemanni and all those murdering, thieving bastards. Ulrich touched his axe handle and swore he would kill them all. He swore to all the gods. He swore to fate. He swore to himself, and he swore, most of all, to Wiglaf's memory.

A small noise drew his attention, and he looked up. Johanne, Gebhard, and Ælfwine, unhurt, were standing at the tree line, looking wet and miserable. He walked to them, embraced the children, and wept.

CHAPTER EIGHTEEN

They buried Wiglaf on a ridge at the edge of the forest. Ulrich did not know what to say. He could not find the words to give voice to what he felt, to give thanks to the man who had taken him in and treated him like a son. Johanne cried and hugged her children tight. Ælfwine and Gebhard were stunned and solemn.

The sun was sinking low in the west as they retreated into the woods. They went to low, marshy ground, hoping to stay hidden from any roving bands of Alemanni raiders. Johanne had rescued some wolf pelts and smoked meat from the looted home, and they spread the pelts on the wet ground, sharing a quarter of pork while they considered their options.

Johanne told the story. She explained how they had first seen the plumes of dirty smoke rising from the south that morning. As new columns of smoke grew closer, she and Wiglaf had gathered what they could save, taken the children, and run for the cover of the trees.

"They came around noontime," Johanne said. "It was pouring rain, but from the edge of the forest, I could see them ride in on their big horses. Dozens of them. Most continued north toward Brunswick, but a few stayed here. What they could not steal, they burned. We thought we were safe in the trees, but some of them came into the woods. We tried to hide in a ditch, but they heard us. Wiglaf told me to run, and he went out to meet them. We made it away, but they killed him. He fought back, but there were too many."

Ulrich shared what they had seen to the south, the new town at Kassel, and the huge army gathering there. "They call themselves the Alemanni," Ulrich explained. "And their leader is a big, red-haired man named Chnodomar."

Johanne frowned at that. "Alemanni? I've never heard of that tribe." Her eyes were still moist with tears, but her face was proud and her mind was sharp.

"I don't think it's a single tribe," Sigmund said. "From what we gathered in Kassel, it sounds like an alliance, a confederation of many tribes. This Chnodomar mentioned a couple: the Suebi and the Marcomanni."

Ulrich shrugged, "The details do not matter. What matters is what they want and where they are going. They said they were going to conquer all Germany, and from what we saw, there are certainly enough of them to think they can try. They must be stopped."

"So, what do we do now?" Ima asked.

There was a long pause before Johanne spoke.

"The ruler of Western Saxony is a king named Erdmann," Johanne said to Ulrich. "He is a good man, and he was a friend of your father's. When we moved here fleeing your wicked uncle, he granted Wiglaf this homestead. His hall is to the north, at a place called Bremen, on the Wesser river. We should go to him and tell him what is happening here. It is his duty as a lord to defend his subjects."

Johanne looked fierce, arms protectively around her children. Ulrich turned to his friends. Sigmund saw his gaze and smiled sympathetically. Tau nodded stoically while Rag dozed, his back to a tree. Ulrich glanced at Ima, who nodded back.

"We will head for Bremen," Ulrich concluded, "but we start in the morning. Tonight, we need rest."

They spent a damp night in the woods, though an outcropping of flat boulders offered some respite from the wet earth. They spread woolen cloaks and furs to make their beds. Ulrich suggested a rotating lookout, using the movement of the moon to divide the night into shifts. Ulrich took the first shift, resting against a tree. He listened to the owls call to one another and fought an overwhelming weariness. When his watch was over, he roused Ima for the second shift; then he collapsed on a heap of furs, instantly dropping into a grateful sleep.

It was near midnight when Ima's shift started, and she began by checking on their horses. The four great war beasts were unsaddled and fast asleep. Two seemed to be friends, and they dozed standing up, leaning against each other. The two others had lain down, and one was dreaming, ears twitching and legs moving slightly as it ran in its dreams. The other woke as she approached but seemed undisturbed by her presence. Its big brown eyes tracked her calmly, and she squatted down and scratched the big animal between the ears. Its eyes closed slowly in gratitude.

Ima had always loved horses. She had grown up with them. Four of the great, gentle creatures had been her childhood companions and a fifth, a curious and gentle foal they named Dainty, had been born on Ima's third birthday. By the time Ima was five she and Dainty were inseparable. She felt as comfortable on Dainty's back, picking her way through the woods about their home pastures, as she did on her own two feet. Dainty had died with the raid that had killed her parents, the raid that had driven her and her grandfather Hugbert to a small subsistence existence far across the land, but still horses gave her joy. They could not afford one of their own, but a generous family across the stream had been happy to employ her to exercise their own fine breeding stock.

Distracted with her own thoughts Ima neglected scratching the stallion's ears, and so the big beast nudged her arm with its nose. "Well you're a greedy one, aren't you," she admonished him gently then resumed petting the animal.

Ima turned at a soft noise to see Johanne walking her way. Johanne smiled and sat next to her, back propped against one of the discarded saddles.

"I am sorry. About your husband. About Wiglaf," Ima said. The words felt insufficient, hollow, but she had no others.

Johanne smiled, but shook her head. "I am sorry about your grandfather," she responded.

Ima said nothing. The loss did not feel real. She had known the kind man her entire life. There was a sudden tightness in her chest. She shook her head. So much had been lost.

"You don't have to come with us," Johanne said gently.

"With Hugbert gone, that home means nothing," Ima replied. "Even if I went back to that place, it isn't safe there anymore."

"You could go west," Johanne offered. "You could go to Rome." By this, she meant the Empire. She knew too that there was a city somewhere in a far away land also called Rome, but typically when somebody said Rome, they meant all the provinces claimed by the vast nation.

Ima shook her head. "I don't know anything about Rome."

"Me neither," Johanne admitted. "But I've heard stories. So many stories."

Rome itself was something of a fable. It was said that the Romans built towers of stone that scraped the clouds. Rome was a place where gods walked among men. They could make the elements bend to their will, send rivers uphill into their towns and harness the power of living fire. Ima was sure that most of the stories were pure fantasy.

"A friend of mine moved to Rome with her husband some years ago," Johanne continued. "She came back once to visit, and she said that women are treated well in Rome. She said there are laws that punish men who hurt women."

Ima frowned. The idea was foreign to her. In the Saxon lands only the kings and their kin were protected by such things as laws.

"That may be," Ima responded, "but the Alemanni are here, and I will not run from them. They killed my grandfather, they killed your husband, and they destroyed your home. Those men, they value only strength and violence. There is no justice in that." She met Johanne's eyes. "What they did to us, they will do to others. I am a warmaiden, and as long as their evil exists I will fight them."

Johanne was looking at her curiously. "Are you religious?" she asked.

Ima shrugged. She could feel the hammer at her breast, hidden beneath her tunic. "There are many gods, and I pray but they never seem to listen. Sometimes I wonder if they take much interest in what we ask."

Johanne smiled. She touched the crucifix which hung around her neck. "I think my God would like you," she said, then she walked away.

Johanne returned to her bedroll, and Ima was left alone with her thoughts. She thought about the companions she had made. She thought of Tau, his eyes blazing with determination to rescue the young boy, Rag. She reflected on how these men had risked their lives to give the hostages a chance to escape. She recalled the tears on Ulrich's face when Johanne and her children were safe. This family loved each other. They were good people, albeit trapped in an evil world.

Eventually her shift was over, and she shook Sigmund awake. The big man groggily nodded and went to relieve himself in the woods.

She lay in the warm spot he had vacated and one last scene, one final memory of this long day, drifted through her mind as she fell asleep.

When they had returned to Johanne's burned farmstead, Sigmund had left the group to go searching around the edge of the field. It was odd to see the big man hunched over, peering into the weeds, and she wondered what he had been looking for. Before long there was some movement in the grass, and a small brown rabbit flashed over to him, standing tall on its hind legs, looking up at him expectantly. Sigmund had carefully picked up the creature, which looked tiny in his huge hands, and petted it gently. Soon enough there were four small kits hopping excitedly around him, and Ima had heard his laugh, clear and deep, from across the yard. It was a strange scene in a day so full of death.

She drifted into a deep, dreamless sleep.

CHAPTER NINETEEN

Up the road, the town of Brunswick had been obliterated. Nothing remained of the place but ash and corpses, and Ulrich and his party gave it a wide berth. They traveled north for ten days. Initially the going was slow, as they avoided roads and kept to dense woods whenever possible. They crossed clearings quickly, sticking to low valleys for fear of any Alemanni raiders that may have come this far north already. For the first two days, the occasional plume of dirty smoke to the south justified their caution. By the third day they had stopped seeing new smoke on the horizon, and by the fifth day, they were able to spend more of their time searching for food. Sigmund and Tau netted nine fat trout from a shallow stream. They dared to light a fire that night and share the meat. On the seventh day, Ima found a nest of rabbits, but left them in peace after seeing the heart-stricken look on Sigmund's face. Luckily, Ulrich speared a large deer, and they smoked the meat. Finally, when Johanne estimated they were only a day's travel from Bremen, they felt brave enough to approach the road for the last leg of their journey.

This far from the Roman border there were no longer old Roman causeways, but instead, simple dirt paths, kept clear of overgrowth by the regular passage of men, horses, and cattle. These paths were clogged with fugitives. Thousands fled north. Carts carried the possessions of families; horses were laden with goods, and people walked, some barefoot, in the muddy ruts left behind. Ulrich and his companions joined the throng and heard many similar stories. People reported that raiders were coming in great numbers. Those who were too slow to flee were killed or enslaved. Towns were being burned and homes lost. It seemed that the razing of Brunswick was just one small tragedy among many.

The town of Bremen reminded Ulrich of his childhood home of Hamburg. It was built of wood and thatch and with high walls to defend against attack. To the west of the city was the deep, fast-flowing river Wesser, rushing north to the faraway sea. A small tributary branched at an acute angle from the Wesser. This smaller stream bordered the town to the east, putting Bremen on something of an island with the two waterways forming natural moats as protection. Above these banks, a wooden palisade protected the king's hall plus two dozen small houses and a handful of barns and stables. The great hall itself, a massive wooden building twice as tall as a house, lay in the center of town and was where the king lived, entertained, and held court. As Bremen had grown, an outer town had appeared. Thatch huts had sprung up outside the protection of the walls, nestled between the palisade and the muddy river banks.

The town, like the road, was flooded with people. The outer town had become a refugee camp filled with tents and hastily built lean-tos. The courtyard of the inner town was packed with supplicants and petitioners, all demanding to see the king. Overwhelmed by the hubbub, Ulrich and his companions elected to camp in the woods beyond the crowded town. They stretched cloaks between branches thrust into the soft ground as makeshift tents. Ulrich and Johanne went into the town the next morning, where a guardsman informed them that the king was busy meeting with his advisors, and no outsiders would be admitted to the hall.

Ulrich was frustrated. "He needs to know what we saw. He needs to know what is happening."

Johanne's voice was reasonable. "I am sure he knows. He has his own scouts, and between them and the refugees flooding north he must be already aware of the extent of the Alemanni threat."

Ulrich was mollified. They waited. The swell of fugitives had fished out the streams and scared off any game, so they were forced to spend money to buy food in the town. Prices were exorbitant from scarcity, and their store of coin was running low by the third day. They were forced to sell one of the horses to buy food. They visited the town often for news and finally, after five tedious days, there was an announcement.

Word said that an advisor of the king would make an address at noon. By midday the courtyard was packed with people. The town gates were thrown wide, and the crowd spilled into the outer town and onto the road beyond. Thousands anxiously anticipated the king's decision.

In front of the king's hall a wooden crate had been placed, and the king's herald stood on the makeshift platform to be seen over the massing crowd. He was in his late thirties, a tall man and gaunt. He was resplendently dressed in a silver-chased cloak, and his long hair was bound with a brightly polished bronze circlet. His voice was clear and loud.

"Every able-bodied man," he announced, "is to muster at dawn tomorrow on the plowed fields east of town. You are to bring what weapons and armor you possess. By order of the king, all those who do not report will be noted, and their lands and holdings will be confiscated. Tomorrow, we march to battle." He stepped down from the crate.

Ulrich had pushed close enough to the front to hear the man speak, but many others further back could not, and so the message was repeated back over the murmuring mass. Ulrich's spirits lifted. Finally, they would fight back. They would take the battle to the enemy, and the Alemanni would finally see just how strong Saxons could be.

In the dark before morning they gathered their belongings and went early to the meeting place. Off a long ridgeline crested by ash trees lay broad fields that had grown wheat and barley. The crop had already been harvested, and dry brown soil showed between discarded yellow stems. It was before dawn, but the place was already swarming with people, milling about in the darkness. Ulrich's family picked a spot near the edge of the woods and settled in to await the events of the day.

They started a small cooking fire and made breakfast. Johanne served a traditional stew of meaty beef bones, barley, and the green stalks of wild spring onions that had grown on the river's banks. While they waited, they used whetstones to sharpen their weapons, and they checked their equipment. Ulrich wore his heavy steel armor, with the feeling that something of Wiglaf still lived in the case-hardened segments. Sigmund and Tau had chainmail shirts which they wore over thick leather breeches. Ima too wore chainmail, the hauberk she had taken from the guard at Kassel. When she had donned it that morning Ulrich had wanted to protest, but Saxon tradition made room for warmaidens, however rare. Tau honed his two long swords, and Sigmund hefted his heavy mace. They carried a set of thick, round wooden shields, even Tau, who reluctantly agreed to use a shield when needed.

The sun peeked over the horizon, and the crowd swelled. Ulrich tried to count the force, but it was impossible as the warriors were interspersed with their children, elders, and occasionally livestock and horses. He made a rough guess that there were two or three thousand people on the fields, of which perhaps half were men of fighting age. It was a vast horde, and still more swarmed from the woods to join the throng.

The sun had been up for an hour when the king's retinue joined the field. In front of a mounted contingent of household warriors rode the king and five warlords, resplendent on fine horses and with silver trappings on their saddles and tack. The warlords wore suits of chainmail, polished and glittering in the morning sun while the king himself wore a gleaming suit of rare and ancient bronze scales, a cuirass similar to what Ulrich's father once wore.

Johanne had been telling a story of her homeland, recalling the blue icebergs that would sail magically down the far north coast. She stopped when the lords appeared.

"There is the king," she exclaimed, "there in the center, in the bronze armor."

The king and his retainers mounted a rise and inspected their army while behind them a hundred household warriors rode. With chainmail, expensive swords, and stout heavy shields, these were the best armed, trained, and armored warriors in the kingdom. The lords had a brief discussion, the king pointing at different sections of the massed crowd, then the men split up. Each of the warlords was followed by ten trained warriors. The final fifty armed men followed their bronze king as he rode down the hill. Thus the great army would go to battle, the Saxon warriors of the kingdom fronted by the lords' chosen guard.

Ulrich's section was commanded by a weathered-looking man of middle age. The warlord looked impatient as he rode toward them. In addition to the fine chainmail that wrapped his torso, he was fitted in a sturdy suit of thick leather armor. Brown leather shoulder guards and gauntlets covered his arms and dark greaves met sturdy boots which were rimmed with steel rivets to provide extra protection. A fine oval shield of red-painted oak hung from his saddle. His ten warriors were likewise on horseback. They followed closely, and once in earshot he began giving orders. The crowd fell silent to listen.

"I am Olfer, and I will be your commander." He gave no title or family name, but from his bearing, Ulrich assumed he was from one of the families closest to the king. Such men often acted as leaders in battle and governors of the lands ruled by the Saxon kings.

The warlord sat on his horse before the mass of humanity. "All that are too young, old, or weak to fight are to leave the field now," he called. "They may follow the army, but they must follow well behind. Warriors may carry only weapons, shields, and armor. All other belongings must go with the baggage." He pointed to the woods and waited as families said their goodbyes. Campfires were stomped out, accoutrements and livestock were collected, and the noncombatants began streaming off the field. Johanne mounted a horse and balanced her children on the saddle. Ima clutched her sword and the lord seemed to catch her eye.

"All women are to go with the baggage as well," the warlord amended in a loud voice. "We have no need for warmaidens today."

Ima growled. She made no move to leave. The lord's eyes and hers were locked in a silent test of wills. The warlord's eyes narrowed and he leaned from his horse to speak softly to the guardsmen behind him. Two began dismounting their horses.

Ulrich could see that there would be violence if Ima did not relent.

"Protect my family," Ulrich said to her. "I know you want to fight, but somebody needs to defend Johanne and the kids in case things go wrong." Ima scowled but Ulrich begged her.

"Please," he said.

There was a long, drawn-out, look of defiance, but finally she conceded. She took Rag, himself reluctant to be parted from Ulrich, and mounted her horse, riding proudly off the field. The lord's men, who had been preparing to push into the crowd, relaxed and returned to their warlord.

Lord Olfer surveyed the field. About three hundred men were under his direct command. The four other groups that clustered loosely around the four other lords were of similar size, making the total army about fifteen hundred Saxon men. As Olfer examined his charge, Ulrich also sized up the men he would be fighting alongside.

Other than the king's guard who waited some distance away, very few of the Saxons had proper arms or armor. What few swords could be seen were short swords, mostly old seaxes in the German style, single-bladed weapons about the length of a man's forearm and made of primitive iron. Many men had axes, mostly for woodcutting, and fully half the host had some form of hunting spear, many of simple wood, others with stubby, iron-tipped blades. There was a scattering of hunting bows and slings among the crowd, but some possessed only sharpened farming implements: adzes, scythes, and pitchforks.

Good armor was in the greatest scarcity. Beyond Ulrich's crew, only the men of the lord's retinue possessed chainmail. The rest of the warriors wore leather hunting shirts or fur jackets as their only protection. These were all strong, hardy men whose daily life was survival in the vast German wilderness. Weakness was bred out of the race by the very harshness of their existence, but with their relatively limited equipment, they looked more like a fierce mob than an army.

The men looked eager but Ulrich felt a nagging disquiet. The Alemanni were just as big, just as proud, but they were better equipped. Nearly every warrior he had seen among the Alemanni wore either chainmail or purpose-built leather armor. They had looted the wealth of a dozen tribes and could afford shields, weapons, and fine horses.

Not only had these Saxon men never met before, they knew little of the enemy they would face, the battlefield they expected, or even this warlord Olfer under whom they would fight. While the Alemanni seemed to have known one another, feasted alongside each other, and were united in a single purpose. Ulrich was apprehensive about their chances.

Olfer spotted Ulrich, Sigmund and Tau in the crowd. He was surprised to see such well-armored men among the mob, and he beckoned to them.

"Can you use those shields?" he asked.

"Yes, Lord," Ulrich said. "We were trained for battle by Wiglaf of Hamburg."

Lord Olfer's eyebrows went up. "Wiglaf the Smith? I know that man. From the days of good King Ædwin."

"I am Ædwin's son. My name is Ulrich. Wiglaf raised me as his own after Edwald took Hamburg," Ulrich responded.

Lord Olfer gave Ulrich a measuring look, then nodded. "I see your father in you now. He was a good man and a good friend. And how is Smith Wiglaf now?"

"He is dead lord. Killed just days ago by the raiders." Ulrich's knuckles went white as his grip tightened on his axe.

Lord Olfer said nothing. He allowed Ulrich's words to hang in the air, but his grave face spoke enough. After a long moment he turned and beckoned to one of his warriors.

"This is Arend, my son," he said, presenting a sturdy looking young man of perhaps eighteen. "He will be standing with me and my household warriors. When the battle begins, I want you and your companions to lock shields with him. Together, we will be the front rank."

Ulrich greeted the lord's son formally and introduced him to Tau and Sigmund. These men would be his war-brothers for his first true shield-wall battle. He hoped that it would not be his last.

CHAPTER TWENTY

By mid-morning the Saxon army was finally on the move. King Erdmann, with his fifty mounted guardsmen, led the procession, and the rest of the army marched on foot behind. Each of the five sections was divided by the warlords' household champions. In the rear straggled the crowd of women, children, baggage carts, and livestock.

They travelled by a wide dirt road that wound across a landscape of dense woods and rolling fields. They went east, facing the rising sun, and it promised to be a cool, clear, fall day. Leaves danced lazily on the gentle breeze, and a dirty plume of dust marked the army's passage.

It was a brief march. Shortly after noon, they stopped. The crowd ahead blocked Ulrich's view, but to right and left stretched a broad grassy field, and the army spread into it. The five lords and their King rode ahead and arranged the army to their liking. In the center, the fifty men of the King's guard rode a short distance ahead and dismounted, giving their horses to boys who led the mounts off the field. They stood shoulder to shoulder and rested their heavy shields on the ground. To either side, the wings were filled in by the five great sections of the army. They lined up at an angle, stretching backward and outward so that the king's men at the center formed the point of a broad wedge. Those men were the best trained and the best armed. They would be the spear point of the Saxon force.

Ulrich, Tau, and Sigmund found themselves on the right flank of the army. Any man with a shield or decent armor was ordered to the front. Ulrich found Lord Olfer's son and planted his shield next to his. Arend was a genial man, with long dark hair and brown eyes who smiled warmly at Ulrich when he joined him. To Ulrich's right, Sigmund crowded in close, and Tau was to the right of Sigmund. To the right of Tau, there were no more shields. This was the edge of the shield wall, although a few dozen more rows of men clustered in a rough mass, mostly bearing axes and spears and wearing rough leather jackets.

Ulrich tilted his shield to gaze up the field. An enemy army was waiting for them. The field sloped gently upward, and men were arrayed along the crest of a low hill about a quarter of a mile away. The midday sun shone from a clear sky and glinted off spear points and shield bosses. Ulrich tried to count the enemy, attempting to estimate its size. It looked like the opposing battle line was about the same width and depth as their own.

"Something is not right," Tau growled.

Ulrich frowned. "What do you mean?" he asked, turning to look at his friend.

Sigmund spoke up. "There are not enough warriors in that army. If that is the Alemanni, where are the rest of them? We saw a force many times that size at Kassel."

Ulrich looked back up the field. Based on what they had seen on the fields beyond Kassel, the Alemanni host numbered many thousand warriors, but this enemy was only about as numerous as the Saxons themselves, so perhaps fifteen hundred. In addition, the Alemanni had been well equipped, with chainmail, brightly painted wooden shields, and long steel swords. The men who faced down from the slope were a rabble clothed in leather and fur and carrying crude axes, spears, and simple slings.

So this enemy was not the Alemanni. The Saxons had marched to this field to fight somebody else. "What the hell is going on?" Ulrich growled.

Olfer was on horseback nearby, examining his command, and Ulrich called out to him.

"Lord," Ulrich called, "who are these men? Whose army do we face today?"

Olfer blinked in surprise. "It is your uncle's army we face today, of course." He raised his voice. "Today, the vile King Edwald will pay for raiding our land and stealing our cattle!" A muted, nervous cheer answered him.

"You mean we are fighting fellow Saxons?" Ulrich yelled back.

"What about the Alemanni?"

Olfer looked at him in amazement. "'Fellow Saxons,' indeed. I would think that you, of all people, would be excited for the opportunity to spill the blood of your treacherous uncle. This is the man who killed your father!" Olfer paused and frowned, "Alemanni? Who are the Alemanni?"

Ulrich was dumbstruck. He had led his friends to this battle eagerly, expecting to fight back against the overpowering threat of the Alemanni, but instead found himself in a petty squabble between Saxon lords. This was idiocy. There was no time for this. Ulrich's blood feud with uncle Edwald was forgotten in the pressing need to defend his people from a greater threat.

A horn sounded, and the enemy army was on the move. Olfer turned and began shouting commands.

"Those men in front," Olfer yelled. "Shields together. Overlap your shield in front of the man on your left. You protect his right. Focus on your shield." There was a crash of noise as the wooden shields slammed together to form the shield wall.

Lord Olfer continued, and his voice began to become strident with the unaccustomed strain of shouting, "Stab down with your spears or up with your swords but do not break the shield wall. Axe men stand in the second row. Your job is to reach over your fellows and shatter the enemy shields."

He turned his horse and rode slowly down the line. "The rear ranks will lend their weight to the men in front. When the shield walls meet, you must drive forward into the enemy. If a man in front of you falls, you take his place. There will be no retreat from this battle. Only victory."

Lord Olfer rode his horse into the line. Men parted to let him pass, and a boy ran from the woods to take his horse as he dismounted. He unclasped his shield from the saddle and took his place to the left of his son.

Sigmund was nervous. "What do we do now?" he asked Ulrich. By this time, the rival Saxon army had already advanced halfway down the field. They beat their weapons against their shields as they advanced. Ulrich's own line was silent and apprehensive.

Ulrich shook his head. "I do not know," he admitted. He looked around. On his right was Sigmund's worried face. To his left stood Arend, who looked confident and proud. Behind Ulrich was a tall, bareheaded man who hefted a logging axe. Green eyes shone from a sun-tanned face. The stranger's only protection was a long cowhide shift that hung to his knees. He was barefoot.

The stranger looked down at Ulrich and smiled, "I am glad that I am standing behind you," he said, slapping him on the shoulder lightheartedly. "That armor looks strong."

Ulrich was glad for the protection of his armor. The steel segments covered him from throat to waist, and metal-reinforced straps protected his groin. Heavy leather boots and gloves would ward off the casual sword thrust, and he wore a stout steel helmet. His shield was clasped tightly in his left hand, and his big axe, honed to a razor's edge, hung low in his right. He glanced at his companions, and while their fine chainmail was certainly better protection than most men had, he felt a sudden pang of guilt that he would fight in equipment that was so much better than his friends'.

Tau swore. "It is utter stupidity to fight one another when your kingdom is under threat," he said. He pointed with his sword, gesturing at the center of the enemy line. "Is that your uncle there? The fancily dressed one?"

Ulrich looked to see that uncle Edwald led the enemy army down the field. The treacherous man was wearing Ulrich's father's distinctive, ancient armor of fine bronze scales. That armor, heirloom of an older age, gleamed like a polished jewel among the dull rabble. Ulrich felt his jaw clench involuntarily.

Suddenly there was no more time for talk. The enemy charged downhill, roaring their battle cries. The defenders yelled back in response, but to Ulrich it sounded more like a scream of terror than one of victory. To his right men began to edge away. Those who were outside the protection of the shield wall cringed in fear of the terrible horde who rushed toward them, but the trained warriors of the vanguard were staunch, and the shield wall stood firm, awaiting the impact.

With a crash of wood and steel, the center of the enemy line slammed into the King's guard. The enemy formed a wedge mirroring their own, with the best warriors at the point of a broad arrow aimed at the center of their shield wall. Because of the staggered formation, it would still be a few moments before the men on the flanks would engage the enemy.

The enemy line had become ragged during the rush downhill, and their shields no longer touched. A man charged Ulrich with his mouth open in an incoherent scream, and Ulrich could count the man's yellowed teeth. Ulrich's mouth was dry, and his heart was racing. This enemy warrior was a pace ahead of his companions and brandished a shield and a short-handled axe. Ulrich could not draw his eyes from its gleaming blade as the man raced toward him. He convulsively gripped the handles of his shield and ducked his head behind the board as the fearsome warrior leapt the last few paces.

The warrior slammed bodily into Ulrich's shield, but that shield held strong. The friendly warrior in Ulrich's second row had leant his weight to the defense, and Ulrich grunted as he met the momentum of the charging man. The attacker, his own shield held like an outstretched battering ram, recoiled from the blow and stumbled backward. He would have fallen except that the swarm behind caught up and pushed him forward. All around was the crash of shield on shield and weapon on wood. Men screamed in terror and pain, adding to the din. Ulrich's enemy had not yet regained his balance. Ulrich lowered his shield, stepped a pace forward, and swung his axe. The blade traced a high arc that ended deep in the man's shoulder. He put all the energy of his anger and frustration into the savage blow. The man's simple leather armor was poor protection against such an attack, and the heavy blade slid through flesh and muscle, smashing down through the man's collarbone and ribcage before finally coming to a rest in his lungs. Ulrich ripped the axe up and away in a fountain of blood and stepped back.

Ulrich locked shields once again with Arend on his left and Sigmund on his right. The man Ulrich had attacked was on the ground, blood burbling at his mouth, and the next enemy warrior snatched up the fallen man's shield. He locked shields with his own brethren, and together they approached more warily.

Arend had cheered Ulrich's small victory, but Lord Olfer was furious. "Don't break the line, you fool," Olfer bellowed in admonishment.

Ulrich complied, feeling ashamed of his mistake. He waited for the next onslaught, which came almost at once. Only two paces away, the enemy line had reformed as a solid mass of shields. Men were peering cautiously over the overlapping boards as they came forward. Ulrich's shield was met by two of the enemy's, and he held his ground as the pressure came on. He leaned into it, and this time the weight did not relent as the enemy pushed forward.

The battle shrank to a tiny claustrophobic space. Ulrich's world existed only behind his shield. To his right and left, Sigmund and Arend grunted, and their shoulders pressed into his own. An axe glanced off the steel rim of Ulrich's shield, and he ducked as the axe searched again and again, hacking at him from above. He had no space to swing his own axe, and he was forced to bring his right forearm up to bolster his shield as the pressure increased.

Ulrich was leaning at a sharp angle, and he swore as he felt his feet slide on the soft turf. His shield slipped for an instant off Sigmund's as he was forced backward. A spear, its wielder unseen, flashed instantly into the vulnerable gap, and Sigmund cried out in pain as its sharp point cut through his mail to scrape into his side. Ulrich strained forward with a furious heave to lock the shields again. The spear was trapped between the shields, and it hung there, bobbing impotently and obscenely in the empty air.

"Are you alright?" Ulrich asked. His face was only inches from Sigmund's, but he had to shout to be heard over the noise of battle.

"It's just a scratch," Sigmund grunted. The big man's face was sheened with sweat and his massive muscles stood out like cords on his bare arms.

The battle had turned into a shoving match. Ulrich had thought he was ready for this. His whole life he had trained to fight in the shield wall, but now he felt nothing but overwhelming frustration. His axe was trapped and useless in the confining space, and all his skills meant nothing in this dense press of battle. An enemy seax was being stabbed under his shield. Its wielder was thrusting blindly, and the blade thrashed about in empty space just inches to Ulrich's left. The man behind Ulrich was swinging his axe in short overhead strokes. The shaft was too short to reach the heads of the enemy, but he could reach their shields, so he kept chopping, driving great splinters of wood into the air as he attempted to shatter the enemy's defenses.

The flow of time began to unravel, losing all meaning in that universe of grunting, straining, and sweating. The battle seemed to go on and on and on. They pushed and stabbed. Axes swung, and men grunted curses. A hawk circled above, apparently insensible to the terrible struggle below, and Ulrich watched it fly, wings outstretched as it rode a thermal ever higher into the blue sky. Something hit him in the stomach, and he looked down. The searching enemy sword had found his torso and began stabbing at it. The blade was unable to penetrate Ulrich's heavy armor, but it stabbed again and again, clinking irritatingly against his segmented steel cuirass.

The futility grated at Ulrich's mind. All their hopes of striking back at the Alemanni were trodden underfoot as Saxon fought Saxon in this pointless battle. Ulrich ground his teeth in frustration. Wiglaf's death, the destruction of their home, the invasion of the Alemanni— these were the things that mattered. Chnodomar was the true enemy, and all would be lost if the Saxon kingdoms weakened themselves here.

A new sound permeated the battlefield. The drumming of hooves filled the air—rhythmic and ominous. Ulrich tried to look for the source of the noise, but he could not see past the sweaty bodies around him or the tall shields in front of him. Suddenly, the enemy line shuddered like a drum struck by a giant mallet.

CHAPTER TWENTY-ONE

Ima watched the battle aghast. She, too, had believed that they were marching to fight the Alemanni, and she had anticipated the confrontation with relish. The Saxons may not have been a proper, well organized battle line, but they were all big, hardy warriors. She had felt fiercely proud as she watched her people march to fight the invaders who destroyed her home.

Seeing that the enemy was not the Alemanni after all but was just a rival Saxon lord, she was outraged. She was in her mail, her sword strapped across her back and Rag behind her in the saddle as she sat on her horse. She held the reins in clenched fists as she watched the shield walls smash into each other in a pointless fight.

For a long time, it seemed very little was happening. A trickle of wounded men limped or dragged themselves away from both sides, but for the most part the two armies pushed and clawed at each other impotently. They were evenly matched and equally stubborn. Ima had ridden out of the trees to watch the battle, and it was she who first saw the unexpected newcomers appear.

On the far horizon there was movement at the tree line. Strange horsemen stepped forward from the shadow of the woods. They were joined by more and more until there were hundreds gathering on the far edge of the field. The hundreds were joined by hundreds more until they became thousands.

In all her years Ima had never imagined that so many men and horses existed in the entire world, let alone on a single field. The field was swarming with them, teeming with them, until they filled the horizon like locusts summoned forth by a vengeful god. It was impossible for her to count them. How many were there? Five thousand? Ten? There were so many horsemen filling the far reaches that the warring battle lines in the foreground looked like a puny scuffle in comparison to the enormous host that had suddenly appeared.

The newly arrived cavalry were Alemanni; of that, Ima was certain. While the Saxon army were a rabble in assorted leather and fur, these men were in uniform. They wore white linen tunics over shining chainmail. All the horsemen wore polished iron helmets and carried long spears with steel tips. Even at this distance she recognized Chnodomar, leading them from the front and center of the horde. He stood out as the biggest man among them, and his size was accentuated as he rode a tall white stallion. From his gleaming steel helmet hung a long red horsehair plume, waving side to side as his horse trotted along the turf.

The battling Saxon armies were oblivious to the new threat. They were blind in the shield wall, each man seeing little more than a few inches in front of his face, insensible of the horsemen that loomed so close. The Alemanni cavalry advanced downhill at a trot, approaching the rear of enemy Edwald's shield wall. The Alemanni horde was huge, and even riding shoulder to shoulder the mass of horsemen outstretched both Saxon shield walls. For a moment, Ima wondered if the Alemanni might have allied with the enemy Saxons, but that thought was quickly put to rest when she saw Chnodomar lean from his horse and casually stab a wounded Saxon warrior who had been limping away from the enemy line.

Kicking their mounts into a gallop the Alemanni center charged, spears lowered, into the vulnerable rear of the enemy Saxon army. Meanwhile, the wings of the cavalry flowed around the battle like an onrushing flood. Horsemen galloped toward the undefended women and children at the edge of the forest, and Ima turned, seeking Johanne and the children in the developing chaos.

The shudder that Ulrich had felt was the Alemanni cavalry charge striking into the rear of the enemy Saxon shield wall. He stumbled forward as the pressure from his opponents suddenly disappeared. He lowered his shield to discover catastrophe. The enemy shield wall had dissolved, and the warriors who had been fighting so fervently a moment before were fleeing in desperation from the unexpected foe. Except there was nowhere to go. In all directions the Alemanni horsemen flowed, spreading death. Three men in front of him, Saxons who had just been Ulrich's enemy, scattered, dropping their shields and trying to run back up the hill the way they had come. They only made it a few paces before being cut down by flashing spears.

Sigmund watched a fleeing warrior die. He had no idea if the Saxon had been friend or foe. An Alemanni horseman, white tunic flapping, charged at the man and stabbed his spear. The weapon slid into the man's back and out his chest before lodging in the dirt. Momentum of galloping horse and horseman snapped the wooden shaft like a twig, leaving the skewered man propped grotesquely in the air. The Alemanni warrior, laughing with the joy of battle, dropped the broken haft and drew a long steel sword to hack at another running man.

Saxon bodies littered the field, horses cantered, and Alemanni shouted in triumph as they wheeled through the broken mass. Ulrich and his closest companions, Sigmund, Tau, Arend, and Olfer, had reflexively backed into a circle, shields and weapons facing outward at the chaos. There were a dozen other such knots as men stood together like breakwaters against this flood of horses and death. For the first desperate moments they were ignored as the Alemanni sought the easier prey that panicked and scattered, but then Ulrich saw two horsemen angle toward them.

These Alemanni had just finished slaughtering half a dozen running fugitives, casually riding at an easy trot and slashing down at the helpless prey. They saw the huddle of five men standing alone, and feeling confident, kicked their horses into a galloping charge.

Ulrich and Sigmund were nearest as the enemy rushed down upon them. One of the men pointed a spear at Ulrich and stabbed forward. Ulrich deflected the blow with the boss of his shield and, as the man galloped by, he swung his axe up to cut into the man's neck, spraying blood. The other man swung an axe at Sigmund who blocked the blow with his shield. Sigmund responded with a powerful counterstroke of his mace, catching the horseman in the stomach. The Alemanni soldier was lifted clear off the saddle by the heavy weapon to thump to the ground at Sigmund's feet.

Ulrich heard a clash of steel behind him and saw Tau stab his sword into an Alemanni horse. The blade drove into its chest, and the animal reared, screaming in pain as it threw its rider to the ground. Just to Ulrich's left, Arend deflected a thrown spear, protectively covering his father with his shield, and Lord Olfer's eyes were wide with fear.

Another man came at Ulrich. He rode as though he was going to pass by on the left, but at the last moment he wrenched the reins hard, meaning to swing his sword down at Ulrich's right side. Ulrich saw through the simple feint. He stepped forward and punched the horse's nose with his shield boss before the turn could be completed. The animal, stunned, tripped sideways, and the rider screamed in panic as he fell. The rider's femur broke with a snap as his mount landed on top of him.

Their private battle waged on. Ulrich cut down another horse and rider as they galloped past. Arend grabbed a fallen spear and threw it like a javelin, skewering a charging horseman who tumbled from the saddle. Sigmund howled in rage and fear as he lashed out with his heavy mace, and the enemy bodies began to pile around the desperately fighting companions.

Nearby, a knot of Saxon warriors was broken as milling horsemen stabbed again and again with long spears. They bled the trapped men until the men no longer had the strength to lift their weapons. Ulrich looked on and knew that he and his friends would die like those men. He put a foot on a dead horse and bellowed his defiance. He brandished his reddened axe and roared, taunting his foe. If he was to die here he would take as many with him as he could.

CHAPTER TWENTY-TWO

Across the battlefield, Johanne and Ima herded women and children away from the chaos. They had seen the Saxon armies broken and knew that the enemy would soon be coming for them. Johanne and Ima told them to take their children and scatter, to stay off the road, to take every horse that could carry them. Many would be captured, but some might still escape to seek shelter in some friendly kingdom.

Johanne balanced Ælfwine and Gebhard in the saddle, and Rag held Ima's horse while Ima helped as many as she could. There were dozens of horses, mostly those that had belonged to the king's men, milling about the edge of the woods. Ima worked desperately to get women and elderly into saddles and to pass children up into waiting, anxious arms. She sent them in all directions, hoping to get many away before the Alemanni horde broke upon them.

Suddenly it was too late. A knot of Alemanni horsemen charged up the slope, dirt and broken stalks of grain thrown in gouts behind the flying hooves. At their head was King Chnodomar himself, huge and terrible, red horsehair plume waving with the wind of his passage. With his left hand on the reins, his muscled right arm hung low, hand gripping a red-dripping sword. His teeth were bared in a grin of victory and his armor was splashed with Saxon blood. Ima cursed and leapt into the saddle, pulling Rag up behind her.

"Go! Go!" she shouted at Johanne, and the race began. They fled for the safety of the trees, frightened horses leaping to the gallop. Ima glanced back to find Chnodomar gaining on them. Johanne, with her two children balanced precariously in the saddle, simply could not drive her horse any faster without risking the children. Ima kept pace with her friend, watching the enemy approach and fighting back the fear that threatened to consume her. There were dozens of horsemen closing in but Chnodomar was ahead of the others. The big man was on a tall, fast horse, and the gap was closing quickly. Ima touched the hilt of her scabbarded sword and steeled her nerves. She was prepared to fight to give Johanne and the children time to escape.

Rag had been sitting behind Ima in the saddle, but suddenly she felt him shift. The boy used her shoulders to steady himself while he rose to his feet, balancing on the horse's rump. Standing, he turned toward the enemy and drew a small knife from a pouch at his belt. Chnodomar was no more than ten feet away now, vicious sneer on his broad face as he lifted his bloody sword.

"Rag, no!" She yelled, wrenching at her horse's reins to turn the beast away, but it was too late. Rag leapt from the saddle. He flew through the air, arms outstretched, and landed like a tree squirrel, all four limbs wrapped about the Alemanni leader's torso. With an adolescent scream of rage, Rag tried to stab Chnodomar in the neck with his knife, but the man's thick fur collar frustrated his attempt. Chnodomar frowned in consternation. He tried to shake the boy free, but with one hand on the reins and the other on his sword, he was momentarily helpless. The big man jerked on the reins, and the confused horse slowed.

The distraction gave Johanne the time she needed to escape. Her horse reached the eaves, and she and her children disappeared into the undergrowth, becoming just another family amid the scattering, fleeing, panicked crowd.

Ima did not escape. Her horse finally responded to the reins, and she turned. She was halfway between Chnodomar and the woods. A horde of Alemanni screamed up the slope behind. Ima drew her long sword.

Rag, meanwhile, had given up on trying to pierce the fur armor at his enemy's neck, and he drew his hand up, slashing the blade across Chnodomar's face in a spray of blood. The Alemanni leader grunted in pain and dropped the reins. He reached up with his now free hand, grabbed the back of Rag's shirt and flung the boy to the ground. Rag hit hard, landing stunned on his back, shocked eyes staring into the cloudless sky. Chnodomar leaned from the saddle. His sword stabbed down once and killed the boy where he lay.

"Damn you!" Ima screamed. She leveled her sword, and

Chnodomar's eyes met hers. Blood ran down his sword and dripped from his cheek and nose. His face was a mask of cold malevolence. His eyes were dark pools of pitiless violence. Behind him more warriors came at the gallop. After a moment of struggle, the rational part of her mind won over her rage. Staying to fight would just be suicide. She sheathed her sword, spat on the ground, and fled into the woods.

Ulrich had seen it all. Framed on the slope he had watched Chnodomar, red horsehair plume streaming from his bright helmet, ride uphill above the milling horsemen. His breath had caught in his lungs when he realized that those distant fleeing figures were his family. He had seen Rag leap between the saddles and Ulrich's heart had stopped when Chnodomar's blade drove down, splashing Rag's blood into the air.

Ulrich bellowed in impotent rage, challenging his tormentors. He was mad with grief and pain. He wanted them to come and fight. He wanted to kill them all, but the enemy was cautious now. Ulrich and his small, huddled band had cut down a dozen Alemanni warriors, and still stood defiant, soaked in their enemy's blood. An Alemanni horseman dismounted and produced a bow and a quiver of arrows. Ulrich considered rushing at the man, but knew that if he did he would be cut down by the watching horsemen. Reluctantly, he returned to the safety of his shield.

The archer picked out an arrow with a deliberate slowness. He inspected it carefully before nocking it to his bow. With a smooth movement, he pulled the string back to his ear and released. The arrow streaked across the field to bury itself with a thump into the wood of Arend's raised shield. The Alemanni cheered. Ulrich's small huddle of men was the only quarry left, and the horsemen were content to sit and watch their prey picked slowly apart. A second arrow flew, this time embedding itself into Ulrich's shield. Another man dismounted and pulled a bow from his saddlebag.

Ulrich and his companions huddled together, protected by their shields as the missiles streaked in from all sides. They were miserable and frustrated, tired and humiliated, and the Alemanni laughed as they toyed with the trapped men. They hid behind the wooden boards as the arrows smashed again and again into the thick oak. They were too tired to talk. There was no escape, no reprieve. More than one arrow sliced a shallow cut into Ulrich's arm as its sharpened

118

head penetrated his shield. Finally Ulrich heard a deep voice raised above the din and the missiles stopped. He lowered his shield to see Chnodomar standing only paces away.

Ulrich snarled an incoherent challenge and stood, dropping his shield to grip his axe with both clenched hands, but a dozen men stood by the Alemanni King with waiting spears, and more archers waited with bows drawn. Chnodomar wore the elation of victory. His handsome face was set in a broad smile. Blood dripped from his long sword, held low in his right hand. He bore Rag's knife wound on his face unflinchingly, a shallow cut running from the bridge of his nose to the angle of his left jaw, and he ignored the slow trickle of blood that dripped onto the fur collar of his heavy cloak. The Alemanni army waited reverently as Chnodomar addressed the companions.

"I remember you!" Chnodomar boomed. He grinned at Ulrich with pleasant recognition. "And how could I forget the black one?" He indicated Tau. "I saw you at Kassel during the feast. My men tell me that it was you who set loose our prisoners that night." The big man sounded amused. "That was a brave move, taking them from right under my nose. Impressive. I like you. You and your men have shown great strength." Chnodomar nodded with approval at the pile of Alemanni corpses that surrounded Ulrich and his companions. He used his long cloak to wipe the blood from his blade before sheathing it.

Off to the west, Ulrich could hear the screams of the women and children who had failed to escape the Alemanni pursuit. All about the field there were the groans of wounded men, but close around them it was quiet. Hundreds of Alemanni horsemen had gathered to watch this encounter, and they sat respectful and silent in the presence of their leader.

But Ulrich was angry. He was not listening to Chnodomar's words but instead was measuring the distance between himself and the big man. He was deciding if he should venture a charge or if he would have better luck trying for an axe throw from this distance. He lifted his battle axe.

"Let me gut the bastard," Tau growled. He dropped his shield to draw his second sword, but Sigmund, wordlessly, held him back.

Chnodomar's grin slowly fell. He looked disappointed. "That is a brave sentiment," he admitted, "but it is highly unlikely that you would succeed." He gestured at the horde of ready warriors. "Your hostility is unreasonable and unnecessary. I invite you brave warriors to join my men. We value strength above all things, and skill like yours will make you lords among my people."

Sigmund answered for all of them. "You may be strong, but it is because of your strength that we fight you. You and your men have uprooted tribes, you have burned homes, you have killed families in your quest for power. On your sword is the blood of a boy, a youth who was like a brother to us. You struck him down without a thought. That is not a strength that impresses us, Chnodomar. Strength should be used to protect the weak, not to dominate them."

Chnodomar frowned in puzzlement. He considered Sigmund's words seriously, but he knew one truth: that his purpose in this life was to entertain Thor and Odin with his valor in war. He believed that the gods put strength into the world to separate the worthy from the weak. A breeze rustled his long red hair, and he looked around. His army covered the field, huge and victorious, and the sight filled him with fierce pride. His gaze turned south, toward Rome, and he thought of how he must enact that evil empire's destruction. Their fall would avenge his forefathers and would be sure to delight the gods. Only victory would ensure Chnodomar's place of honor in Valhalla. His frown was driven away by a fresh swell of purpose.

"Take them," Chnodomar ordered, turning away. "Keep them alive."

Ulrich, Tau, Sigmund, Arend, and Olfer were confronted with the leveled spears of an army. They dropped their weapons.

CHAPTER TWENTY-THREE

Having achieved the destruction of the northern Saxon kingdoms, the victorious Alemanni army returned south. Ulrich and his companions were relieved of their armor, weapons, and boots and left barefoot, with only with their woolen nightshirts as protection against the gathering autumn chill. Their wrists were bound with coarse rope, and the ends of these ropes were tied to the saddles of their captors' horses. For the first few hours, the Alemanni made game of them. They took turns kicking their horses to a run, yanking the captives to be dragged along the rough ground. Thankfully the Alemanni soon tired of this and were content to let the prisoners, bruised and humiliated, slog along behind the walking horses.

Ulrich took the opportunity to inspect the enemy. He was surprised to find that many only bore simple spears or axes and wore leather armor or fur. Not every man of the Alemanni actually had chainmail coats and fine steel swords; it had only seemed that way because the best-equipped men were the ones who led the charge. Even so, Ulrich was disheartened. He guessed there were six thousand horsemen in this army. Even the combined might of Saxony, had they been united rather than fighting each other, would have been overwhelmed by such strength. He wondered at the fabulous wealth required to mount and arm such a force. How many other tribes had these Alemanni conquered already?

There were other captives besides Ulrich and his band. Captured Saxon warriors, likewise bound and yanked along, were scattered among the moving horsemen. Carts from the Saxon baggage transported women and children who were doomed to a life of slavery. They did not bother to bind these prisoners on the carts. After they unceremoniously speared the first few children who tried to escape, they had no more trouble from them.

Ulrich searched those carts desperately for Ima, Johanne, Ælfwine, and Gebhard but they were nowhere to be seen. He hoped that meant they had escaped and were not lying dead somewhere in the pitiless Saxon hills. He did notice his father's old bronze scale armor. As the mass of horses moved, he spotted a man wearing the distinctive cuirass in the group riding closest to King Chnodomar. The man was a tall, blond warrior, and the armor was sheeted in blood that was quickly turning into a black stain. Ulrich wondered if that meant his treacherous uncle had finally met his end at the hands of the Alemanni. The thought gave Ulrich no joy but only emphasized the totality of the Alemanni victory. Chnodomar, after having him stripped of his possessions, had tried on Ulrich's own steel cuirass, but finding it too small for him, had gifted it to another one of his chosen warriors at the head of the column.

They rode south for ten days. The Alemanni seemed to be in no hurry. They rode brazenly along the roads. During the day the defeated walked and stumbled behind the horses, and at night, they huddled together under heavy guard. The Alemanni ate at dawn and dusk, and the prisoners were tossed the leftovers of these meals.

Finally the fortress town of Kassel heaved into sight. The city had swollen with people. Crowds flooded the streets, cheering their victors. The prisoners were paraded down the avenue before the roaring masses. They were thrown in cages near the town square, and queues of men and women formed to gloat and insult the captives. They seemed to particularly enjoy gawking at Tau. A black-skinned man on display was a novelty in the German hills. Ulrich and his companions were caged together, and there were half a dozen such cages, each similarly packed with captured Saxon warriors.

They were tired, bruised and hungry after the brutal march, but once they were back to the town, they were at least better fed. An elderly woman was tasked with keeping the prisoners alive. She kept a large kettle nearby, bubbling over an open fire where she stewed broth constantly, adding beef, chicken, and barley to keep pace with the prisoners' needs. Still, conditions worsened as the fall air was turning cold, and the prisoners huddled together at night for warmth. Meanwhile a festival erupted as Kassel celebrated its warriors' victory.

By the third day of their imprisonment, the celebration began to die down, and a slave market opened. Near their cages was a broad open field, and on the far quarter of this field a high wooden stage was arranged. One by one the Saxon women and children were brought to that stage to be auctioned off to the highest bidder. It was Sigmund who noted that not all the patrons were Alemanni.

"I think that the Alemanni are just the ringleaders. Most of the people here represent various different peoples," Sigmund said. He pointed out strangely attired men and women of the milling throng, ones with different accents of German and with darker or lighter tones of hair, skin, and eye color. "I cannot identify them by name," Sigmund admitted, "but I think I can count at least five different tribes gathered here."

"So what does that mean?" Tau asked.

"It means that the Alemanni strength comes from its alliance of tribes, not from a single tribe." Sigmund's intelligent eyes turned to his companions. "It could also be a weakness. If the leaders lose their popularity their allies may abandon them."

Ulrich shrugged. "I just wonder what they have planned for us next."

"I have a guess," Tau responded. "They are not selling us in the market. They are saving us for something else. I think they intend to make us fight for their amusement. Why else keep us like this? But I know one thing." Tau flashed white teeth. "The man who gives me a weapon is going to regret it."

Tau's prediction was right. On the fifth day, the fights began. It was a chill fall morning, and the sun rose in a cloudless sky. Ulrich had slept fitfully. His rough shirt was his only protection from the cold nighttime air. He awoke and relieved himself in the clay pot provided for that purpose then received a bowl of hot soup gratefully. He watched a team of slaves clear the field.

The slaves swept away fallen leaves before drawing a circle of chalk. The circle marked an empty space about twenty paces across. The ground sloped down here, making the field something of a natural amphitheater, and people began to file onto the slopes. They brought furs and blankets, food and wine. They appeared to be settling in for a pleasant picnic. A dozen empty chairs, the largest a veritable throne, were set up on the wooden auction stage.

At noon the entertainment began. It started innocently enough with a series of wrestling matches. For two hours, Alemanni warriors squared off against each other. Bets were placed, and combatants were cheered. Victory went to the man who either pinned the other or forced their opponent out of the ring of chalk. Ulrich was starting to doze when the roar of the crowd, rising to a fever pitch, woke him.

Chnodomar stood before his throne. Armed men guarded the stage, and the other elevated chairs were now filled. Ulrich guessed that those men who found seats on the platform were the lords of allied tribes, for they were resplendent in gold and silver arm rings and wore a motley of brightly colored tunics and furs. In contrast, Chnodomar was bare chested against the cool, late-autumn day, dressed in leather breeches and a wolf's-fur cloak clasped with an iron chain. A dark scab had formed over the wound on his face, and his long red hair was unbound, flowing in an unruly mass to his shoulders. He dominated the scene.

The crowd cheered him wildly until he threw up his hands for silence.

"Friends and allies," he addressed the crowd in a booming voice. "All of Germania is now ours."

The cheering erupted once again, and the big man waited patiently for it to die down before continuing.

"The Saxons are our slaves," Chnodomar said, "and soon, we march on Rome. You have seen their cities of stone; you have seen their fertile fields; you have seen their strong fortresses. Imagine those are your cities and imagine those are your fields and imagine those are your fortresses." He clenched his fist, his voice angry now. "You have seen their treachery, and for their betrayal, they shall pay dearly."

Ulrich did not know what treachery Chnodomar was referring to, but the crowd responded to his words. Discontented grumbling sounded among the gathered men and women.

Chnodomar paused, and as quickly as it had come, his anger disappeared, replaced with a broad smile, "Besides, have you ever seen a Roman?" He held out a hand at chest height. "They are only this tall. How can they defend their walls when they cannot even see over them?"

This comment was greeted by laughter. "But today is a day of celebration," he said cheerfully. "Enjoy your next entertainment." He waved his hand at the cages where the captured Saxon warriors were penned. He returned to his throne, sitting comfortably, an expectant look on his genial face.

A dozen Alemanni soldiers approached the cages. Each man wore fine chainmail and carried a long spear. They selected the cage two down from where Ulrich and his companions were penned and opened it. The Saxon prisoners were forced out and ushered forward into the ring of chalk. The man on Chnodomar's right stood.

"I am Serapio," he said, introducing himself more to the crowd at large than to the five unlucky men. "I am nephew and liege-lord to the king. You should know my name."

The man who spoke did bear some passing resemblance to Chnodomar, but where the king was red-haired and broad faced, Serapio was dark and thin. If the Alemanni king were a lion, Serapio was a snake. He wore a copper circlet in his brown hair, and his fine linen tunic was whitened with chalk. He addressed the prisoners in the circle.

"The only reason you have survived this long is because of your strength in battle," he said. "He among you who proves to be the strongest will have won his life." He signaled with his long fingers, and five daggers were thrown to the dirt in the middle of the arena.

The prisoners hesitated. They were strong-looking men to Ulrich's eyes. Based on their simple clothing, he guessed they had been farmers at the time of the catastrophic battle rather than members of the Saxon king's retinue. Still, Saxons were a hardy breed, and they were natural fighters, even if they were not trained warriors. But now fear showed in their eyes, and all five seemed frozen in indecision.

Serapio snapped his fingers impatiently. Alemanni soldiers advanced on the men with leveled spears. In response, the prisoners gingerly stooped. Each selected a knife and stepped back. The Alemanni spears were withdrawn, and the Saxons looked fearfully at each other.

There was a long, tense silence. Ulrich and his companions watched horrified from where they stood, trapped in their own cage.

"My God," Olfer said softly, sitting heavily on the cage floor. "They can't really…"

Olfer never finished his sentence because, as he watched, the bloodshed began. One of the Saxons glanced too long at the man to his left, and another saw his chance. His knife flashed to sink into the man's back, and blood splashed bright into the clear autumn air. The fight was over in a horrible moment of knives stabbing again and again into unprotected flesh. Ulrich could only stare, speechless.

When the horror was over one man was still standing, but he swayed on his feet. The crowd roared their approval. The man had been the biggest, tallest and heaviest of the five prisoners. He was dripping blood from a dozen deep wounds. He tried to take a step and staggered.

Serapio clapped politely, addressing the wounded man. "Well done. To you I give a final choice. You may take your freedom and leave, or you may join my entourage as a chosen warrior of the Alemanni. What is your answer?"

The Saxon man did not respond. His eyes wandered crazily. He looked as though he were going to speak, then he suddenly bent forward and vomited blood. He collapsed in a heap on the ground. Chnodomar exploded with laughter, and the crowd joined him in his mirth.

Serapio looked offended. "Well, that was impolite," he said testily. He waved a hand, and a team of slaves cleared away the bodies. Ulrich heard retching and turned to see Olfer vomiting into the dirt of the cage. His son, Arend, was comforting him, but Arend was looking distinctly green himself.

"Next," Serapio commanded.

The next cage in line was opened. Those men were brought to the chalk circle, and this scuffle got off to a much quicker start than the first. Knowing what to expect, the five Saxons raced to grab knives from the bloodstained ground before leaping back, eyeing each other warily. The victor of this round won handily. He was a small man, but he was very fast, leaping in and out of the reach of the others to plant blow after deep blow. When it was over he stood tall above the four bodies that were once his companions. He was breathing hard, but other than some shallow slashes, was unwounded. The crowd cheered.

Serapio smiled and stood. "You understand the offer. Will you stay with us for victory or will you run away, only to be defeated later?"

The victorious Saxon hesitated. "Will you feed me?" he asked.

"Of course. All Alemanni warriors feast like kings," Serapio responded. His voice held an edge of annoyance.

This Saxon chose to join the Alemanni. He bowed low and offered the knife, hilt-first, to Serapio. The thin prince did not deign to step down to accept the weapon, but instead ordered a soldier to escort him away. The man went willingly.

Now it was their turn. The twelve spear-armed soldiers escorted Ulrich and his companions out of the cage. They went to the chalk circle as the crowd looked on.

CHAPTER TWENTY-FOUR

A rend and Olfer looked ill as they walked to their doom. Tau bore a look of proud defiance, and Sigmund was strangely placid. Ulrich walked straight to the pile of blood-slick knives and snatched one up, but Ulrich did not turn on his friends. Instead, he hefted his knife and glared up at the stage. He bared his teeth in a savage grin.

"Tau, I believe you are getting your wish," Ulrich said.

Serapio was confused. Certainly these prisoners were not foolish enough to try to fight their way out of this? He glanced at his uncle, but Chnodomar was not looking at him. The king was gazing down at the prisoners, an enigmatic grin slowly growing on his face. Serapio snapped his fingers, and the spear-bearing Alemanni soldiers advanced once again.

Sigmund chuckled, "If I had known we were going to be fighting the whole Alemanni horde today, I wouldn't have pissed myself earlier. I would have saved it to piss myself now."

"It is an honor to die alongside you men," Olfer said, his voice somber.

"Let us just see how many of them we can take with us," Tau responded savagely, then he threw himself upon the enemy.

Tau attacked. With an upward slash, he struck the nearest spear point with his knife. The metal blades rang together, and the strike was so fast and so sudden that the spear was deflected in the Alemanni soldier's hands. Truly, the heavy spear, with its much greater mass, did not move more than a few inches, but Tau had caught the man off guard. The brief instant of surprise was all he needed, and he used it to duck under the sharpened blade. He lunged forward and slashed his small knife through the soldier's unprotected neck, spraying blood. Just that quickly, the count of their enemies was down to eleven.

Meanwhile, Ulrich had been sizing up the enemy nearest to him—a tall warrior with a dark beard who faced him with a leveled spear. Ulrich saw the warrior's eyes flicker to the left, heard the crash of steel as Tau attacked, and watched his opponent's eyes widen with surprise. With his free hand, Ulrich grabbed the shaft of the man's spear and pulled. The Alemanni soldier stumbled forward, and Ulrich stabbed with his knife as he pulled. The blade punched clean through the Alemanni chainmail and implanted itself to the hilt in the man's chest. The look of surprise on the man's face had turned to shock and pain. He coughed blood. As the dying man's grip weakened, Ulrich yanked the spear from his grasp and turned it on the enemy. He brandished the weapon and stepped forward, snarling at the surrounding Alemanni warriors.

In the next instant, four more of the Alemanni went down. Tau, with his customary quickness, danced into the enemy and slashed a second soldier's throat before the enemy could even react. Sigmund somehow bulled his way past the spears, and barehanded, began smashing two of the Alemanni warriors' heads together. Lord Olfer dropped his knife and grabbed the haft of an enemy spear in each hand, struggling with two of the men. This pinned them in place while Arend moved in and killed them both with his knife. The half-dozen remaining Alemanni recoiled from the unexpected attack.

Tau laughed. He taunted the enemy, dancing in and out of range while stabbing at their faces with a stolen spear. Sigmund had dropped his two senseless foes and held a spear like a club. He was roaring as he swung his weapon at the enemy, trying to fend them off with sheer ferocity alone. But despite their momentary advantage, Ulrich knew they were in trouble. All around him were cries of indignation as the crowd rose to its feet. He heard the distinctive sound of hundreds of swords rasp ominously from hundreds of scabbards. An alarm was going out, and more soldiers would be here soon.

Suddenly, three of the Alemanni soldiers found their courage and rushed at Arend and Olfer. The three enemy spearmen stabbed forward together, and one of them sank his blade deep into Olfer's abdomen. The old man gasped with pain and doubled over. Arend cried out in fury and launched himself at the men, receiving two spear points deep in his own chest. Arend coughed blood and collapsed.

Ulrich moved forward with a snarl, but fresh warriors appeared to threaten with naked swords. The crowd pressed in from all sides. Ulrich, Tau and Sigmund were forced into a tight knot in the midst of a tightening, vengeful mob. Ulrich knew he was going to die and felt a strange sense of calm as a hundred blades came forward.

"Stop," Chnodomar's massive voice boomed. Men were shoved out of the way as the big man pushed through the crowd. He stood before Ulrich and his companions. He had no escort and carried no weapons. He folded his massive arms on his barrel chest. Ulrich was a tall man, but Chnodomar towered over him. He was even bigger than Sigmund. Muscles stood out on his broad shoulders and across his naked torso. He was, incongruously, grinning at the three men. His guileless face showed genuine humor as he spoke.

"What are your names?" the Alemanni king asked with a smile.

Ulrich, still in a rage, growled and took a step forward, but Tau, realizing that they were being given a chance at life, stepped in front of him.

"I am Tau, prince of Ghana," Tau allowed. "This is Ulrich prince of the Saxons, and my other friend here is named Sigmund. Would you like to arrange a truce, or shall we continue slaughtering your men?"

Chnodomar laughed then. "Once again, you have beaten me," he said. He turned to the crowd. "Three cheers for our champions, Tau, Ulrich, and Sigmund," he roared out.

The crowd roared back, raising their voices to a raucous cheer as they shared in their leader's mirth. Men stamped their feet and beat their weapons on their shields. Chnodomar grinned at the three men until the crowd quieted down again.

"I do not suppose you have changed your mind about joining me?" the Alemanni king asked.

Ulrich spoke then, and his voice was bitter and full of fury. "I would never join you, you bastard. You killed Rag."

Chnodomar frowned. He did not know who or what Ulrich was talking about, and he was momentarily at a loss. Unconsciously he ran his hand across the scab on his face.

"I'll kill you," Ulrich growled. He was seeing red, thinking of the cheerful youth. "I swear that I will kill you if it is the last thing that I ever do."

Chnodomar's face was serious, and he nodded gravely. His voice was lower now, intended only for them. "That is a warrior's oath, and I have respect for a promise like that," he responded. "And I should probably murder such a determined enemy." He paused, considering Ulrich and his companions for a long moment. He looked thoughtful, and the crowd murmured. Finally, the Alemanni king made up his mind. "But no. You will live today," he decided finally. "You are clearly loved by the gods. They would be displeased if I killed you before your time. I will not disappoint Thor and Odin of their entertainment."

Chnodomar raised his voice so the whole crowd could hear. "In recognition of these men's strength, I grant them life. But, in return, they are to do us a service. They will go to the Romans, and they will carry a message. They will tell the treacherous Emperor Constantius that the Alemanni are coming for him. That Chnodomar is coming for him." He turned away and stretched his arms in the air as he called out to the gathered mob. "The Romans will fear our coming, and they will know the purpose of their own destruction. They will know it was for their treachery that they perish."

And the crowd roared.

CHAPTER TWENTY-FIVE

Ulrich, Tau, and Sigmund struggled out of the town. Arend was dead. Olfer lived, but he was badly hurt. The spear blade had gone deep into his abdomen. While the bleeding had stopped, the pain was incredible. The old man could walk only with great difficulty and a steadying hand. He wept over his son's body and insisted that they carry Arend to be buried in Saxon soil. They went north, limping away from their enemies, wounded and tired, with no supplies and little protection from the cold fall nights.

The day turned overcast and bleak. The night was moonless and windy-cold. Even the usually irrepressible Sigmund was burdened and somber as they trudged deeper into the German wilderness. They were lucky on the second day, coming across a devastated settlement from which they scavenged a handful of flints, two rusty knives, and a pile of cured pelts that had been somehow overlooked by Alemanni raiding parties.

But by that night it was clear that Olfer was not going to recover from his wounds. He spent the night shivering and sweating, falling deeper into a feverish delirium where he ever cried out for water or called to his son. They tended to him all night, keeping him near their small campfire for warmth, but in the morning, with a last, heart-wrenching moan, he departed to join Arend in the afterlife.

The rising sun found them finally among the dense forests and low hills of the ancestral Saxon lands. They buried father and son side by side on the verge of a grassy field, filling the graves with Saxon soil, and fulfilling the last wish of a dying man.

Ulrich, Tau, and Sigmund sat on the turf beneath the dull gray sky, disheartened and silent. The fresh mounds of disturbed earth were like scars on the green land. Ulrich felt empty.

"What do we do now?" Sigmund asked. His voice was hollow and flat.

Ulrich did not answer. He was tired and cold. His eyes looked unseeing into the gray sky.

But for Tau no future was so bleak as the years he had spent as a slave. At least he could stretch his arms without feeling the binding chains. "This isn't over," he said. "While we live this is not over. We have to keep moving," Tau insisted.

"Where would we go?" Sigmund asked.

"We could go to the Romans," Tau suggested.

"The Romans turn away outsiders from Germany," Sigmund said. "All along the German border they have built tall walls and strong forts to keep us out."

Tau was stubborn. "We have no weapons. There are only three of us. We are no threat to them. They will not turn us away." He looked to Ulrich for support.

Ulrich realized that both faces turned to him for an answer. He forced himself to focus, to consider their options. On one hand it was possible that not all the Saxon lands had succumbed to the Alemanni, perhaps a kingdom survived in the far north, and they could seek asylum there. But then he remembered how Chnodomar had spoken of the Romans, and a flicker of hope flashed in his mind. Chnodomar hated the Romans. He meant to fight them, and Ulrich knew on which side of that fight he wanted to be. The enemy of his enemy would be his ally.

"We cross to Rome," Ulrich said.

So the three of them started west. After some time they reached a crossroads. The milestone read Colonia Agrippina, 107 miles. Ulrich did not know what kind of place Colonia Agrippina was, but with little else to go on, they headed in the direction indicated by the weathered stone. The journey took four days, during which they walked through an empty, ravaged countryside. They lived off the land as they went, spearing fish from streams with sharpened sticks, stopping each night to build a fire and cook their meager meals. Scavenging in a few more ruined homesteads provided some additional necessities, and they kept moving.

Finally they reached the Rhine. They did not know the name of the river then, but they did know that their journey was at an end.

The Roman road stretched through the hilly countryside straight as an arrow. On its junction with the river stood a massive fortress.

Ulrich and his companions found themselves walking toward the largest standing structure that any of them had ever seen. The fortress was an imposing square of narrow brick, one hundred paces per side. Six rounded towers faced out of a broad wall as tall as five men. The place was in the midst of being rebuilt. Piles of broken masonry lay in scattered heaps around the wall's base. Whole lengths of rampart had been pulled down, leaving ragged scars that ran deep into the structure. The wooden gates that crossed the roadway were of fresh, green wood, betraying their new construction, and Ulrich could see busy crews laying new stone along the broken sections. Watchmen moved among the stone crenellations at the wall's top. As they drew within shouting distance, a challenge rang out.

"Halt and state your business," a voice called. It spoke in German, but with a strange dry-twanging accent that Ulrich had never heard before. Armored soldiers watched them approach from above the high wooden gate. Their brightly polished helms had long nose guards and cheek pieces which were strapped tightly under the chin. The sentries were clean shaven, carried long spears, and had short swords strapped about their waists. Two wore segmented heavy armor of the same design that Wiglaf had taught Ulrich to make, lorica segmentata. The rest were in chainmail.

"My friends and I are refugees from the Saxon lands." Tau answered. "We flee the Alemanni and bear a message for a Roman king named Constantius."

After a brief consultation, the doors opened. Six horsemen in identical Roman helmets, fine chainmail, and long lances galloped out of the gateway. They rode in close order and flew past the three men. They raced up the road before fanning out into the open countryside, scouting for any threats. Within the open doors a single man stood waiting, hands clasped behind his back.

Ulrich led his companions through the gates. The thickness of the walls turned the passageway into a shadowed tunnel. The Roman at the end was a black silhouette framed against bright daylight. They stepped out of the shade of the gateway into a wide courtyard.

Within the courtyard, feverish construction was at work. Brick masons worked from scaffolds all about the tall walls, while the grounds of the fortress was a military camp. Leather tents stood in orderly rows beside the path, and twenty archers practiced in a yard at the opposite corner. A dozen horses were stabled to the right, and a company of soldiers drilled in formation nearby.

"I am Legate Severus of the Fifth Legion," the Roman stated flatly. "What news do you bring of the Alemanni?" The officer, like many of his men, was dressed in segmented steel armor, but was distinguished from them with a brilliant red cloak which he wore clasped about his neck. Ulrich noticed, with some surprise, that the man's legs were bare. Rather than trousers, the Roman officer wore a short tunic beneath his armor. The red of its loose cloth ended above his knees. His feet were strapped into leather sandals. Ulrich looked around, and every single Roman soldier that he could see, from the men practicing archery to those holding shields in formation, had legs and arms bare. They seemed to be unfazed by the chill fall day.

Tau spoke again, "We were prisoners of the Alemanni king, Chnodomar. He released us to carry a message to Constantius."

Severus shook his head. "Emperor Constantius is not present in this province. You may tell me what you know, and I shall determine the value of your message."

And so, standing before the officer in the fortress's courtyard, Ulrich and his companions summarized their tale, starting with the Alemanni raids into the Saxon territories, the overwhelming defeat of the twin Saxon armies, and their brief, but violent, imprisonment in the Alemanni base. Severus stood stoically. His face betrayed no emotion as the events were recounted. The man was older than they were, perhaps thirty or thirty-five years old. He had a thin face, short brown hair, olive-colored skin, and dark eyes. He stood much shorter than all three men, perhaps five or six inches less than Ulrich's six feet, but he projected strength and confidence as he faced the three big men alone in the midst of the Roman camp.

When the story was over, Severus nodded. "Caesar of the West, Flavius Claudius Julianus represents Rome in this province. He will wish to hear your news himself, and he may have further questions for you. I will take you to him. But first," he pointed across the yard at a freshly built wooden storehouse, "if you are hungry, the quartermaster will provide you with a ration. I will meet you in one hour." Without another word, the legate turned sharply and walked away.

Ulrich, Sigmund, and Tau were now, quite suddenly, alone in the middle of the Roman encampment. Between the soldiers training and the craftsmen working, the camp hummed with activity, but the three of them were entirely ignored. The six horsemen who had raced to scout the countryside at their arrival rode back in and dismounted, leading their horses to a nearby stable.

"They don't seem to like pants," Sigmund observed. "How are they not cold, though?"

"And they really are as short as Chnodomar said," noted Tau.

Ulrich, meanwhile, was marveling at the precision with which a nearby troop of soldiers was drilling. They paced across the yard in perfect unison, all holding identical tall, rectangular shields at chest height. They marched, turned in step, and marched again. There were a hundred men in the close-packed group, forming a square of ten rows of ten men each. At each turn, a different side of the square was now leading the formation. They marched an even twenty paces, then turned again for another side to lead. Suddenly, an order was shouted, and the formation responded, turning from a dense square into a broad shield wall, a line two men deep and fifty men across. The change was accomplished faster than Ulrich would have believed possible, and he looked on as fifty shields in the front row slammed together into a perfect unbroken aegis. A fraction of a second later, fifty more shields became a roof, lifted by the men in the second row to cover the heads of the men in front. The speed and precision of the move was breathtaking.

"So, that officer mentioned food," Sigmund prompted his companions, and the three of them left the main street and walked toward the aforementioned building. They arrived to be greeted by a portly older man who wore a dark green toga. He sat perched on a tall stool and was flanked by three large tables covered with parchment. Pausing from whatever he had been writing, he smiled cheerfully at the three men.

"Welcome, welcome," the heavyset man spoke in German. "I assume I will be feeding more barbarians today at our good Legate's behest." His tone was friendly. He blinked when he saw Tau. "And an African gentleman too. My goodness you certainly are far from home!"

Tau, for a rare moment, was taken aback. He was used to being treated as some sort of oddity, to pique the curious, if not to be outright feared. People thought he was an aberration, a devil. He had not been recognized as African in decades. "You know where I am from?" he asked with surprise.

"Of course, I do," the man responded with a casual wave of his hand, "I spent half a decade with the Legion in Africa and another dozen years in Asia. I've seen men of all different colors." He smiled. "What is most important now though is getting you something to eat and drink." He turned and spoke in quick Latin to a servant who had appeared at the warehouse door.

In another moment a large wooden platter appeared, brought out by two boys in white linen tunics. On the platter were three round loaves of bread, a small bowl of sweet honey, and a tall clay flask of fragrant olive oil. The quartermaster cleared a space for the tray among his scattered documents. Soon, the food was joined by a jug of red wine and four simple copper cups. Three stools were produced, and they sat across from the quartermaster as they ate, dividing up the bread with their hands and sharing the honey and oil.

Introductions were made, with the quartermaster, Marius Fulvius, raising his cup to each man in turn.

"You mentioned 'more' barbarians earlier. Have others come before us?" Ulrich asked.

"Oh, yes, for the past few weeks, there have been a great many fugitives fleeing from the wilds of Germania. Hundreds in fact. Mostly Saxons but with a fair number of Chatti and Frisians mixed in too. The rumors are inconsistent, confusing, with each tribe having its own story. I am only a mere quartermaster, but much of what I have heard has revolved around these 'Alemanni.' It seems that they are stirring up quite a bit of trouble beyond the walls." Marius's eyes lit with curiosity.

Ulrich felt a lift of hope. With all the Saxons fleeing to Rome, perhaps Ima, Johanne, and the children had made it here as well. Maybe they were safe. "Where did they all go?" He asked. "They were all let into Rome?"

"Our benevolent General Julian, bless his heart, has a soft spot even for savages, it seems, and he has allowed a veritable tide of refugees into the city," Marius answered with a smile.

"City? What city?" Ulrich asked, confused.

Marius blinked at Ulrich for a moment, then shook his head. "Why, Cologne of course! I should have expected. You barbarians don't even know where you are. Here. Let me show you. I will draw you a map." He turned and shouted a command, and soon a boy appeared with a wooden tray with shallow vertical sides. Before he allowed the boy to put the box on the table, the quartermaster carefully rolled up his precious parchments and put away his ink and reed pen. The box, when placed before them, proved to hold a layer of fine sand. Marius began drawing in the sand with his finger as he talked.

"You find yourself, gentlemen, on the northern edge of a grand empire. Civilization ends at these walls." He pointed with his finger at his drawing. A small box corresponded to the fortress where they sat. He continued tracing lines in the sand. "To the west, the Roman province of Gaul stretches to the North sea, and across that sea are the British Isles, where we drove back the savage Picts. To the south, the vast Mediterranean sea is a Roman pond, bordered on its southern shores by our rich African colonies. Far to the east, war simmers with the Persian Empire, but up here, up in the north," he circled the first area once again, "we have a crisis of German barbarians, and the Emperor Constantius has turned his personal attention to this area. He even sent his own cousin Julian to sort things out." Marius's voice was proud as he described the vastness of the Empire known as Rome.

Marius wiped a hand across the sand, smoothing the big map into nothingness. "I will give you some more detail. Here is the River Rhine," he continued. He drew a diagonal line into the fresh grains. The line cut from the labeled northwest to the southeast of the makeshift chart. "Everything to the west of the river is part of Rome, specifically the province of Gaul." He paused, then corrected himself, "Well, some of the land to the north here is settled by the uncivilized Franks, but they are not important," he said dismissively. "We are here." He redrew the small square on the eastern side of the river. "This is Castellum Divitia." He waved his free hand around at the fort in which they sat. "This fortress guards the bridge across the river Rhine. A bridge that leads to the Roman city of Colonia Agrippina, or Cologne." He drew a great semicircle on the west side of the river. "Cologne and Divitia represent the final outpost of civilization into this wilderness," he concluded.

Ulrich suddenly felt very small. He looked at the massive walls of the fortress and realized that he had lived his entire life on the edge of a much bigger world. His perspective was reworking itself in his head.

Sigmund spoke first. "But how did it all begin?" he mused.

"You mean the Empire?" Marius shrugged, "Now that is a bigger question than I feel I have either the time or the competence to answer. I am no philosopher. I manage the supplies for three legions, and that is plenty enough to occupy my time."

Tau had always known the world was big. In fact, he figured he had probably rowed across most of it, but he frowned at the quartermaster's sandbox. Even on the larger map, he was certain that Marius's drawing had not included his long-lost birthplace of Ghana. He felt a pang of homesickness at the thought and wondered just exactly how far from home he was.

"I have another question," Sigmund said. "Why does nobody around here wear pants?"

Marius laughed. "You German barbarians and your trousers. Well, to a Roman, pants are the mark of a savage. No truly civilized person would wear such a crude garment, rubbing and chafing between your thighs. And sleeves? Sleeves are feminine. A true man shows his toughness by bearing bare arms and legs against the cold."

Their discussion was interrupted by the approach of Legate Severus, now flanked by two escorts on horseback.

"I am glad to see you have eaten," the officer said. "We will go to the general now. Follow me."

Ulrich, Tau, and Sigmund thanked their host, who waved genially as they stood to go, unrolling his parchments once again on the swiftly-cleared tables. The companions followed Severus as he turned and walked briskly toward the west end of the fortress. The two horsemen followed behind at a respectful distance.

"Remind me of your names, so that I can introduce you to the general," commanded the legate without turning.

They complied, and the officer merely nodded to show that he had heard. He led them across the camp and through an identical gate at the far end. They passed the gloom of that passageway to find themselves stepping onto an enormous bridge. Twenty massive stone pilings stood out of the rushing water, supporting a broad wooden span a full quarter-mile in length. The surface of the wooden pathway was wide enough for two carts to pass easily and was made of smooth-sanded oak. Ulrich was in awe of the massive bridge. There was more wood here, and more skillfully fitted together, than in the greatest Saxon hall. He felt a curious sense of vertigo as he walked across the long span, watching the water rush past, deep and fast, swirling about the stout pilings.

At the end of the bridge lay the city of Cologne. "My god," Sigmund breathed in amazement. The wall that encircled this city was every inch as high as the tall bastion of Divitia, and it stretched left and right for a great distance along the western bank of the River Rhine. He marveled at the amount of effort it must have taken to build such walls, with high stone and brick towers—a wall protecting the entirety of a city and all the people living within.

Severus must have heard their gasps of amazement because he chuckled. "Welcome to Rome," he said.

CHAPTER TWENTY-SIX

They passed into the city of Cologne.

"What happened here?" Sigmund asked, shocked. Now that they were within the walls they could see evidence of destruction all about them. Inside the city, great chunks of the wall had been smashed, and rubble lay about the inner ramparts. They stood on a high point where the causeway rose to meet the bridge, and further damage could be seen deeper in the town. Burned out wooden buildings, empty stone foundations, and jagged vacant frames were evident throughout, although the destruction had seemingly spared many elegant houses and buildings. As they walked on, they passed a semicircular stone theater several stories high where light colored stone betrayed recent repairs. Everywhere, like in Divitia, construction crews worked busily.

"The Franks happened." Severus sighed. "We had some…difficulties here a year or two ago, and the Legion was forced to pull out. In the meantime, those savages had the run of the place." He shook his head. "It matters not. Whatever they damage, we will rebuild. Such problems are trivial to an empire." He waved his hand as if to dismiss the issue.

He stopped walking. "We are here," Severus announced. They had arrived at a fine two-story building of white granite. Elegant marble columns framed bright, red-painted, double doors. He turned to the three men. "You will go inside and you will speak to Caesar Julian. You will speak honestly. If any of you speak a single falsehood, I will kill you myself." The legate's eyes were flinty as he held the gaze of each of the three much-larger men in turn. Ulrich was left with the impression that the Roman officer was serious. They walked up a short flight of granite steps and pushed open the doors to the house.

Inside was an ornate entryway. Brightly colored murals covered the walls, and the floor was a mosaic of painted tiles. Sunlight flooded the room through skylights in the high ceiling. Despite the coolness of the day, the interior of the house was pleasantly warm. The floor felt warm on his bare feet. He knelt and touched the tile. This building was somehow heated through the floor itself. Legate Severus had moved on, and he beckoned to them from the far hallway. Ulrich stood and followed.

They passed through another set of doors and into an outdoor courtyard. There, reclined on couches, were five men wearing white togas. One man had been speaking enthusiastically when Severus led the three men into the yard. He paused to inspect the newcomers. Severus spoke to the group. Ulrich supposed that they were being introduced because he heard their names but, not speaking Latin, understood nothing else.

The one of the men nodded and sat up. He spoke to the other men in togas, who bowed and let themselves out. Severus gestured at the couches, and Ulrich and his companions sat. Severus pointedly stood between the barbarians and his general. His hand rested casually on the hilt of his sword. Coals glowed dully in a brazier between them, warming the open space.

"My name is Flavius Claudius Julianus," said the toga-clad man, speaking German with an easy fluency. He looked to be in his mid-twenties. His animated, lively face was slender, and looked very Roman, with dark brown eyes and tan skin. But while most of the Romans were clean shaven, he wore an untidy beard, trimmed roughly at his neck and which ran up the sides of his face to meet a mop of soft, unruly, brown hair. He was dressed in a long white toga, though his arms were bare, and around his waist he wore a red sash. "I am Caesar of the West, General of the Legion, and cousin to Emperor Constantius. You may call me Julian. And you are Ulrich, Sigmund, and Prince Tau," he said, acknowledging each of them in turn. "Come now. Tell me your story, and please start at the very beginning."

They recounted once again the events of the previous weeks and, this time, in much greater detail. Julian listened with great interest, interjecting often with questions or requests for clarification. By the time they reached the end, the coals in the brazier had been refilled twice by servants, and the sun was settling toward the horizon.

When the tale was done, Julian sighed and sat quietly. After a moment of reflection he stood abruptly. "Thank you, gentlemen," he said. "You provide us with military intelligence of great value. The activities of the Alemanni are of prime importance to the Empire. You have permission to come and go as you please within our lands. Much of the town has been vacated recently, and my magisters are assigning lodging to refugees in the undamaged houses of the southwest quadrant."

Julian produced a sheaf of parchments from a pouch in his sash. The papers were crossed and crisscrossed with script. He rifled through them for a moment before selecting one, dyed almost black with written and rewritten words. For a moment he looked as though he were going to tear off a piece of the parchment, but then he thought better of it. He beckoned to the three men and led them back into the house.

They entered a candlelit study. An unfathomable quantity of stored wisdom filled this room. The walls were lined with shelves bearing hundreds of scrolls and weighty codices. On two oak tables lay a dozen more codices, pages open to the dry air, among scattered parchment and wax tablets covered with script. Julian took a small square of blank parchment from a nearby drawer and scribbled hastily on it before handing it to Ulrich.

"This script will guarantee you lodging within the city. Bring it to any of my magisters to be assigned a place to stay. Thank you for bringing me information on the enemies of Rome. Severus, please show these gentlemen out." As Ulrich and his companions left, Julian sat down at the nearest table. He produced an iron stylus and began writing furiously, tracing the Latin letters deftly into the soft wax of a folding wooden writing tablet.

Ulrich, Tau, and Sigmund were led out into the torch-lit streets. Without another word, Severus summoned his waiting sentries and stalked away, leaving the three visitors blinking in the twilight. The urgency of the past days was draining away, and Ulrich felt curiously disconnected. Too much had happened. Even the awe of the walls of Rome had a hollow quality to it. Wiglaf was dead. Rag was dead. His home was gone. Even vengeance on his uncle had been stolen from him. So much had been lost.

The three of them stood for a moment in shared silence, but a silence that gradually filled with the sounds of the city. The distant banging of hammers rang from where masons labored at the city walls. There came the hum of voices from a nearby marketplace and the clatter of hooves and the rumble of wagon wheels on paving stoves. Shutters banged open and shut, and from somewhere, the soft notes of a lyre wafted across the empty spaces between the houses.

"Well," Ulrich spoke, "let us go see what this gets us, I suppose." He held up the scrap of parchment the general had given him. "And perhaps Johanne and the kids made it here too."

"And Ima as well," Tau interjected. "They were not among the prisoners at Kassel."

They walked west, along a wide avenue that led deeper into the city's heart. They came across a busy marketplace. Even at this late hour the square was bustling with activity. A dozen stalls sold food and drink. Fresh-baked bread, fruits and vegetables, and smoked meat and raw fish was traded for coin. Pottery, tableware, tools, clothing—Ulrich had never seen so many wares at one market. A trader displayed horses in front of a large stable on one end, while on the other an official-looking government warehouse bore the imposing inscription SPQR. Musicians gathered their coins and packed away their instruments in leather cases while a dozen children played, kicking a leather ball across the paving stones in the center of the square.

They had just entered the open space when Ulrich heard his name called. Two small children were running toward him, and Ulrich's eyes filled with unexpected tears when he recognized Ælfwine and Gebhard. The boy reached him first and leapt into his arms. Tears were pouring down his face as he lifted Gebhard to his shoulders and hugged him hard. He was laughing and crying at the same time as he tousled the grinning boy's hair. Ælfwine, a year older, stood nearby. She tugged on Sigmund's breeches.

"Pick me up, Sigmund," she ordered seriously, and the big man complied, seating her on his broad shoulders. Ulrich smiled at her, and she reached out solemnly, shaking hands with Ulrich in the snapping way Tau had taught her.

"Where is your mother?" Ulrich managed to ask, smiling through his tears.

"Right over there," Gebhard pointed across the marketplace, still in Ulrich's arms. "She is buying fish."

Ulrich could not see Johanne through the crowd, but he hoisted the boy to his shoulders and began walking in the indicated direction.

"Mother sold the horses. She said we needed the money for food," Ælfwine reported. Her voice was filled with disapproval.

"I liked the horsies," Gebhard said helpfully. "I named them. They were named Fussy and Greedy."

"I am sure she did the right thing," Ulrich responded automatically. He was hardly listening, still overwhelmed by his sudden happiness.

"But we got a doggie," Gebhard informed him.

"We got a dog." Ælfwine corrected, sitting tall and straight-backed on Sigmund's shoulders as they threaded through the crowd.

The crowd parted, and Ulrich saw Johanne standing at a stall. Her back was to them. She was holding a basket of groceries as she paid the shopkeeper in coins. Ima stood beside her. Ima turned and saw them first, and she nudged Johanne, who turned her head. Her face showed first surprise, then joy. Johanne and Wiglaf had raised Ulrich from a boy and Johanne was like a mother to him. Ulrich gently placed Gebhard on the ground and went to embrace her. He hugged her tight. She looked tired. Her face was more lined and drawn than when Ulrich had last seen her, but she looked otherwise healthy and well. She had cut her long hair short and was wearing a simple green linen tunic.

"I'm so glad to see you," Johanne said. "To find you all safe."

As Johanne greeted Tau and Sigmund, Ulrich turned to Ima. He swallowed against a lump in his throat. She was dressed plainly in a yellow tunic and with her long blonde hair drawn back, but nothing could disguise her beauty. Her blue eyes considered him quietly.

"Thank you for protecting my family," he said awkwardly.

Her eyes flickered away. When she met his gaze again, Ulrich could see the hurt that lay within them. "I am sorry I could not save Rag," she said.

Ulrich shook his head. "That's not your fault," he said, knowing that the words were inadequate.

Tau stepped forward and shook Ima's hand with his customary aplomb. He stepped back. "Don't worry," he said, slapping Ulrich on the shoulder companionably. "I know it will not bring the boy back, but we will kill the bastard responsible. I promise you." His words were savage, but his grin was genuine.

"Thank you, friend," Ulrich responded. He cuffed away a stubborn tear. Meanwhile a large dog, a mastiff, loped out of the crowd and greeted Johanne's children. Sigmund bent down to pet the beast and laughed as the big dog licked his face.

"Come on," Johanne said. "That nice man, Julian, is letting us stay in a great big empty house in the city. It is far bigger than we need. You must come stay with us."

Reunited, friends and family walked into the torch-lit evening.

CHAPTER TWENTY-SEVEN

The house Johanne had been assigned was indeed impressive. It was a beautiful one-story affair of stone, brick, and tile that shared walls with similar residences on both sides. Myriad windows and broad square skylights were paned with a translucent, blue glass—glass that filled the rooms with an aquamarine brilliance of shifting light. Johanne demonstrated how a cleverly-designed wood-burning stove, low in an open courtyard behind the marble entryway, generated a rising column of heat that was vented throughout the hollow walls and floors of the entire house. This warmed the residence while keeping the smoke and soot of the burning wood out of the living spaces.

The courtyard was the centerpiece of the house. It was also home to a small garden and a pool that was kept filled by clear rainwater collected off the roof by a series of slanting pipes. There was a stone and iron grill in a small kitchen bordering the courtyard, vented by a flue that let smoke out, but was cleverly curved to keep rainwater from getting in. Fresh water for drinking was piped through the house by a concrete pipe that came from the main aqueduct, and wastewater flushed an indoor lavatory that emptied into a covered sewer in the alley.

Three spacious sleeping quarters opened onto the courtyard. These rooms, on which feather-filled mattresses adorned low wooden couches, filled out the remainder of the house. Johanne had established herself and her two children in one room, and Ima had been sleeping in another, so Ulrich, Tau, and Sigmund, all unaccustomed to such incredible luxury, comfortably bunked together in the final room. There was plenty enough space here for all of them, so Ulrich gave Julian's parchment to Johanne, who gave it away to another, less fortunate, family of refugees.

It seemed that the calamity that had racked Cologne had been sporadic in its destruction. Some buildings bore the marks of scorching by fire. Some stone houses had been pulled down into rubble, but other places were curiously untouched. Most of the city's inhabitants had fled the Franks but had not returned, leaving much of the town empty, which was fortunate for those refugees allowed to stay in the vacated residences. Roman guards patrolled the streets day and night, and crime was nearly unheard of in the heavily garrisoned town.

The refugees were mostly Saxons with a good mix of Frisians, Cheruski, Chatti, and other Germanic tribes who had fled the advance of the Alemanni. To assist in the integration of the newcomers into civilized society, a government ministry was established to instruct them on matters of money and finance. They offered advice and assigned appropriate employment to the generally unskilled "barbarians."

A new month began peacefully. Johanne, having sold the valuable horses for a hefty number of Roman coins, was confident the family had enough wealth to afford food through the winter, and the children were delighted to have the run of the town. Ulrich and his friends, though, quickly began to feel restless as the empty days drifted by. Ima had found work caring for the horses of the garrison Auxilia. These auxiliaries were the army of supporting troops that trained and fought alongside the Legion. Not being true Roman citizens, each soldier was paid only a third as much as a legionnaire, but they were fiercely proud nonetheless. It was not typical practice to employ women, but the captain of the Auxilia cavalry was desperately shorthanded in the care of the five-hundred-odd horses of his command, and he paid Ima handsomely for her skill.

Ulrich found his employment at the blacksmith's forge of the Auxilia quartermaster. Contracting for the work, the overseer of the supplies agreed to pay him on a per-item basis for the repair of broken and bent swords, spear blades, armor plates, and other accoutrements. There was no shortage of maintenance to be done. Ulrich went to work striking hammer to anvil, using the skills Wiglaf had taught him so well.

Tau became an assistant to the Legion engineer corps, always in need of hands capable of moving heavy equipment. He was fascinated with the Roman artillery. He watched closely as the ballistae and catapults of the Legion were exercised in the open ground to the west of the city. His charm found him in the good graces of a Legion artillery commander, a weathered, patient man in his late forties, and Tau began to actually learn the Roman art of siege craft. He returned every night to the house, eyes sparkling as he described some arcane bit of physics that gave the Romans such mastery over time and space. Sigmund, meanwhile, made a new friend.

It had been a dark, windy night in the city, and Sigmund was fast asleep. In his dreams he was back at his family's home on the river Wesser. The warm sun fell on his face as he sat on the muddy riverbank. His daughter crouched nearby, gathering pretty clamshells. The hem of her pink dress was wet from the damp sand. He opened his mouth to call her name.

His eyes snapped open, and he found himself wide awake. He sat up in the dark chamber. Ulrich and Tau were sound asleep on their respective beds. He strained his ears and looked around, but could identify nothing that would have woken him. Only Ulrich's soft snoring droned on, quiet and even comforting in the still room. The memory of the dream evaporated, leaving only a profound sense of loss.

The need for sleep was gone. Sigmund slid from the bed and stood up. He had discovered that the linen tunics fashionable among the Romans were much more comfortable than the rough leather and fur he was used to. He doffed his nightshirt and pulled one on. He slipped out into the courtyard. The night was chill, so he walked across the courtyard, went into the marble entryway and retrieved a cloak from a hook near the front door. He clasped it about himself as he went out into the night.

The city slept. Many torches had been allowed to burn out in their sconces. A full moon hung bright in a cloudless sky while short gusts of chill wind ruffled the cloak against Sigmund's ankles. Dawn was a long way off. He looked up and down the street. So much of this city was still curious to him. He was intrigued by the range of exotic goods that arrived each day in the market, hinting at a transport system that allowed fast travel over incredible distances. He was impressed by the supply chain implied by the well-equipped legions, and he was impressed by the supremely efficient messenger service that delivered written messages and parcels throughout the city and beyond. It all implied a level of organization and forethought of which he had not thought people capable. Despite all that had happened, he was glad to experience Rome. He felt a strange kinship with this foreign race of engineers and clever architects. They, like he, were thinkers. They, like he, were planners. They, like he, were philosophers.

He moved off down the street. The city wall drew him in, and after a few blocks, he stood before it. He gazed up at the expanse of fitted brick, feeling curiously small, but also safe, like he was in a cocoon. That thought struck him. This must be how the Romans felt, how they wanted to feel. Inside the walls was safety, security, control. The walls held the dangers of the night at bay. Building walls and guarding them was difficult, but so was ploughing a field or fending for your family in the harsh German wastes. It was planning, not effort, that separated this civilized world and barbarism. Through the application of forethought and intellect, the Romans had carved out places to feel secure in a violent world. He turned away.

Besides the wall, the most impressive edifice in the city was the huge concrete and marble theater at its center. Sigmund wandered that way. The windswept streets were empty, and he was glad to have the night to himself and his thoughts. Four stories of stone loomed over his head as he approached the building. Its polished facings were decorated with intricate marble carvings, and a broad frieze adorned the entablature. A high archway led into the structure, and he followed it. Stairs led upward, and he found himself high among the empty wooden benches. The wind hummed as it swept through the hollow structure. Sigmund sat on one of the benches, savoring the surreal vertigo the towering walls engendered. Suddenly he realized he was not alone.

In the center of the theater stood a man. He wore a dark robe that hung to his ankles and a linen hood drawn up over his head. He was pacing back and forth in the low space before the stage and appeared to be considering the many decorations and inscriptions that covered the wall there. Sigmund, drawn by curiosity, stood and made his way down through the auditorium. He left the archways and entered the flat, empty space behind the pacing man. As he walked into the open area, the stranger noticed his approach. He turned, and Sigmund saw his face framed in the moonlight. It was Julian.

Julian stood patiently, watching the big man approach. His reserved expression brightened when he recognized his visitor.

"Sigmund, is it? The Saxon," he said with a smile, snapping his fingers.

"Caesar Julian?" Sigmund asked, curiosity evident in his tone. He was surprised to see the commander of the Roman army out here, all alone, in the middle of the night.

Julian seemed unflustered by the intrusion. He turned back to the stage.

"What do you think of this?" he asked, pointing.

In front of Julian was a recess in the stage's foot. Inside the small space was a statue. Sigmund stepped closer and considered it carefully. Perhaps two feet tall, there stood a figure of brilliantly painted marble. Transfixed in stone was the image of a man. The man held a red lyre in his left hand, wore a green circlet of leaves on his head, and had a golden scarf loosely thrown about his shoulders. His heroically proportioned body was naked.

Sigmund glanced at Julian, but the general's face was carefully expressionless. Julian was watching him closely. Sigmund realized that this was a test. The Roman general would not expect a German to know Roman art by rote, so Julian must be testing his ability to reason, to deduce meaning from clues. Sigmund arranged his thoughts carefully. The naked figure was muscled to the very limit of possibility for the human frame. But Sigmund had noticed that depictions of historical events throughout the city showed their subjects dressed in togas or armor; nakedness was reserved for religion and myths. He considered the accoutrements and the context, then ventured a guess at the meaning.

"This statue depicts a god," Sigmund answered. He turned to look at Julian. "A god of music."

Julian smiled. "An excellent deduction. This is Apollo. Are you familiar with Apollo?" Sigmund shook his head, and Julian continued. "Apollo is a complicated god. From Mount Olympus he oversees the gifts of acting, music and truth. Although, according to Plato, those are all the same thing." Julian frowned and looked back at the statue. "If the Christians have their way, I'm sure he'll be smashed and replaced with a cross or with one of those dour images of their own God being tortured."

Julian shook his head sadly at the thought. "Walk with me," he said, and led them out of the theater.

"I suppose you are wondering what I am doing out here in the middle of the night?" Julian asked.

"I'll admit it piqued my curiosity," Sigmund responded.

"Alexander the Great didn't sleep more than a few hours each night, so neither do I," Julian responded proudly, stifling a yawn. "Besides, I do some of my best thinking at night."

They walked down the dark streets. Julian was leading them on a long circuit of the city.

"Tell me," Julian continued, "what are the gods of the Germans like?"

Sigmund did his best to answer. He told him what he knew: of Wodan and Donar and the Aesir and Vanir, of the unceasing battles in planes beyond earth and of the continual intrigues of the many gods who toyed with the mortals for their entertainment, of fortunetelling and the divination of augury, of the role of animal sacrifice in harvest times and the great differences of belief from tribe to tribe. Julian seemed already quite well versed in the pagan pantheon and interjected with a lively exuberance. They completed one entire lap of the city before the story was half done.

"Ah, yes, brilliant," Julian spoke, his eyes shining. "Like those of the Olympian gods, each pagan tale has a moral. Each teaches a lesson. And together they serve as a recording of our own primitive history. There is so much richness to it, and so much to be learned." His face fell. "I fear that my uncle, Emperor Constantine, did a terrible thing when he allowed the cult of Christianity into the empire. Christianity is destroying the old ways, replacing them with their new mysticism. Rome is built on tradition, and those traditions are being eroded. Truly, I fear it may be our final undoing."

Julian stopped and peered at the moon, judging the time of the night by the moon's position in the sky. "I am afraid that I must leave you now." He put on a wry grin. "Many of my lieutenants disdain the company of non-Romans, but I sense you have an agile and perceptive mind. I appreciate a new perspective on the old questions. In anticipation of further discussion, I leave you with a contemplation. Consider: what if the plurality of the gods was itself both true and an illusion?" Julian smiled. "This is the exact question that Plato asked seven centuries ago. Give it some thought, and if you find an answer, come and dine with me tomorrow at sundown. I will look forward to your response."

With that, Julian turned and paced away down the dark street.

CHAPTER TWENTY-EIGHT

Sigmund and Julian quickly became friends. Julian explained to him that he had spent his whole life as a scholar in Athens and only recently became burdened with the governance of Gaul at the behest of his cousin, the Emperor of Rome, Constantius II. He had brought the army of Gaul to Cologne to repair it from the damage done by a recent incursion of Franks, with whom he had just signed a treaty agreeing to leave each other mutually in peace. Julian's chief concern now was the Alemanni, who were threatening to push into this Roman province.

Julian trusted the daily affairs of the Legion and Auxilia to his seasoned staff, including Severus, four other legates, and the myriad Auxilia commanders. The Franks seemed to be respecting the treaty, and the rebuilding of the city was progressing on schedule. Julian divided his time between making plans to stop the Alemanni from crossing the Rhine and maintaining his feverish study of philosophy and history. It was regarding this last pursuit that Sigmund and the general found common ground.

What Sigmund lacked in book learning, he made up for with sharp reasoning and strong intuitive sense. He aptly deduced deeper meaning behind philosophical treatises, and Julian valued him for his practical logic and the freedom from bias he could bring to so many hidebound schools of thought. Sigmund became a regular at the lively discussions Julian would hold with the educated men of the city, and Julian hired a tutor to begin teaching him to read and write in Latin.

Meanwhile, the Roman army was encamped on the fields west of the town. Grass-covered hills rolled around dense stands of woods. Orderly lines of tents dotted the hillsides, and the Legions drilled constantly. Troops of cavalry rode in orderly formations, riding knee to knee and practicing mock charges up and down the gentle slopes. Archers honed their craft, arcing their arrows into targets of woven hay, and the siege engineers worked their massive equipment, launching boulders and barrels with incredible accuracy across vast empty fields.

Tau was with the artillery. A dewy morning found him sighting a ballista, essentially a massively oversized crossbow on a gimbaled wooden mount, onto a target almost half a mile away. Ima, exercising a young horse, cantered over to watch. Tau gazed carefully down the flat ramp of the weapon. Two men winched the thick rope back against the twin torsion springs that gave it power. Once the massive crossbow was drawn, Tau placed a bolt, a thick, heavy arrow four feet long, into the groove and pulled a lever. The rope snapped forward, and the bolt whipped into the air, soaring high in a graceful arc before plunging down toward the target. A puff of yellow dust betrayed where the missile smashed through the chosen haystack.

"Not bad," Ima admitted.

Tau smiled. "If I had known you were watching, I would have tried a harder target."

Ima hopped off her horse to inspect the weapon. The three soldiers assigned to the ballista grinned at her amiably as she walked around the wood and iron contraption. A stack of missiles rested nearby.

"Would you like to give it a try?" Tau asked.

Ima shrugged. "How does it work?" she asked.

Tau pointed at the iron torsion springs. "It comes down to these. These iron bars are flexible, but they were originally forged straight. When they are bent they want to return to their previous shape. When the tension is released they snap forward and pull the rope, flinging whatever is on the ramp downrange. I'll show you. Pick a target."

Ima looked down the field. There were a half dozen haystacks laid out in a scattered pattern on the far hillside. She pointed at the farthest one. "Let's hit that one."

Tau nodded. "The base of the weapon articulates. Turn it like so." He showed her then stepped back to let her do it herself. "You'll want to aim higher than I did since the target is even farther away. There is a bit of a breeze coming in from the west. Aim a hair to the left to compensate."

Ima aimed the weapon with her best guess then nodded to Tau. He signaled to the foot soldiers who winched the rope against the springs. Ima loaded the arrow as she had seen Tau do and grasped the firing lever. After a moment's hesitation she pulled it, and the bowstring twanged. The missile sped off down the field to strike plumb into the center of the target. The soldiers, enjoying the moment, gave her a cheer, and Ima grinned at Tau proudly.

"Beginner's luck," Tau teased her.

"There is no such thing. I'm a natural," Ima insisted. She suddenly felt warm and realized that she was blushing as she looked at Tau's dark, handsome face. She turned away. "Well, I'll leave you to it," she said.

She climbed back on her horse and rode away. Tau watched her go, suddenly transfixed by her comely figure and long, soft hair. The Roman soldiers were grinning at him knowingly.

"What are you smiling at?" Tau asked, embarrassed. He shook his head and went back to his work, but the damage was done.

That evening the whole household had dinner together. Johanne had learned to cook Roman bread, and with the bread she served them a feast of her traditional stew, this time mixed with beef and cabbage, all flavored with green onion. The meal was lively, the children laughing and running around the courtyard with the big dog while Sigmund propounded philosophy, but Tau felt awkward. He was intensely aware of Ima's gaze as she lounged on the couch across from him. Her light blue tunic brought out the blue in her eyes.

"What do you think about the Romans?" Ulrich was asking Johanne.

"I like them!" Johanne responded energetically. "Despite all the scary stories about them in battle, they seem very gentle. The soldiers in the square always smile at Gebhard and Ælfwine when they play with the other kids."

"There are a lot of other kids here," little Ælfwine explained. "Many more than in Brunswick. We have to teach them all the good games." She looked very serious.

Johanne smiled at her daughter before turning back to Ulrich. "I feel safe here. The walls are comforting, and there is very little crime in the city."

Ulrich nodded. Within the walls of Rome arguments were settled in court rather than with the sword. Food was plentiful and cheap, and theft was uncommon. In nearly a month, he had not heard of a single murder or witnessed a duel in the marketplace. It was remarkable.

"We saw a show in the theater today," Gebhard informed Ulrich. Sigmund poured olive oil from a small amphora onto the boy's plate, and Gebhard dipped his bread in it as he talked. "There were men in masks, and they ran around hitting each other with wooden swords."

The shows in the theater were free, and they were popular, ranging from humor to tragedy to circus performances, but most were plays of some sort.

"And the buildings are so beautiful," Johanne breathed. "I could spend a lifetime just wandering the city and enjoying the artwork. That poor old Chatti next door, the one who lost his family to the Alemanni, he spends all day staring at all the statues."

"Is there anything about living here that you don't like, though?" Ulrich asked. He was probing, in part, to explore his own feelings.

Ima spoke up. "Women are inferior to men in Rome. In Germania, there were matriarchs. My mother was a warmaiden. But here there are no woman governors or woman soldiers. Here such things are impossible because they are against the law." Ima frowned. "In fact, there seem to be laws for everything. From where you can stable a horse to where you can throw your trash. It can be overwhelming. The refugees are having the hardest time with it. The legal court is constantly full. The judge is daily admonishing petty infractions or administering fines."

Tau nodded. "In some ways it seems that the Romans have thrown off the yoke of savagery, only to be drowned in laws." Ima's face turned towards him, and he felt warm.

Sigmund spoke up in defense of Rome. "Four centuries ago there was a Roman named Cicero who said, 'the good of the people is the greatest law,' and the Romans have built their civilization around this idea. I know it seems like there are a lot of rules, but I truly believe they are trying to do what is best for everybody."

"It sounds like you're turning into a Roman," Ulrich noted, but there was no criticism in his voice, only curiosity.

Sigmund shrugged. "The Romans are different from us. They have spent so much of their history questioning, building, making philosophy, and exploring the world. I like it. They give me hope that humanity can do better. That we can be better." He smiled ruefully at his friends. He felt embarrassed, like he had revealed too much.

Ulrich put a friendly hand on Sigmund's shoulder. "I'm glad you're my friend, Sigmund. Your optimism gives me hope, and I hope you're right," he said.

After dinner, Tau lay in bed. He was alone in the darkness. Ulrich and Sigmund had long since fallen asleep, but Tau was wide awake. He lay there for a long time, staring at nothing. Finally, he stood and exited the chamber, crossing quietly to Ima's room. He put his hand on the door, but before he could knock, it opened from the inside. Ima stood in the doorway, her blue eyes staring into his. He kissed her, and she drew him into the room, closing the door behind them.

CHAPTER TWENTY-NINE

The end of the month heralded the beginning of winter, and the Roman army made plans to move out. Sigmund was present at the planning meetings with Julian. They left the city and went to the camp, where the general called his lieutenants to order. A map of the region was spread out on a broad wooden table, and Julian opened the discussion. The warm campaign season was drawing to a close, and having all the army concentrated in one place was becoming a drain on the local economy. Under Julian's command were five Roman Legions of a thousand men each, ten auxiliary regiments of five hundred men each, and three thousand cavalry. Maintaining the long supply lines, especially wine, meat, and bread for this army of thirteen thousand was a monumental effort and would only become more onerous as the winter months drew on. Redistributing to the heart of the province would ease the effort.

As Julian noted, the army had already accomplished their objectives in this far province: First, they had forged a truce with the northern Franks, and second, they had rebuilt Cologne as a bastion of the Empire. He proposed that, leaving a hefty garrison in the reclaimed city, they should now withdraw to the interior of Roman Gaul, wait out the winter, and anticipate starting the final decisive campaign against the Alemanni the following spring. The general, in true form as a scholar, believed in the virtues of debate, and he opened the forum for discussion.

Present at this meeting were the thirteen chief commanders of Julian's army. Legate Severus was there, studying the map intently, as was the blonde Briton Eogan, commander of the Auxilia, but the most senior officer present was Marcellus, the Magister Equitum. He was a tall, grave man with close-cropped, gray hair, a proud demeanor, a long military career, and a short temper. He had been commander of this army long before young Julian arrived.

Once Julian finished, Marcellus took the floor. He had been visibly impatient while his general was talking, and he swelled with self-importance as he spoke.

"This coming year will show us victory over the savages," he addressed the crowd. "Emperor Constantius's army under the great General Barbatio will march from Italy in the spring, and we will crush the Alemanni between our two fronts."

"My only remaining concern," Julian responded, nervously toying with a stylus, "is that the Alemanni will march early, or even attack this winter."

Marcellus frowned. "Our spies assure us they are already settling in for the season. Their warriors have gone home and have scattered across all of Germania to wait out the winter."

Julian still fidgeted. "I would feel more comfortable if I had use of the whole army. If Constantius had trusted me with Barbatio's twenty-five thousand men in Italy, we could have finished with this threat long ago."

Marcellus restrained a scoff. The idea of this puppy leading the entire army of the Western Empire was laughable. He was confident that the rest of the council felt the same way as he did.

Severus, who had been intently studying the map, looked up. "It does us little good worrying over what might have been, General. We have our thirteen thousand soldiers. We know that Chnodomar can raise at least twice as many, and he has many allies besides. Taking direct action against those odds is inadvisable. I agree that we should wait out the winter, anticipating reinforcements in the spring."

Julian nodded. "Thank you, Severus. All right let us focus on the matter at hand. We shall redeploy the army to here and here." He pointed to the map. "My headquarters shall be Sens with Marcellus headed to Reims, and our supplies can—"

"Pardon me, General," Sigmund interrupted. He was uncomfortable. Julian had invited him personally, but he was self-consciously aware of being the only non-Roman at the meeting. Furthermore, his grasp of Latin was not yet perfect. Still, he felt compelled to speak up.

"Can we really be so sure that the Alemanni won't march this winter?" Sigmund asked hesitantly, looking at Marcellus.

Marcellus was astounded. It was bad enough that Julian made friends with savages, but now he was allowing one of his pets to speak at a military council? "The barbarians," Marcellus said, instilling the word with as much contempt as he could muster, "never march in winter. They are too scared of the cold." This drew a small chuckle from the gathered council.

Sigmund shook his head. "When my companions and I escaped from their camp a little over a month ago, they had gathered in great strength. They showed no signs of dispersing or settling down for the winter." He looked at Julian. "They are a fierce army—a proud force and well organized. They genuinely intend to destroy Rome. I think they will strike while they are strong. They will not wait for spring."

Julian looked indecisive. "What do you think, Severus?" he asked the Legate.

Severus hesitated for a long moment before answering. He shrugged. "I am sorry, Sigmund, but Magister Marcellus is right. In my experience, the Alemanni have always been loath to fight in the winter."

Julian turned back to Marcellus. "How much do you trust the reports of your spies?" he asked.

"My spies say the Alemanni are dispersed, General," answered Marcellus.

Julian nodded. "All right," he said decisively. "We will redistribute the army in Gaul." He leaned over the map, and using wooden markers to represent each of the regiments, they discussed the retiring of the army to winter quarters.

When the counsel was completed, Julian sought out Sigmund to speak privately. The high table was removed, and couches were brought in. Julian always insisted on eating only what the common soldier was served, and so two standard rations of bread, smoked meat, and diluted wine were brought into the tent for them to share while they talked.

"Thank you," Julian began, "both for coming to this meeting and for speaking up during it. I know that was not easy." Sigmund shrugged, and Julian continued. "Many of the patricians disdain my friendship with a German, but I value a fresh approach. Socrates says to always consider both sides of an issue thoroughly." Julian looked reflective while he chewed on a piece of bread. "How I wish I could have spoken with that man," he said wistfully. "Socrates I mean." He swallowed his bread. "Besides, almost half of my army is German auxiliaries now. It's always a good idea to know how your men think."

"Tell me more about the Alemanni," Sigmund said, changing the subject. "They harbor such a deep, intense hatred of Rome. It's unsettling."

Julian sighed. "Perhaps they are right to hate us. There is much dark history there."

Sigmund frowned. "I remember Chnodomar mentioned two Romans, Caracalla and Constantius. Who were they?"

Julian nodded. "The first, Caracalla, was the Emperor of Rome a century ago, and the Alemanni grudge began with him. Caracalla promised the Alemanni protection, but it was a trick. He betrayed the Alemanni, and subjugated them instead, using them for his own selfish means." Julian shook his head. "The second man is my cousin, the current Emperor of Rome, Constantius the Second."

Julian paused to take a swig of wine before continuing. "I honestly don't know all the details of Constantius's dealings with Chnodomar and the Alemanni, but I do know he has been conducting business with them for a long time. The reason I was pulled from my studies in Athens and appointed as the Emperor's representative in Gaul is because my cousin is running out of people to trust. Too many deals have gone bad. There was a revolution in Cologne six years ago. A Roman usurper named Magnentius seized control of the city, and Constantius encouraged the Alemanni to attack him. Knowing my cousin, he probably promised Chnodomar a lot of land and silver to do it but then later broke his promises."

Julian was quiet for a long moment, looking deep in thought. A gentle breeze rustled the tent flaps, and the two men shared a companionable silence as they finished their small meal.

Julian broke the silence. "Did you know that he murdered my family?" He said. His voice was sad.

"What?" Sigmund asked. He bolt upright and stared at the young general. The words were so unexpected that he did not know if he had heard correctly.

"Constantius did," Julian responded. "The Emperor had my family killed. My father. My mother. My grandfather. I even had an older brother." His voice was small. There were no tears on his face, but the pain was there nonetheless. "He feared they would challenge his claim to the throne. I still don't know why he spared me." He shook his head sadly. "I was just six years old at the time. I suppose he thought a small boy was no real threat." Seeing Sigmund's concern he gave a wan smile. "Don't worry my friend. This is ancient history."

"I'm so sorry," Sigmund stammered. He felt heartbroken and shocked by his friend's sudden, terrible, revelation.

Julian waved it off. "Don't be. Don't be. It doesn't matter. Marcus Aurelius told us that we must meet the challenges of the world with logic, not passion. The world is as the world is, and it is our duty only to be virtuous. My cousin is the Emperor and my life's duty is to Rome." He turned to his friend, smiling suddenly, and said, "And that is a great duty indeed."

Their talk returned to lighter subjects after that. Sigmund had become enraptured with Aristotle, but Julian preferred Plato. The friendly argument continued long into the night.

Sigmund got home just before dawn. At breakfast Sigmund brought the news of the army's plans to decamp to the family. They ate indoors now, as it had become too cold to comfortably dine outside.

"We should go with them," Sigmund insisted. He yawned hugely, then shook his head, fighting sleep.

Ulrich was reluctant to blindly follow the Romans. His employment was as an independent artisan; thus, he had no firm allegiance to the Legion or the Auxilia. He was not sure yet just how far he could trust them. He frowned but said nothing.

"If the army is withdrawing deeper into their empire, how do we know this city will be safe from the Alemanni?" Johanne asked anxiously. Her priority was the safety of her two children.

Sigmund briefly considered stoking her fears in the hopes that she would agree to follow the army with him, but he decided that was dishonest. "They have rebuilt the walls and the defenses, and they are leaving a sizable garrison here. Now that they have gone through the work of securing the city, they will not allow it to fall again," he admitted. "You will be safe if you choose to stay here."

Tau looked thoughtful. "If we follow the army, we risk becoming entangled in whatever conflicts follow them," he pointed out.

"Conflicts? They are determined to fight the Alemanni, are they not?" Ima said.

Sigmund confirmed with a nod. "Julian said that the primary focus of the next campaign season will be the total neutralization of the Alemanni threat." Sigmund said. "They mean to destroy them utterly."

Ima leaned back, satisfied. "Good. If they are going to destroy the Alemanni, I want to be there. I want to help them do it," she said savagely. "I have unfinished business with those bastards." She looked to Ulrich for support.

Ulrich looked thoughtful but still did not respond, so Tau spoke up. "Ulrich, you saved my life and freed me from slavery. I swore my swords to your service, and I do not take such oaths lightly. I will go with you wherever you decide."

Ulrich smiled at his friend. He thought in silence for a long moment. The family looked to him for a decision. "I agree with Ima," he decided finally. "We owe the Alemanni a debt of blood for the death of Wiglaf, for the murder of Rag, and for the destruction of our home. I do not wish to stay in Cologne and wait out the coming conflict. If the Romans plan to fight them, I will do what I can to help."

Johanne sighed. "All right, then. I guess it's decided. If you all are going with the army then I feel safer coming with you than I do trusting Ælfwine's and Gebhard's safety to the garrison alone."

The family packed its belongings and made ready to travel. They had few possessions, just those clothes they had purchased in the city and what coin they had accrued. Ima helped Johanne sell the house furnishings, and they set off on foot behind the marching army.

CHAPTER THIRTY

In the winter of the year 356 Julian divided the Roman army and spread it around Gaul. He trusted the bulk of the army to Magister Marcellus, who was emplaced in the strategic town of Reims. Marcellus was given orders to strike at any bands of Alemanni that might, despite the winter snows, venture across the border, and he was given orders to reinforce any bastion of Gaul that came under attack. Julian kept only a small force—one Legion commanded by Severus, and one regiment of auxiliaries under Eogan. After breaking off from Marcellus in Reims, they moved deeper into Gaul, and the army settled in for the cold months.

Sens, Julian's chosen headquarters, was an old, abandoned fortress standing to the east of a languid river. When Julian's army had arrived, it consisted of little more than a big wall, twenty-five feet tall, enclosing a rectangle of empty space and broken foundations. Within weeks, a wooden town sprang up. The Legion, skilled engineers that they were, dropped their swords and armor, picked up hammers and axes, and went to work. Granaries of timber were constructed and filled with grain. Barracks were put up in stately rows, and stout wooden doors filled the long-empty gates. The deep ditch outside the stone walls was freshly filled with sharp wooden stakes, and the empty fields beyond were cleared of brush so no one could sneak close. A grid of residences was built in the center of town to house artisans, officers, and the Legion's friends and dignitaries.

Ulrich had become a trusted craftsman to the Auxilia. The staunch Legion, made up only of Roman citizens, was notoriously disdainful of outsiders, but the smaller Auxilia support regiment was a place where foreigners could prove themselves in the service of Rome. It drew men from all tribes beyond the empire, including Germans, Frisians, Franks, and even faraway Britons. This regiment of Auxilia, called the Petulantes, was a 'balanced regiment,' which meant they formed their own contingent of archers to complement the light infantry that filled its ranks. They also had their own cavalry, but that wing would hardly fit in the small fort of Sens, so they were barracked with Marcellus in Reims. The Auxilia's commander, a Briton named Eogan, was a genial man who appreciated the service of a talented smith. He paid Ulrich well for his services.

Ulrich had been saving his earnings to buy a replacement cuirass of segmented armor, but the Petulantes were issued only chainmail, not the heavy steel lorica segmentata. Meanwhile, the heavy Legion, which had plenty of sets of lorica segmentata, was not in the business of selling it to barbarians, so Ulrich would have to make his own. His forge smoldered, and the case-hardened segments began to stack in a corner of his workshop. The room rang with hammer blows as a new axe, bigger even than the one Wiglaf had forged for him, began to take shape. It was a slow process, but he had spare time as the work sent to him from Eogan was increasingly sparse as winter settled onto the land. Ulrich was able to spend a good deal of time with Johanne and the children as well.

Ælfwine and Gebhard continued to grow like weeds. For Gebhard, Ulrich made a toy buckler and wooden sword, their grips sized for the small boy's hands. For Ælfwine he forged a fine steel chain necklace, its delicate links carrying, to Johanne's approval, a small iron cross.

Ulrich got to know Sens as winter rolled in. Stone stairs climbed through round towers leading to the broad tops of the thick walls. Ulrich strolled the ramparts every day, enjoying the gorgeous vistas of the rolling countryside. The defenses were jointly manned by the Auxilia and by the Legion. The legionnaires were polite but distant. He found companionship easier with the auxiliaries, many of whom were Saxons and spoke wistfully of their ancestral homes. They shared Ulrich's anger and sorrow at the ravages of the Alemanni, and many sought him out to hear his stories from beyond the border.

Snow fell on the land, and traffic along the roads became sparse. The storehouses of grain were rationed by the army quartermasters. No news came from the frontier, and hopes were high that it may be an uneventful season. Perhaps that is why few took much notice of the small crack that developed along the north wall. Ulrich, despite his regular visits to the ramparts, failed to notice it at first. It was easy to miss, just a fine trace a hair's width wide that slithered along the wall's surface. It lost itself in the vertical grain of the coarse stone. An anomalous rain on a November day gave way to a frozen night, and ice covered the world in a thick sheen. The next morning the crack had widened into a fissure. It was now a finger's-width wide and slashed all the way down the outer face of the wall. Commander Eogan brought it to Julian's attention, and the general came to see the problem for himself.

Julian ordered a full inspection by his best engineers. It was obvious that the problem was getting worse. By the end of the week, the fissure was a hand's-breadth wide and widening by the day. The Legion engineers noted that the ground beneath that wall was soft. The heavy stones were sinking into the weak earth. The only way to prevent further collapse was to tear down the whole section of wall, reinforce the foundation with new timber pilings and poured concrete, and rebuild the wall once again from the ground up. Julian ordered it done, and work began immediately. The wall's stones were carefully chiseled out one by one from the old mortar and stacked for reuse.

Another week found a fifty-foot stretch of the wall deconstructed. The Legion, under the direction of their engineers, worked around the clock. A massive pile driver, as tall as the wall itself, was constructed, and new logs were driven deep into the ground, hunting for bedrock.

That was when the Alemanni struck.

CHAPTER THIRTY-ONE

The attack came without warning. Night had fallen on a wintery day, and from the darkened sky dropped a storm of razor-sharp arrows. Twenty legionnaires were working in the gap, driving wooden pilings and mixing concrete. Half a dozen men were wounded before they even knew they were under attack. The Legion made a habit of laboring in full armor, and several other men were saved by their protective steel. The soldiers dropped their tools and ran for their shields and swords. A warning was called, and the wooden doors at the fort's east and west entrances were slammed shut.

Julian had been writing in his study when a runner brought the news of the attack. He dressed hurriedly, donning a second tunic against the night's cold. By the time the general reached the wall, the work had ground to a halt. The unseen enemy was hidden by the shadows of the forest. Fifty legionnaires filled the gap in the wall. Together they made an impenetrable mass, with a wall of shields blocking the night and a roof of shields overhead. This was the testudo formation, a dense, protective shield wall that looked much like the turtle for whom it was named. Arrows, invisible against the dark sky, flew from the dark woods and rang futilely against the protective shell, bouncing and scattering like angry hail.

Julian, seeking a better vantage point, dashed up the stairs to the wall's top. The sentries made room for him to peer out into the night. His eyes, blinded by the firelight of the town, could make out nothing against the inky blackness. Sigmund joined him.

"Can you see anything?" Julian asked.

Sigmund peered into the dark woods. "I can see the shapes of many men moving against the tree line. I can't tell how many there are. They are scattered across the whole face of the woods."

Julian turned, looking back into the town. He spotted his legate standing calmly behind the Legion testudo, hands clasped behind his back as he watched his men weather the impotent storm. "Severus," Julian shouted down. "Bring pitch and hay to the battlements. We need light."

Severus nodded, and called to several of his soldiers. Bales of tightly-wound hay were brought up the stairs. They were soaked in pitch, set alight, and thrown into the empty space beyond the wall. Their light was bright against the gloom, and in its glare, Julian could see there were at least two hundred enemy at the edge of the field, about a hundred paces away, with more moving deeper in the trees. Severus joined his general at the ramparts.

"Have we confirmed the enemy's identity?" Julian asked the legate. Although in his mind there was little doubt.

"They are Alemanni, General," Severus confirmed. He carried a pair of the enemy arrows in his hand. He held them up; they were thick and heavy, tipped with narrow steel points without barbs. They looked brutal and wicked compared to the Roman archers' elegant missiles, which had long, thin shafts and broad, triangular heads. "These arrows are definitely Alemanni in origin. They may look primitive, but they craft them with great precision and skill. The shafts are weighted, and the arrow heads are hardened and narrow. They trade ranged accuracy for penetrating power. In fact, they are especially designed to penetrate our heavy armor. Still, at this long range, they are of little use against good shields."

Julian looked out into the darkness. He felt a sudden chill. Why had no scouts warned of this attack? Had the outposts already fallen? As he looked into the windswept night, light of the living town at his back, monsters of the darkness at his fore, he pictured for a moment that his garrison was all alone—the last bastion of Rome against the barbarian hordes. He shivered.

"General," Severus prompted, "your orders?"

Julian turned away from the night. Standing before him was Legate Severus and next to him was Commander Eogan of the Auxilia.

Julian hesitated. He looked down from the high wall. The Legion still huddled beneath its shields, and the sound of bouncing arrows was now a continuous drumroll.

"Can we attack them?" he asked his lieutenants.

"Absolutely, General," Severus responded. "My Legion is at your disposal. If we leave a small force in the gap, we can march the rest of the men against the barbarians immediately."

Julian nodded. He felt reassured by the legate's confidence. "Can your Auxilia support him Eogan?" he asked.

"That's what we do best," Eogan said, grinning ear to ear. He slapped Severus on the back enthusiastically. "My swordsmen will cover your flanks, and my archers will be on your heels. Together we will teach this rabble what happens when you attack Rome."

Julian nodded. "Let's do it," he said.

Within ten minutes the small army was organized. Roman soldiers marched into orderly files behind their centurions. They filled the empty space between the wall and the town. Severus stood before his men in full armor. He was joined by a standard-bearer holding aloft the eagle pennant of the Legion.

Ulrich, Tau, and Ima had joined Sigmund on the wall. "Can we do anything to help?" Ulrich asked.

Tau shrugged. "They seem to have it all under control," he said.

Ima slid her fingers between Tau's discreetly. He smiled at her. Together, they leaned over the wall to get a better look. Nearby, a small brown cat stood on the crenellations, ears alert and attentive. Sigmund, always a lover of animals, gently scratched the cat beneath the chin. The cat purred appreciatively, but its yellow eyes stayed watchful.

It was easy to spot the differences between the Auxilia and the Legion when they were arrayed side by side. The soldiers of the Legion carried large square shields and wore heavy steel cuirasses. They carried the short sword, the gladius, and stood in close formation. The Auxilia infantry, in contrast, wore light chainmail and carried smaller oval shields. The longer sword that they carried, the spatha, was more awkward in close combat but more useful in skirmishing and better for defense against cavalry charges. The Auxilia archers were also in chainmail. They had no shields but carried recurved composite bows of the most modern Roman design.

At an order from Severus the Legion streamed out of the gap in the broken wall, followed immediately by the Auxilia. They picked their way carefully across the ditch with its sharpened stakes and formed up in the empty ground just beyond. The heavy legionnaires made a shield wall and led the advance while the lighter Auxilia infantry spread out on the wings. The Auxilia archers were in a loose formation immediately behind, nocking arrows to strings as they marched forward.

The sentry to Ulrich's right coughed nervously. He was a handsome man with an open, genial face and close-cropped brown hair. He wore the uniform of the Auxilia and held a long spear. He recognized Ulrich and flashed a quick, self-conscious smile, but it faded instantly, replaced by a worried look.

"I wish we had our cavalry with us," the sentry said, watching the small Roman army move up the field. Enemy arrows were still falling steadily among the advancing ranks.

"Where is the cavalry?" Ulrich asked.

"They've been stationed with Commander Marcellus in the town of Reims, about ninety miles to the north because there is more grain storage there." He shook his head. "A hundred lancers could clear those bastards out in moments."

The man had spoken in German with a strong Frankish accent. He spat over the wall, cursing the Alemanni. Ulrich was surprised at his vehemence.

"Have you fought the Alemanni before?" Ulrich asked.

The sentry nodded. "We fought them at Augustodunum and at Noviodunum. And they almost destroyed two legions at Decem Pagi before we chased them away at Brotomagus. All that was just last summer."

Julian's voice came from close behind. "The Alemanni are not like the other German tribes. They are better equipped, better organized, and dead-set on our destruction." The sentry snapped to attention, and Ulrich moved aside to let the general lean on the parapet.

"We created this enemy," Julian continued. His voice was flat. "We betrayed the Alemanni—conquered and enslaved them. Then we liberated them, thinking they would be grateful, only for another generation of emperors to take advantage of them all over again. We have given them cause to hate us, all the while teaching them how to fight."

The Romans had advanced halfway across the field. They were holding their shields over their heads as the arrows continued to fall. In the center, the Legion, with their sturdy armor and heavy shields, was weathering the storm of missiles, but on the flanks, the missiles began to take their toll. Among the lightly armored Auxilia, arrows were sliding past shields and cutting through chainmail, and bodies were falling onto the field. The army was leaving a scattered trail of casualties behind the advancing wings. The Roman archers began firing, launching their arrows over the heads of the Legion, but they were shooting blind, and it was impossible to see what effect their missiles were having in the dark. The enemy retreated into the trees.

As they approached the woods, the army left the light of the burning thatch. Torches were lit among the leading ranks of soldiers, and in their light, the enemy could be seen moving beneath the trees. In the shifting torchlight their shadows morphed and danced, shifting like demons as they ran to and fro.

At the edge of the woods, the Legion stalled. The enemy had melted away, moving deeper into the forest, and Severus was loath to send his men into its blackness. The strength of the Roman army lay in its ordered discipline and even ranks. That advantage would be lost in a scuffle among the broken underbrush and scattering trees.

While the army hesitated, the Alemanni, sensing their enemy's indecision, launched their missiles with a renewed vigor. The arrows came down in a torrent, and at this close range, spears, javelins, and sling stones were mixed into the deadly hail. The Legion held formation, crouching beneath their shields to weather the storm, but the Auxilia suffered. They were meant to be supporting troops. With their smaller shields and lighter armor, they had the advantage of mobility over the heavy Legion, but in a standstill that light armor was a deadly liability. The Auxilia quivered under the constant bombardment. Every few seconds, a man fell as a lucky missile slipped in, seeking soft flesh.

"Bastards," the sentry on the wall muttered angrily. "They won't come out and fight us like men."

General Julian said nothing. His jaw was clenched tight. His knuckles were white where he gripped the battlements.

Far across the field Severus, standing in the midst of his beloved Legion, came to a decision. On his order the Legion, keeping formation, began to edge backward. Severus signaled Eogan, who thus ordered a full retreat among the Auxilia. The light soldiers fell back from the deadly barrage. They broke formation and moved fast, sprinting out of range of the arrows, leaving the stoic heavy Legion to take the brunt of the attack. The Auxilia soldiers rescued their wounded as they went, carrying them on their shoulders as they returned to the wall.

The slowly retreating Legion was left alone on the field, and they looked small and vulnerable as they packed tightly together. They were in the testudo formation once again. With their shields covering all possible angles of attack, they looked to all the world like a moving hillock of painted wood on the gently sloping turf. The testudo was famously impregnable, but in this formation they moved with painful slowness, and the enemy, emboldened, came from the woods in a scattered mob, throwing spears and launching arrows at the retreating Romans.

The tide of enemy lapped about the Legion but steadily the testudo creeped implacably along. The enemy encircled them and taunted them, threw spears and launched arrows at the wall of shields yet were wise enough to stay out of range of the short, lethal gladius. Not a single legionnaire fell and eventually the Legion was in the shadow of the wall. A hundred or so of the overeager Alemanni feared their prey would escape. They ran close to press the attack, but they paid for their impetuosity. The Auxilia archers rushed up the staircases to line the wall, and their advanced bows cut down the rushing barbarians with murderous precision. The lightly armored Alemanni fell in droves as the lethally accurate Roman arrows cut into them. In seconds, dozens of bodies littered the field, and the remaining Alemanni ran back out of range. The Legion returned ponderously to the gap, blocking it with a solid wall of shields.

Julian sighed, unclenched his hands from the parapet, and went down to the yard.

CHAPTER THIRTY-TWO

The harassing attacks continued all night. Eogan and Severus rotated their men in short shifts to keep them fresh. Enemy were seen on all sides. The fortress was surrounded, although the fighting remained concentrated on the broken section of the wall. At one point, after a few hours of uneasy quiet, two hundred Alemanni warriors launched a surprise attack. After covering themselves in mud and crawling unseen across three hundred feet of empty ground, they rose suddenly from the ditch and threw themselves on the legionnaires that blocked the gap. The attack failed. The steady Legion bore the blow without a waver, and the reckless warriors were cut down by stabbing gladii and Auxilia arrows, adding their bodies to the scattered piles of corpses before the walls.

All through the night, firelight appeared in the woods as the Alemanni gathered in ever greater strength. Snow fell, and by morning the smoke of a thousand cooking fires rose into the chilly air. At noon Chnodomar himself appeared. He was riding a tall white horse, and the red horsehair plume on his helmet hung limply down his back.

He led a massive horde to battle. Behind him, ten thousand warriors in mail and leather stepped onto the snowy field. They carried spears and swords and were ringed by a screen of archers. The hooves of a thousand barbarian cavalry horses stamped the turf. Chnodomar curbed his horse just out of Roman bowshot and turned to his men. His speech was inaudible to the defenders, but every Roman braced himself for the inevitable attack. Every soldier of the fortress was at his station. The wall was lined with archers, and the gap was filled tight with the shields of the legionnaires. The fortress held its breath.

Ulrich looked on as, with a roar, the Alemanni finally came. White tunics flapped over glistening chainmail. Leather boots pounded the dirt. Weapons were held high in anticipation of the killing blow. They came in a mob, driven on by their own fierce hate and their warrior pride. The most eager sprinted ahead, and some, in their haste, impaled themselves on the sharpened stakes of the ditch. The rest ran on, and the Roman archers loosed their arrows. Men fell by the dozens, but it made no difference; ten thousand Alemanni warriors rushed the fortress and slammed into the Legion soldiers holding the gap.

There were too many in the massive Alemanni horde for them to all attack at once. The Romans were packed in tight, and the Alemanni, in their haste, had no discipline to their charge. The front row of legionnaires faced a mob of loosely scattered warriors, and the leading Alemanni died quickly, cut down by the ready and waiting swords of the Legion. The next wave was no more fortunate. They were so closely followed by their compatriots that they ended up crushed against the Roman shields by the pressure of the men behind. They had no room to swing their weapons. The face of the mob was so broad that the flanks of the leading ranks were forced hard against the cold stones of the wall itself, to hack and pull uselessly at its unyielding surface.

The bulk of the Alemanni horde was somewhere in the middle of the pack, unable to see forward, unable to move back, and some unable even to breathe due to the crushing pressure of the mass of men. The air was forced from their straining lungs, many were crushed to death by the weight of their own assault.

The Romans guarding the gap were having a much easier time of it, buttressed by the steady support of the waiting legionnaire file. For every man holding a shield against the Alemanni horde, ten more stood firm in the ranks behind and leant their weight into the press. The Romans also had better traction in this shoving match. The Alemanni were trying to push uphill against snow-covered, muddy turf and slippery grass. The Romans stood level, their sandals on the flat, dry, paving stones of the fortress of Sens, and they held their ground.

The Roman archers on the high wall had easy targets. They drew, aimed carefully for unprotected faces, looked for helmetless men, and placed their shots deliberately. Ulrich climbed to the bastion, but he found that the Romans needed no help from him. Eogan was there too, walking the wall and instructing his men calmly.

"No wasted shots, archers," the Auxilia commander said in an even voice. The barbarians might rant and roar, but the Romans fought quietly, conserving their breath. Thus, Eogan's voice carried well, even in the din of battle. "We don't have enough arrows to kill them all. Just aim for the biggest and ugliest ones."

Eogan saw an arrow fly right into the eyepiece of a closed steel helmet. The Alemanni warrior must have been killed because he dropped his arms and stopped moving. His head lolled on his neck, arrow sticking up and out of the eyepiece. Morbidly, he did not fall. The density of men was so great that he stayed in place, propped up by the close-packed men on either side. The dead warrior wobbled obscenely as the mob jostled his corpse. Eogan walked to the archer responsible, a tall young Briton who was stringing another long Roman arrow.

"Good job, Oscar. Very nice shot," Eogan said, patting the man on the shoulder. Oscar grinned and loosed another arrow, which smashed into the bare skull of a closer man, spraying blood and brains in a grotesque fountain of death.

On the ground within the fort, Julian stood with Sigmund and Severus. Incongruously, on this day of battle, the general wore a loose white toga, the dress of a philosopher. His arms were crossed on his chest, and he spoke pedantically, gazing toward the solid mass of legionnaires holding the gap.

"I would not bet one of our men in single combat against one of theirs." Julian was saying. "The Germans are bigger, stronger, and have been bred for generations to survive the harsh conditions of the wilderness. Our men are raised in the pampered comfort of cities. But still Rome wins its battles against such barbarians. Why is that? The difference is that the barbarians are warriors, while our men are soldiers." Both Severus and Julian were watching the Legion struggle, but neither seemed particularly concerned.

"The enemy's fierce appetite for combat may be intimidating to other tribes, but it is not how pitched battles are won," Julian continued. "It is discipline that distinguishes the soldier from the warrior, and a properly led team of soldiers can fight and defeat many times its weight in warriors."

"Yes, General," Severus responded dutifully. In truth he was only half listening. His thoughts were consumed with strategies and contingency plans. He did not mind Julian lecturing him about things he already knew. He had grown to rather like the young general. Julian might be more scholar than soldier, but Severus knew that Julian was no fool. Julian trusted the advice of his seasoned lieutenants.

A commotion in the other direction made Severus turn. There was a crash at the eastern gate and the sounds of men shouting. Without a word, Severus sprinted down the street in the direction of the sudden noise. Ulrich, curious, followed behind.

Severus arrived at the gate to see that it still held. The thick timbers were unbreached, but they shuddered under the impact of unseen attackers. Severus climbed to the parapet to find that a mob of Alemanni was trying to break down the gate. This attack was smaller than the one at the gap, but there were still well over a thousand warriors clustered outside. Some swung axes at the wooden gates, others shot arrows at the defenders. A few of the attackers were even trying, by standing on the shoulders of their companions, to scale the sheer face of the stone wall.

Severus sighed. He gave a command to one of his captains, and archers were diverted to reinforce this section of the battlements. He walked into the guardhouse. In the space immediately above the gateway holes were open in the floor, and Severus could see the tops of the heads of the enemy who hacked at the gate. Pots of red-hot sand were baking over open fires, waiting for just this moment. He ordered them poured slowly down through the floor. Screams and the sickly-sweet smell of burnt flesh rose through the murder holes.

Severus noticed Ulrich standing nearby, watching the carnage below. "They'll never get through this way," the Roman legate reassured him. "They need siege equipment. Battering rams, siege towers, artillery, even simple ladders would be something. But as far as I can see they have none. They are impetuous. Even as sophisticated as the Alemanni are, they still lack foresight. Other than that one gap, this old fortress is virtually impregnable against such a simple assault."

"How old is this fortress?" Ulrich asked curiously.

Severus thought for a moment. "Honestly, I do not know for

sure." He squinted at the stones around him. Just then an arrow streaked in the open stone window, flew inches from the legate's unprotected head, and clattered harmlessly against the opposite stone wall. Ulrich jumped, but Severus did not so much as flinch.

"I would say at least three hundred years," Severus said, finishing his thought. "It may have even been one of the forts built by Julius Caesar himself, which would make it about four centuries old, but the Roman stonework is no less stout for its age," he said proudly. He thumped the arched entryway with his fist. "Maybe stouter."

The fighting went on all day. Severus reduced the active defenders to a third of his force and let the other two thirds rest and eat. Those on the wall and at the gap were rotated out every few hours, keeping the defenders fresh while the Alemanni tired, and the pressure gradually slackened.

Julian called a conference that afternoon. Severus and Eogan joined him at a broad tent erected just behind the gap. Marius, the portly quartermaster, was also there, as was Sigmund. Two Legion centurions, Antonius and Valerius, each a junior commander of five hundred men, were eager to be part of the fight.

Julian, long, white toga just brushing the paving stones, began the discussion in his customary open-ended fashion. "We need a solution to our current plight. Suggestions from all are welcome," he said.

Severus, used to his general's scholarly way of speaking, offered context. "The enemy siege, in its current form, would have little chance of breaking through our defenses given an unbroken wall, but the situation in the breach is tenuous. Our soldiers have held firm so far, but given that we are outnumbered almost ten to one, a single mistake in the gap could spell instant disaster."

"In addition," Eogan put in, "my archers are running desperately short of arrows, and we lack the necessary materials to make replacements. We have resorted to firing their own missiles back at them, but even those are limited."

"There is some good news." Marius spoke up, ubiquitous papers and scrolls filling his hands. "We have enough grain and preserved meat to last all winter. The well produces clean fresh water, and there is even enough wine for all, provided we dilute it at least..." He paused, shuffling through papers. "At least four to one."

"Thank you, Marius. That is good news indeed," Julian said, nodding.

"If only we had our cavalry, we could clear them out from the woods easily," Eogan mused.

"Some artillery would have been nice too," the centurion Valerius said. He was a burly Italian. A veteran of a decade of battles, he was a reticent and serious soldier who had a reputation for fierceness in battle and for writing somewhat mediocre poetry.

"That is my fault," Julian said with regret. "The cavalry could not have been reasonably stabled here because Sens lacks the grain storage, but we should have at least brought the Legion's ballistae." He shook his head ruefully. "I didn't think we would need it."

"None of us expected this, General," Severus said. "But we cannot make plans for what might have been. We can only work with the resources at our command. Regret gets us nowhere. We must focus on making plans to survive the winter."

"Truly, though, we may not have to wait all winter," Julian said optimistically. "Marcellus has the bulk of the army at Reims, only ninety miles north, and he has orders to strike at any Alemanni that enter Gaul. He must have news of this attack through his scouts. I am sure he will be here to relieve us soon."

Sigmund spoke next. "The Alemanni presence here raises questions of its own," he said. "How did they get this deep within Gaul without being challenged? Why did no scouts report their crossing of the border? And why, of all places, did they choose Sens to besiege? They had to actually bypass Marcellus and the main army at Reims to get here." Sigmund had the full attention of the council now.

"I think, General," Sigmund continued, "that we must at least conclude that Chnodomar must have known that you would be here."

"That would explain why they are here and not at Reims," Valerius said with a frown.

"Also," Sigmund went on, "I believe it likely that Marcellus's failure to respond and Chnodomar's knowledge of your location might be related."

A long silence greeted that revelation. Severus shifted uncomfortably, and Eogan coughed. The implication of treason was impossible to miss, but nobody was ready to delve into those dark waters just yet.

"It does not matter," Julian said, breaking the silence. "We must make plans based on what we do know and use what tools are at our disposal. Our greatest weakness is that gap, so we must continue to rebuild our wall." The general's statement invited no rebuttal, and the soldiers, engineers all, began to draw up new plans.

By evening, the Alemanni grew tired of throwing themselves at the unshakeable Roman defenses and retreated to the edge of the ditch. They were still within bowshot, but the Roman archers had ceased firing to conserve their ammunition. The Alemanni contented themselves with hurling insults and the occasional desultory sling stone. Most of the attacking force had returned to the woods to cook and warm themselves by their fires, so it came as a surprise to the Alemanni when, at twilight, the Roman Legion suddenly burst from the gap to form up in a semicircle a dozen paces from the fortress. They made a shield wall, and above them, with surprising swiftness, a sloped construction of timber planking was erected on tall wooden supports. This freestanding scaffolding touched the wall's crenellated top at one edge and slanted steeply down to form a low roof where the legionnaires stood at the ditch's verge.

The Alemanni, seeing this new development, attacked with renewed vigor, but they were no more successful breaking the new Roman line than the old. In addition, the timber roof protected the Romans from the storm of arrows, which embedded themselves impotently into its slanting surface. The thump of hammers and the grinding noise of chisels betrayed where the Roman stonemasons went to work rebuilding the wall in the shade of their protective wooden ceiling. Julian, seeing the effectiveness of his plan, breathed a sigh of relief and went to bed.

CHAPTER THIRTY-THREE

U lrich, restless and rising early, woke to a frigid morning. The sun was just below the horizon, casting its glow into a clear sky. A thin mist filled the snowy woodlands beyond the wall as the light grew. Ulrich leaned on the battlements and chewed meditatively on dried beef and a hunk of cheese. The Auxilia sentry next to him dozed standing up, eyes closed, leaning on a long spear as he snored softly. The clank of hammer on stone still rose from below as the laborers worked tirelessly on the broken wall.

Ulrich heard the enemy artillery before he saw it. From the edge of the wood came a strange noise. It sounded like a massive door, creaking slowly on ungreased hinges. Curious, he peered into the wan pre-dawn light to see what kind of thing made such a sound.

Suddenly, there was a thump and a twang, and a huge missile sped from the woods to smash through the wooden roof that protected the men who labored in the gap. A scream pierced the morning air, and splinters were launched forty feet into the sky. He looked down into the fortress to see that one of the stonemasons had been struck by an enormous arrow. The arrow had broken clear through the wood and flung the man back to the closest row of wooden houses. Four feet long, the wooden shaft with its steel tip had ripped the man in half. It had then rebounded off the flagstones and carried what remained of the mangled body in a smear of blood along its destructive path.

The dawn light was just reaching the woods, and Ulrich could see that the missile had come from an enormous ballista. It was being crewed by a team of five Alemanni in their distinctive white tunics. As he watched, two more ballistae were dragged forward alongside

181

the first. The first machine was reloaded, and another big arrow streaked in across the snowy field. This one struck lower, smashing through the clustered legionnaires that formed the shield wall at the base of the sloped roof. At least three men were hit, and a fan of blood splashed back from the missile's impact.

The dozing sentry was wide awake now. "Where the hell did they get ballistae?" he said. He swore, brandishing his spear angrily.

Without a word Ulrich spun on his heels and raced into the fortress. He took the stairs from the wall two at a time as he sprinted toward his temporary home. In his mind he saw the Alemanni breaking through the ruined Roman defenses. He saw Johanne and her children sold into slavery. He saw his friends dragged behind horses until their skin was torn to ribbons. He saw them nailed to poles until they died of thirst. He saw gentle Sigmund's throat cut and Tau's body displayed for curious gawkers. He was angry and scared and knew that the Romans, for all their skill and discipline, had planned poorly. The Legion had already shown that it was too weak to cross that open field. Unopposed, the artillery would slowly grind the defenders to dust. Unless somebody did something, they were all doomed.

He and his friends shared a house at the center of town, and at its door he stopped. He slowed his breathing and calmed his nerves. He pushed the door open as quietly as he could. In the front room, Sigmund slept in a bed in the corner, and Johanne's big dog snored on the floor. Past this was a hallway, and he crept into it. He padded silently past where Ima and Tau shared a small room. Johanne and the kids' room was at the end of the hall but this next door was his own, and he opened it. Inside was his finished suit of armor, still glossy and untarnished. He lifted the heavy steel cuirass and buckled it about his torso. The feeling of security of the heavy armor settled his jangling nerves. He pulled on a long hunting jacket of rough leather to cover the conspicuous garment. This mission would require subterfuge. He buckled on a sturdy steel helmet and hefted his new battle axe. Making pains to leave as quietly as he could, Ulrich slipped back out the front door and into the waxing winter day.

Shouting filled the dawn air, and armored soldiers ran toward the beleaguered gap. The crash of splintering wood and the screams of men were evidence that the enemy ballistae were still performing their deadly work. Ulrich ran the other way, toward the fortress's east gate.

"Are there any enemy outside this door?" he shouted up to the sentry. It was Oscar, the skilled young archer who, recognizing Ulrich, responded at once.

"No, it's all quiet. All the barbarians look to be enjoying a nice peaceful breakfast in the woods over here." Oscar glanced toward the gap where the noise of the siege engines boomed and echoed. "What's going on over there?" he asked Ulrich.

Ulrich ignored the question. "Let me out, Oscar," he commanded.

Oscar hesitated. "Why?" he asked curiously.

Ulrich growled impatiently. He hefted his axe. "Because I'm going to go kill those bastards."

Oscar blinked. He hesitated for another instant then shrugged. "I can't argue with that," he said. "Good luck. Kill a lot of them." He grinned down at Ulrich and ordered the big locking bar lifted. The door opened just a fraction, and Ulrich slipped out. The heavy door slammed shut behind him, and he was all alone, stranded on the wrong side of the wall, facing no-man's land before a hostile army.

He knew the enemy was watching, so he dashed to his right, and holding his axe in both hands, leapt into the spike-lined ditch. The bottom of the ditch was not very deep, but it was rimmed with ice, and he landed on it heavily. Fortunately, the spikes were all aimed away from him, directed toward an attacker, and the thick poles served to steady him. He planned to walk south in the ditch, paralleling the wall. He knew that he would have been seen exiting the big gates, but he hoped that, if he circled far enough around the fortress before crossing the empty ground toward the trees, the defenders there would assume he was a German scout and not a Roman spy.

Just then, with a creak, the big double doors opened again. Ulrich turned back and what he saw made him swear. Tau, Ima, and Sigmund were exiting the fortress. All three were wearing mail and carrying swords. The door slammed behind them, and they jumped down into the ditch to join him.

"You bastards! What are you doing here?" Ulrich hissed.

Tau was grinning. "That's what I was going to ask you," he said.

"I'm going to destroy those ballistae," Ulrich explained. "We have already seen that the Romans cannot sortie into that empty field without getting overwhelmed. I plan to circle around the fort, cross into the woods and attack them from behind."

"This is a suicide mission," Sigmund said, aghast.

Ulrich felt a sudden pang of anger and sadness. He gritted his teeth against the tears that threatened to come. "That's why I didn't want any of you to come," he said. The tears came anyway. "Please go back in," he pleaded. "I don't want you to come with me."

Sigmund frowned. "And how are we supposed to live with ourselves knowing that you went off to die alone?" he asked. His eyes were wide and his question plaintive.

Ima chimed in. "Your chances of doing it alone are impossible. Together we are more likely to succeed." Her voice was matter-of-fact. "You idiot," she added, teasing him with a smile.

Tau laughed, a rich sound that broke the somber mood. "Finally, there is some action," he breathed. "I grow restless cooped up with nothing to do all winter." His smile was wide as he clapped Ulrich on the shoulder. "Come on. Let us go rescue these poor helpless Romans from the mess they've gotten themselves into."

Ulrich grinned back. He was suddenly glad to have his friends at his side. The thrill of battle filled him, and he hefted his axe.

"All right then," he said. "There's no time to waste."

Together, the four friends worked their way along the ditch. Their heads were below ground level, and they were invisible to the Alemanni in the woods. Oscar must have passed around word of their presence, for while the sentries on the wall looked down on them curiously, nobody fired on them.

"Where did you get those weapons and armor anyway?" Ulrich asked.

"Eogan lent them to us," Sigmund grinned. "Or at least he would have lent them to us if he knew that we had borrowed them."

Ulrich shook his head ruefully. He realized that he had been shaking, but now his hands were steady. Together they made their way to the southeast corner of the fortress and turned the right angle. They followed this ditch all the way to the next corner and stopped. They had arrived at the farthest point from the action, and what would hopefully be the quietest part of the field. The beleaguered defenders of the gap were far across on the north side of the fortress, and the gate they had exited was similarly distant to the east. Gingerly they climbed out of the ditch and began crossing the snowy field.

Their footprints were fresh in the icy snow.

They had almost made it to the tree line when there was a shout from somewhere ahead. An arrow flew from the woods to strike, quivering, in the snow just to Sigmund's right. Ulrich swore. They had been spotted by the Alemanni. He raced for the cover of the trees, his companions following close behind.

There was no enemy visible directly in front of him, so Ulrich kept running. Another arrow thrummed through the branches from the right, zipping past into the undergrowth. A copse of trees was in their path, and they burst into it, surprising a dozen warriors who squatted around a cooking fire. The Alemanni gawked at the interlopers, but Ulrich did not break stride. He rushed out the other side of the copse and stumbled down a steep embankment onto a frozen stream. His friends were on his heels. The arrows had stopped, but there was angry shouting behind, so Ulrich led his companions in a sharp left turn up the stream and through some dense undergrowth. After fifty paces, they left the streambed and entered a wide clearing.

Hundreds of Alemanni were camped on the frozen ground. This deep into the woods, the early dawn sunlight had not yet broken through the trees, so this whole division of the enemy still slumbered. Cloaks, fur pelts, and leather blankets were heaped across the sleeping men. Ulrich hesitated. He glanced around, looking for a way to escape. Suddenly a hand grabbed his ankle, and he jumped. He looked down to see Ima beckon to him. She had concealed herself underneath the edge of a nearby blanket, becoming just another lump within the formless mass. Tau had already followed suit, and Sigmund and Ulrich hastily threw themselves on the ground as well.

Ulrich slid under a blanket to find himself face to face with a sleeping man. The warrior was a huge swarthy man with an unkempt shaggy beard and foul breath. The man was snoring noisily, and Ulrich twisted away to watch the woods from whence they came. He saw that Ima, Tau, and Sigmund were now just shapeless forms in the cloaks and furs, hidden amongst the sleeping enemy. He froze at the sight of movement in the shrubbery nearby. He closed his eyes and tried to slow his breathing to match that of the snoring man beside him. He half cracked one eyelid to watch twelve Alemanni warriors step from the woods with drawn longbows. They walked onto the scene warily and scanned for their prey. The nearest one stepped close to Ulrich, his booted foot only inches from Ulrich's face. As Ima had anticipated, the enemy was scanning the field for fleeing men, not looking down at the sleeping warriors. After a tense moment the patrol went back into the woods and noisily continued up the frozen stream bed.

For a minute, neither Ulrich nor his companions moved. From a nearby heap of furs, he could see Ima's big blue eyes, wide and anxious, staring at him from beneath two layers of blankets. Ulrich waited until he thought they were safe, then he counted to one hundred to be sure. Finally, he crawled out of the blankets and stood. The swarthy man groaned and rolled over to fill the warm spot that Ulrich had vacated. The four companions were alone among the sleeping enemy.

Without speaking, Ulrich motioned for his friends to follow. They crossed the field, picking their way between heaps of blankets and sleeping men, and entered the woods on the far side. Once safely in the undergrowth, Ulrich let out a pent-up sigh of relief. Sigmund looked worried; Ima looked confident, and Tau was exuberant. Ulrich felt energized. He realized that he had been restless, frustrated to wait passively while the Romans had all the fun. It felt great to be back in the fight.

"All right, we probably look enough like the Alemanni or their German allies to not arouse too much suspicion from here," Ulrich said. "Now we just need to circle around to the ballistae and disable them."

"Oh, good. I'm glad the hard part is over," Sigmund said drily.

Tau clapped Sigmund on the back. "Come now, friend. Don't claim you aren't having fun." Sigmund grinned back ruefully and shrugged.

Ima was looking at the sky thoughtfully, judging the position of the sun. "The ballistae are that way," she said finally, pointing to the right. Ulrich had lost his bearings during the rush through the woods, so he was grateful for her sense of direction. They started moving.

They crossed a war camp that was larger than any of them had imagined. It was as if the entire population of Germania had travelled into Gaul to assault this fortress. Banners of all shapes and sizes flew above camps big and small. Even as they watched, new wagons came up roads and cow paths bringing supplies and equipment. Raiding parties rode in from far afield with plundered food, weaponry, and newly captured slaves. Some of the larger encampments could have passed for moderate-sized towns, even bearing hastily built wooden dwellings. Circles of carts made lively, makeshift marketplaces from which wares were bought and bartered.

Through it all they kept moving, and the noise of battle grew louder. The loudest sound of all was the thrum of the ballistae. The big weapons sounded like giant harp strings, plucked at a note almost too low for the human ear to hear. Ima led them assuredly on, and finally they found their targets. The three ballistae were perched at the edge of the forest and were firing constantly, each crewed by five competent Alemanni warriors. The missiles hummed as they flew off their perches, propelled forward by the clever torsion springs. Ulrich could see that the Romans were suffering badly. Their protective roof was little more than splinters, yet the Legion still huddled miserably in the gap. The bolts from the ballistae were striking with deadly precision into that mass of soldiers, and Ulrich could only imagine the death and pain they were causing there.

There was a crowd of Alemanni onlookers around the weapons, and they cheered at each impact. Men, women, and children together were enraptured at the sight, gloating as the missiles wreaked their devastation among the hated Imperials. Tau sidled up to one such onlooker, a tall Germanic warrior who leaned casually against a nearby tree.

"Where did these ballistae come from, friend?" Tau asked nonchalantly. The man turned, then jumped when he saw the dark face. He was speechless for a moment, as this was his first time ever seeing a black man. Then, sensing no danger, he recovered enough to answer.

"We took them from a small outpost east of here," the Alemanni warrior answered, still blinking in surprise at the dark visage. "Fifty cowardly Romans died at our hand."

"How many ballistae are there?" Tau asked.

The man gestured. "Just the three you see here," he responded.

Tau nodded and turned away. Sigmund discreetly walked to a tree where a huge two-handed sledgehammer was leaning. He hefted the heavy tool and nodded at Ulrich. He was ready. All four of them strolled to the nearest weapon.

Ulrich stopped with Sigmund at the first ballista. Tau and Ima walked on to the next one. Tau had unsheathed both his swords and was holding them low. When he got to his chosen target, which was the middle weapon of the three, it was being loaded. The cord was being cranked by two men, and a third was hefting a heavy bolt to place in the slot. Tau reached out, placed his sharpened sword blade on the oversized bow string and gently slid it back. The cord split apart, its ends flapping uselessly forward with a wheeze. The warrior who had been cranking the weapon began, with an offended look on his face, to protest. Tau's sword came up fast into the man's open mouth, silencing him forever.

At that same moment, Ulrich and Sigmund took action. The man in front of Ulrich was watching his prior bolt shot fall and did not see Ulrich approach. Ulrich drove the sharpened upper point of his axe blade into the man's unprotected spine. The man fell forward with a scream, and Ulrich ripped the weapon back in a spray of blood. An Alemanni warrior to Ulrich's left started to draw his sword but never finished drawing it as Ulrich swung the axe back to slam into the man's torso. He leaned all his weight into the blow to throw the man to the ground. Meanwhile Sigmund unleashed his massive strength in a vicious attack on the ballista, smashing it again and again with the big hammer. Ulrich moved to cover his friend as he destroyed the weapon.

Meanwhile, Ima and Tau worked together to fend off a counterattack from the next ballista's crew. Tau was moving with his customary quickness, dashing in and out of range of the men who came at him with drawn swords. Two men came at Tau at once and he, with a speed almost imperceptible to the eye, slid his right blade into the forearm tendons of the Alemanni on his right. The man's weapon slumped, and Tau swung his left sword sideways at the other man. That warrior brought his own sword up in a desperate parry but was instantly struck down as Ima lunged forward, her two-handed sword taking the man in the throat.

The rest of the ballista's crew fled in panic from the unexpected foe, and Ima and Tau moved on. The final weapon's crew saw them coming, and all five men were standing with weapons drawn. Ima lunged into a sprint. She hurtled toward the waiting enemy. At the last second she dropped to her knees to slide underneath the guard of a big man who carried a long axe. Her outstretched sword drove into his stomach, and he howled in pain, dropping his weapon. Tau came close behind, swords flashing, and the remaining men were driven

188

back by the fury of their assault.

Sigmund and Ulrich followed and smashed axe and hammer into the second ballista, reducing the device of precision engineering into a useless pile of splintered wood. Finally, all four of them stood at the last weapon. Practiced in this business now, Ulrich efficiently cut the slide in two with his axe, and Sigmund smashed the weapon's mount into splinters. The crowd, frozen with shock, stared at them aghast. All three ballistae were destroyed, and the four companions stood defiant with weapons bloody and teeth bared.

With a howl, the Alemanni mob surged. Sigmund was the first to step forward to meet them. There was a broad shield lying discarded against the base of the nearest ruined ballista, and Sigmund dropped his hammer to snatch it up. He stood between his friends and the mob with the round shield in both hands, leaning into the wood like a man leaning against a gale. The enraged enemy slammed into him.

Ima rushed to his side. She crouched and stabbed beneath the shield, slicing into the legs of a warrior who hacked at Sigmund with an axe. The enemy fell and another took his place and Ima stabbed again. To their left, Ulrich held his ground. He was a bulwark in the flood. His axe whistled like a living thing as it threw men back in bloody death. He ignored the blades that glanced off his heavy armor as he swung again and again. Tau was a whirling dervish on their right. At once unpredictable and deadly, he flowed from defense to attack, parrying blows to create openings for his striving blades.

Overrun and hopelessly outnumbered they fought desperately to survive. They acted automatically, on instinct, screaming in defiance as they parried and cut, attacked and dodged. Ulrich was in a berserk rage, insensible of the wounds he received; a spear flashed in to graze along his left thigh, an arrow sliced a shallow cut into his cheek. He drove the haft of his axe into a man's face, back swung to parry a sword thrust, and dropped the axe's heavy blade to cleave an attacker's skull in half. They had accomplished their mission and saved the fortress, but now inevitable death came for them. There was no time for fear, no time for regret, only time to howl and struggle as the blades came in.

Suddenly, Sigmund went down. The blade of a fast-swinging war axe glanced across his skull, and he stumbled. He dropped his shield, stunned. He was defenseless on hands and knees before the raging horde. Ima grabbed up the shield and stood over Sigmund. Shield in one hand, sword in the other, she was a goddess of war, defiant in the face of all odds. Ulrich and Tau stood back to back, snarling and bloody in the maelstrom of blades and death, inviting the enemy to come and die.

But the enemy hesitated. An Alemanni warrior looked past Ulrich with an expression of surprise, and Ulrich took advantage of his distraction to slice the man's hand off at the wrist. The man screamed and fell but no warriors took his place. Ulrich sneaked a glance over his shoulder to see what the man had seen, and what he saw made him laugh with joy. The Romans were coming.

At double-speed, the fast-moving Auxilia regiment slammed into the Alemanni horde. They attacked in skirmish order, their round shields held level, and their long swords stabbing forward. They parted to pass Ulrich and his companions, reforming to drive deep into the disorganized Alemanni mob. The Auxilia fought like men possessed, and they howled like barbarians as they killed. They were keening and laughing, and even outnumbered, they slaughtered the unprepared Alemanni. Eogan, following close behind, laughed and grabbed Ulrich in a massive embrace.

"You crazy bastards," Eogan yelled joyfully. "You reckless idiots!" He lifted Ulrich bodily into the air and shook him like a child. "You did it. You really did it!" He put down the Saxon.

"But we can't stay here," he said. "Get back to the fortress. Run! Run, you silly fools before you get murdered." Eogan yelled an order to his men, and they halted their advance. The Auxilia tightened their formation and began backing slowly in a defensive shield wall. Meanwhile the Alemanni was forming for a counterattack. Thousands and thousands of savage warriors were flooding out of their camps, and the small force of Romans would soon be overwhelmed. The companions fled.

From the fortress, the soldiers of the heavy Roman Legion advanced to join the beleaguered Auxilia. Ulrich saw Severus leading them as they moved, slowly and methodically, in the impregnable testudo. Ulrich and Tau supported the stunned Sigmund between them, and they hurried, with Ima, past the living bulwark of shields and back to the safety of the wall.

The light Auxilia fled to safety from the Alemanni swarm, and the Legion took their place. The testudo absorbed the massive Alemanni counterattack without a flinch. Once again, the fierce German warriors flowed around the Roman formation, and again, the Romans weathered the storm. They reversed their march, returning implacably back to the fortress, fighting every step against the massive press of enemy warriors. When they reached the wall, the gap was sealed tight with Roman shields and swords, and the Alemanni tide was thwarted. Eogan allowed a single flight of deadly arrows to slice down from above, and the Alemanni backed off. Alemanni dead littered the field.

And the fortress of Sens was saved.

CHAPTER THIRTY-FOUR

"Thank you," Julian said.

His face was somber. More than a hundred of his soldiers had been killed in the bombardment and many, many more were wounded. The Roman medics were overwhelmed, treating their own soldiers, so Ulrich and his friends bandaged their own, thankfully minor, wounds. Sigmund's head was throbbing, but his skull was intact. Together they were sitting around a cooking fire in the yard when Julian found them.

"I wish to ask you a favor," the general said stiffly. He turned and beckoned across the courtyard to Eogan, who had been checking on his own wounded Auxilia. When Eogan joined them, Julian continued. "You have proven your skill and courage, and we have a great need for brave men," Julian said. "I invite you to join my auxiliaries and to fight as friends of Rome."

Looking on, Eogan, commander of the Auxilia, beamed benevolently at the companions, and Julian stood silently waiting for a response. All eyes turned to Ulrich, and after a long moment he finally spoke. "I am no soldier," Ulrich said. Julian's expression did not change but Eogan looked downcast.

"However," Ulrich continued, "I will fight alongside you until Chnodomar is defeated and the Alemanni are destroyed. Once that task is complete, I would ask to be a free man again."

Julian looked to Eogan. The Auxilia commander shrugged, and Julian nodded in turn. He turned back to Ulrich. "I agree to your terms," the general said. "You shall be a privileged soldier of the Auxilia of Rome, but you shall be honorably discharged at the conclusion of the present conflict, if that is what you wish."

Ulrich gave a sideways glance to his friends. He hoped that they would join him, but he tried to keep his face impassive. He knew that this was a decision they must make on their own.

"I will go with you," Tau said at once, "just as I have always promised." Ulrich smiled at his friend.

Sigmund gave a wry grin. "I feel like I am deep enough in this mess to want to see how it ends," he said. "How sure are you that we will win?"

"We will win," Julian said confidently. "Marcellus will come from Reims with the Army of Gaul and rout this rabble. Together we will pursue them to the banks of the Rhine. Then we will join with Barbatio's Army of Italy. By the spring, the Alemanni will be destroyed once and for all."

Ima had not yet spoken but Julian caught her eye, and his face fell under her knowing gaze. He shifted his weight uncomfortably. "For you, Warmaiden Ima, I am sorry. You have also shown your bravery, but we do not allow women to fight. Women have no place in warfare among a civilized people."

Ima smiled, but not without cynicism. "What about Bellona?" she replied evenly. "Is Bellona not your Goddess of War? Does she not lead your men into battle? I was led to believe that you were a man of tradition. If you are truly a servant of the old gods of Rome, then you are a hypocrite if you pay homage to Bellona the Warmaiden yet deny women the right to serve in your army."

There was a pregnant pause while Julian stared at Ima with a surprise that slowly transformed into a look of grudging respect. "You are right," he mused finally. "I've never thought about it like that... I don't..." He was momentarily speechless. He looked to Eogan for support, but the Auxilia commander, wide eyed, threw up his hands in surrender.

"It's all right," Ima said with a laugh, breaking the tension. "I do not want to be a part of any organization that doesn't want me in it anyway. I am going to tag along and watch you destroy the Alemanni, but you don't have to worry about me running around corrupting your precious troops with my breasts."

Eogan was turning red with embarrassment, but Julian nodded seriously.

"Thank you," the general said with a bow. "And I appreciate what you have done for us. You have saved us. You saved Sens, and you saved my men, and Rome does not take such service lightly."

Ima nodded in acknowledgement, and the two Roman commanders turned and walked away. The companions looked at each other as Johanne refilled their bowls with a thick barley stew. Johanne's two children were playing knucklebones on the ground a few feet away with a young Roman boy about their age.

Ulrich breathed out a long, pent-up sigh. "What have we gotten ourselves into?" he asked, addressing nobody in particular.

Tau chuckled. "Don't act like you didn't secretly want this to happen. You've wanted to join the Roman army ever since you saw the big walls of Cologne."

Ulrich grinned ruefully. "The Romans are formidable," he admitted, "and it's just too good of a fight to miss."

The broken fortress wall was rebuilt in a week, and Sens was secure. The Romans huddled behind their fortifications, ate their rations, and waited for Marcellus to march from Reims to break the siege. But Marcellus never came. All that winter, Flavius Claudius Julianus, Caesar of the West, with only a handful of men at his disposal, was trapped in a tiny fortress and besieged by his most hated enemy. Chnodomar's Alemanni threw themselves again and again at the wall, each attack more desperate than the one before. They probed for weaknesses, but the fortress held. Winter turned to spring, the frost melted, and one day, the Alemanni were gone. The dawn rose on empty fields and silent woods.

A lone Alemanni deserter pounded at the front gates.

The man was disheveled, gaunt and hungry. He was a Suebi tribesman named Fulco, and he promised to tell everything he knew in return for a flask of wine and a haunch of meat. Julian agreed, and the traitor was paid. Through ravenous bites of smoked beef he explained that the Alemanni had gone home because they were starving. The army was too big to feed. The forage parties had gathered every morsel of grain for a hundred miles in every direction. Chnodomar led his people back east to regain their strength in the rich lands about the Rhine River.

Julian sent out scouts, and they corroborated the deserter's story. They found a blasted, desolate landscape. Farms were stripped bare, homesteads were razed, and any un-garrisoned towns had been torn down to their very foundations. No fish swam in the rivers, and no

194

deer ran in the woods. A perceptive eye would notice that even the songbirds were missing from the trees. The only food in the land was stacked safely in the storehouses of Sens.

With some trepidation Julian unlimbered his regiments and began preparations to move. They would march north and discover what had happened to Reims, to Marcellus, and what fate had kept the Army of the West from relieving its Caesar throughout that long winter.

CHAPTER THIRTY-FIVE

As newly-registered soldiers of the Auxilia regiment *Petulantes*, Ulrich, Sigmund, and Tau were introduced to their new equipment. First, they were provided with new weapons. The swords used by the Auxilia were called spatha, and they were different from the legendary gladius used by the Legion. Spatha swords were slightly thinner, but half again longer than the gladius. They traded the gladius's stabbing efficiency in the tight shield wall for the ability to slash in a skirmish and to fend off horsemen. The weapon seemed appropriate to the savage, high-energy flavor of the Petulantes. Javelins, called pila, were also part of their new equipment. Two of these long, thin weapons were carried strapped across the back and could be held like spears for fending off enemy cavalry or could be thrown to add a ranged bite to the massed charge. Finally, each was given a sheath with five short missiles, and they were like nothing that Ulrich had ever seen before. These were hand-launched darts called plumbata, each close in size and shape to a short fat arrow, and each with a lead weight at its waist to give the weapon its heavy striking power.

"Fighting with us will be quite different from what you have experienced before," Eogan said.

It was an unseasonably warm evening in February, and all four men were sitting on the ground with the weapons spread about them. Stacked to the side were the broad oval shields which, in contrast to the imperial eagles of the heavy Legion, bore the Petulantes' curiously barbaric horns of a Celtic beast, blue on a yellow background. All had been given standard-issue steel helmets, chainmail, and the blue and yellow tunics of the regiment, although Ulrich was allowed to keep his personal lorica segmentata as it closely resembled standard-issue Roman equipment.

Eogan spoke to Tau, Ulrich, and Sigmund. "Become familiar with your new equipment, and later today, you will muster to train with the Auxilia. You will find that when we fight, there is no fencing with the enemy, no dancing about. You just hold your shield level with your neighbor's and stab your sword into the enemy's belly. If you do it properly, it is a tedious business, not very exciting at all."

At the morning muster, all five hundred soldiers of the Auxilia were gathered at the broad flat training field when the three companions approached. There were broad smiles visible on the faces of the nearest soldiers. They had seen the companion's heroism that winter, and they welcomed their new recruits gladly. At the simultaneous order of the five Auxilia centurions, a deafening cheer of welcome greeted the three men. The regiment slammed swords on shields and roared a Latin salute to welcome their new members. Tau, Sigmund, and Ulrich, embarrassed, stood grinning in their new gear, already feeling like a part of this proud unit.

Their own centurion was a tall, fair Frank named Clodovicus. He was an energetic man in his late twenties and was overjoyed to meet Ulrich and his companions. The junior officer led a hundred men of the Auxilia and would be placing the three newcomers in the very front of his line. He gave each of the three a Roman handshake, right palms clasping forearms tightly, and introduced himself. After a quick muster, each of the five centuries, or sections, of the regiment split up to practice drills.

For the first few examples, Clodovicus had Sigmund, Tau, and Ulrich stand nearby to watch. They caught on quickly. This Latin order meant "raise shields;" that Latin order meant "unsheathe swords," another word meant "prepare javelins," and so on. Even without speaking Latin, the sequence was easy to follow, and the three men practiced with their regiment until lunch was served. After their meal of bread, meat, and diluted wine, which was taken sitting in the middle of the parade ground, the afternoon was given over to missile practice.

Ulrich found this exercise to be particularly interesting. The Roman pila, or javelins, were just as effective as thrown missiles as they were as melee weapons. They flew truer and farther than Ulrich had ever seen a spear fly before, and after only a few hours, he felt that he could place the weapon with nearly as much accuracy as any of the veterans around him. The plumbata were even more intriguing. Thrown overhand, the heavy darts were even farther-ranged than the javelins, and Ulrich could launch one nearly the length of the fortress, although without quite as much accuracy as the heavier javelins. He was skeptical of their utility, light as they were, but he was assured that they were quite effective, especially against cavalry.

Ulrich was surprised to find that their day's training was over by late afternoon, leaving him with the rest of the day to his own devices. On Wiglaf's farm, he had been accustomed to hard labor from before dawn until after dusk. He, Sigmund, Tau, and two new friends from the regiment had a companionable supper, and then Ulrich went to his workshop to finish an order of spearheads for the Legion.

Sigmund found the training to be tedious, but he was happy to be alongside his friends. At least the repetitive drills gave him time to ponder questions of philosophy, and he left that evening to seek out Julian to discuss an esoteric epiphany of Plato's Republic. Tau, meanwhile, had found the exercises to be fascinating. Even if he would not stay with the army in the long term, as a prince of Ghana he recognized the utility in understanding the inner workings of the greatest military force in the world.

When Julian's small army left Sens in the spring, Julian paid the three men back-wages as though they had been a part of the Auxilia for a whole year. Ulrich had never seen so much money. Many of the coins were solid gold. He would have shared it with Johanne, but she no longer needed any charity from him. Sometime that winter, she had fallen in love with a young, handsome, black-haired, Italian legionnaire named Lucianus who adored her and her children. They had been married within a month of meeting, and Johanne was happy. Ulrich was happy for her.

When the army was on the march, they carried all their own armor, weapons, and food, but Ulrich was glad to be out of the cramped fortress of Sens and stretching his legs. Sigmund and Tau walked companionably alongside him, and the rest of the Auxilia, mostly native Germans, were good company. Every night Sigmund went off to chat with Julian, and Tau snuck away to be with Ima, but Ulrich camped comfortably with his regiment. Gebhard and Ælfwine were happy and healthy, playing with the other children of the convoy, and his friends were safe and free. He felt imbued with new purpose as he imagined this Roman army bringing punishment to Chnodomar, defeat to the Alemanni, and vengeance for Rag and for Wiglaf.

CHAPTER THIRTY-SIX

The march from Sens to Reims, a distance of ninety miles, took a leisurely ten days. They could certainly have covered the distance faster, but the Roman army marched in a curious fashion. Each evening, after the day's march, if a fortress was not immediately available to camp within, they built one. The construction was astoundingly fast. In a handful of hours, depending on the terrain, how hard the earth was, and the availability of lumber, the army built an entire fortress.

It was a wooden affair, with tents thrown up inside in an orderly arrangement. Four entrances always faced the four cardinal directions, and the fort looked the same every time. Each man knew his job and did it quickly, some digging the ditch, others filling it with sharpened stakes. Some men cut trees, others drove them into the ground to make a tall palisade. Some days they were lucky, and Julian would take them to an existing stone or brick outpost, but, regardless, the army never once slept without a protective rampart.

Julian was leading his force, and with nervous anticipation, approached Reims. Over the prior months, the failure of Marcellus to lift the siege of Sens had caused Julian first to feel annoyed, then curious, and then, after some time, very concerned. He suppressed the fear that Reims had been crushed by the overwhelming Alemanni force. If Reims had fallen that winter, he would have failed the thirteen thousand soldiers who counted on his leadership in Gaul.

Julian's consternation was absolute when the gates of Reims admitted him to an untouched fortress. The great Roman Army of the West waited within the town's high walls, and they had not so much as left their posts all winter. Julian sat his horse at the

200

crossroads of Reims, but Marcellus did not come to greet him. Before Julian went to seek him, he interviewed the soldiers of Reims.

"Yes," they said, they knew that the Alemanni were loose in Gaul. "Yes," they knew that Julian had been besieged in Sens, just down the road. "Had there been an order to attack any Alemanni that entered Gaul?" Julian asked. "Well, not that I know of, but I'm sure that's more of a question for my superiors, sir." "Had Marcellus sent any men to attack the Alemanni?" "Well, no, not at all. There were no orders like that. We stayed at our posts, and it was a quite boring winter for us all, I'm afraid to say."

Julian was incensed. He appropriated a stone manor in the center of the town, brought Severus and Eogan with him, and impatiently sent a messenger to summon Marcellus.

Marcellus, the Magister Equitum, appeared in full battle dress. His bearing was sullen, his face defiant. He refused to look Julian in the eye, but being the taller of the two, stood straight-backed and gazed over his head.

"What is the meaning of this, Marcellus?" Julian asked. His voice was choked with anger. "Before we established winter quarters, I gave you direct orders to respond to any attempt by the Alemanni to cross the Rhine. They rampaged through Gaul, and you did nothing!"

Marcellus sneered, "You are no soldier. What do you know of war? You are a pampered scholar. I should not have to take orders from you." He still did not meet his commander's gaze.

Both Severus and Eogan stiffened. Julian's eyes blazed but carefully he mastered himself. After a long moment he spoke evenly. "Did you not swear to serve the Emperor? My cousin Constantius? Do you not acknowledge that he appointed me his personal deputy in the West?"

"I swore to serve Constantius, not you," Marcellus replied. "He is a true soldier. You should never have been sent here. If you knew what was good for you, what is good for Rome, you would return to your studies and leave the fighting to the real men." Marcellus sniffed, then delivered his final verdict. "You care more about being liked than about being respected. You are already a failure as a general."

Julian considered him quietly for a long moment. Finally he sighed.

"Marcellus, your career is over. Pack your things. I am sending you back to Milan to face the Senate for your choices. I will write to my cousin and tell him that you are coming." Julian turned to Severus. "Legate Severus, you are hereby promoted. You will take Marcellus's position as the senior commander of the Legion of the Roman Army of the West." Julian turned back to Marcellus. "You are dismissed, Marcellus." His voice was heavy with disappointment, as though discouraged by an inattentive student.

After Marcellus left, Julian sat heavily. "I still don't understand why he did it," he said, shaking his head. "Why not lift the siege? He had to know that disobeying my orders would ruin his career."

Severus stood rigid. His face was severe. "I met someone who might shed light on the situation," he said. He walked to a back door of the manor and opened it, allowing in an older man, tall and gray headed.

"My name is Eutherius," the gray-haired man said without preamble. "I am Marcellus's chamberlain." Julian raised an eyebrow at Eogan who, although similarly surprised, nodded to confirm the man's identity.

"Go on," Julian prompted him.

"Marcellus was hoping that you would die at Sens," Eutherius said. "He thought that if you were out of his way, Constantius would promote him to your position as Caesar of the West."

"Do you have any proof of this?" Julian asked, eyes narrowing. A thought ran through his mind, something that Sigmund had said that winter—he had suggested that somehow Chnodomar had known that he would be in Sens. It was a terrible thought, and he recoiled from it.

"I only know what I have heard with my own ears," the older man replied stiffly. "He has also been spreading pernicious rumors that you plan to overthrow Constantius and claim the title of Emperor for yourself."

Julian whistled. True or not, if that rumor was spread in Rome, his paranoid cousin would certainly have him beheaded for treason. Julian shook his head.

"What do you think, Severus?" Julian asked.

"Honestly, I have no idea," Severus responded flatly. "I have no taste for these underhanded games." He sounded disgusted. Julian looked at Eogan who just shrugged.

Julian sighed. "All right, Eutherius, I appreciate you bringing this to my attention. I want you to follow Marcellus to Milan and testify to the Senate. I ask for no personal favor. Simply tell the truth. Can you do that?"

"Of course, General," Eutherius responded dutifully. He bowed deeply and saw himself out.

"What a mess," Julian said to Eogan and Severus when it was just the three of them left.

"I would rather be in battle," Eogan said.

"And me as well, friend," Julian said smiling. A table and a map were brought to the room, and the three Roman commanders began plotting the destruction of the Alemanni.

CHAPTER THIRTY-SEVEN

A t Reims, the Roman Army of the West was reformed as a unified whole. Ulrich's unit was joined by its sister regiment, the Celtae, and together they were reinforced by five hundred light cavalry. The nearby camps of legionnaires, Legion archers, and heavy cavalry filled the hills and valleys outside the city until a full thirteen thousand soldiers waited for battle. Ulrich did not know all the details, but the news of Marcellus's rumored betrayal and subsequent dismissal trickled down the ranks. Severus's promotion and new expanded duties brought him to all the camps of the army, and he took the time to explain the season's plan of campaign to each of the units in turn.

Severus stood on a wooden podium in front of the Petulantes. The soldiers were silent, listening. Ulrich sat in the front row with his friends.

"We are just a small part of the force that will march on the Alemanni." Severus said. He was speaking in German, knowing it to be the conversational tongue of this Auxilia unit.

"General Barbatio is on his way from Italy with twenty-five thousand men, and together at the Rhine River, we will trap Chnodomar and his Alemanni between us. Fight well friends, and this threat to Rome will be destroyed before summer's end."

He stepped down from the podium to the cheering of the men. He moved along to the next unit to repeat his short speech, this time speaking in Latin to the Herculiani, an old and much-decorated Legion ten centuries strong, that waited patiently beneath its eagle standard.

The army moved out the next day. They travelled east along the great Roman causeway that passed through civilized Gaul and toward the German border. Small homesteads here and there had been destroyed by the Alemanni occupation that winter, but it seemed that most of the populace had been able to flee to nearby Roman fortresses. Protective stone forts dotted the landscape, patiently watching over the Empire's holdings as they had for hundreds of years. The army passed through a fertile countryside in which homes were being rebuilt and fields were being plowed in preparation for the spring planting. Stout stone bridges carried them over streams swollen with spring rains. But even in this safe countryside, the army either found a fort to occupy, or built a wooden one wherever they camped. No self-respecting Roman soldier would be caught defenseless in open ground.

In two weeks, one hundred and seventy miles passed beneath their boots. Finally, the army stopped at a deserted old fortress and went to work. This place, now called Saverne, but which Clodovicus said had once been called Tres Tabernae Cesaris, was little more than a broken foundation. At the easternmost edge of the flat plains of Gaul, it sat at the base of a steep incline. From here the road led into the high hilly lands of the ancient limes Germanicus, the line of fortifications that had once bounded the frontier of Rome.

The stones of what buildings may have once graced Saverne had been scavenged and carted off long ago, so kilns were erected, and new bricks were fired out of the local dark clay. Lime was brought in and mixed with aggregate and water to form mortar, and the construction began. Julian oversaw the first stages of construction personally. He was especially interested in three small buildings that adjoined the road. He called them Julius Caesar's taverns, and he insisted that they be rebuilt in a very particular and ancient style. This site seemed to hold a special, almost holy significance to him, and he breathed with satisfaction when the work was done. He left the construction of the defenses to his engineers and lieutenants.

Morale was high, and the soldiers sang as they worked. There were many songs, some in Latin, many in German, and even a few in the strange and haunting Celtic tongue. Sunny spring days alternated with days filled with warm spring rains, and Ulrich was happy. The work was soothing, almost meditative in its monotony, and the hours flowed by as he troweled mortar and stacked bricks on high defensive walls, clean new granaries, and cleverly designed Roman residences.

Meanwhile, the fast-riding scouts of the army ranged far and wide. By summer, word came that a horde of Alemanni had crossed the Rhine upstream and attacked the city of Lugdunum, or Lyon as it was called in the modern tongue, far to the south. But the garrison had held them off, and the battered enemy was now retreating back to Germania. In response, Severus headed out with half the army's cavalry to cut them off.

From the walls of the newly built fortress of Saverne, Ulrich watched the force leave. There were thousands of them—some with shields and long spatha swords. Still more with the composite Roman bows that could be fired from horseback; their arrow-bags bulged with fresh missiles shipped from the factories of Italy.

The most exotic cavalry came last. Ulrich gazed upon the very largest horses the skilled Roman breeders could field. In fact, they looked more like plow beasts than nimble warhorses. They needed to be big, however, because they were draped in heavy armor. The horses were living hillocks of steel. Sheets of polished metal scales hung about their flanks and reflected the evening sunlight. Their riders were likewise heavily armored, their own metal clothing blending into that of their mounts.

"The armored cavalry are called cataphracts, and Julian says they are his secret weapon," Sigmund told Ulrich from where they stood atop the new high wall. "He says that they are unstoppable."

Ulrich was skeptical, it seemed to him that the whole point of cavalry was speed and surprise. Loaded down with hundreds of pounds of case-hardened steel, he wondered if the beasts could even gallop. But he shrugged and assumed that the Romans knew what they were doing. They usually did.

News of the cavalry's victory came a few days later. Messengers reported that Severus successfully ambushed three retreating groups of Alemanni raiders. At the same time, however, it was discovered that this enemy was smaller and weaker than expected. Only about a thousand Alemanni were captured or killed, and neither Chnodomar nor any of his lieutenants were among them. The real enemy still lurked to the east, waiting across the Rhine.

Severus was still a day's ride away, returning in triumph when news of a great tragedy reached Saverne.

Julian's campaign plan depended on catching Chnodomar between two forces. Julian would come from the west, and Barbatio's bigger army would come north from Italy, and the Alemanni would be trapped between them and destroyed. Julian had been waiting these last weeks for confirmation that Barbatio, commander of twenty-five thousand men including the Emperor's elite guard and the Great Army of Italy, was on the move. Once he had word of this, his own army would disembark, and the gears of war would begin to turn. But on that warm summer night a tired messenger, horse lathered in sweat, trotted exhausted into the camp. He brought the news that Barbatio had been ambushed. The Emperor's Guard had been routed, and Barbatio had fled. The plan of the campaign was in tatters, and now the enemy was coming west.

"The Alemanni are limitless," the terrified messenger said. "They cover mountains with their shrieking hordes and charge in endless swarms of terrible warriors. They fell on Barbatio's twenty-five thousand and threw them back in bloody carnage. Barbatio is retreating in disarray, and the Alemanni, victorious, vicious, and drunk on conquest, are now headed this way."

The messenger, upon discharging his duty, left the camp. He leapt on his horse and fled west, headlong panic taking him deeper into Gaul on an exhausted mount as he ran from the tide of savages he had seen flow from the dark forest. The Alemanni were coming, and they seemed unstoppable. All the western Roman Empire was under threat of being overrun.

Julian did not act immediately. His scouts at the Rhine had not yet reported any Alemanni movement into Gaul, and he knew that Severus was only a day's ride away. He would wait until his senior officer had returned before taking action. He spent that night alone in meditation, trying to imagine what Alexander the Great would do.

The next dawn, scouts at the river began to report Alemanni warriors crossing from Germania into Gaul in great numbers. Worse, an Alemanni scout was discovered within bowshot of the walls of Saverne, spying on the new Roman defenses. Midmorning finally brought the return of Severus and his cavalry, and Julian called an urgent council. Severus, Eogan, and all the senior centurions and commanders were present. Ulrich, Tau and Sigmund were even invited, and Ima was given a place of honor next to Julian as a sign of his respect. None of the small buildings of Saverne were large enough for this group, so they gathered at the training grounds outside. A large sand table was present with a well-drawn diagram of the countryside from Saverne to the Rhine.

Julian explained the situation briefly, and without giving his own opinion, waited for input from his commanders.

"If Barbatio's twenty-five thousand, the Great Army of Italy, was so quickly defeated, we would be hard-pressed to defeat them with only thirteen thousand men," offered Severus cautiously. He was still dusty from the road, but his stoic face showed no hint of fatigue.

"Do we know how many Alemanni we face?" Eogan asked.

"Barbatio's messenger guessed that the enemy number between thirty and forty thousand warriors," Julian replied. He produced a piece of paper from his robes and glanced at it before continuing. "And our scouts report that the enemy is massing near the town of Argentoratum. At least twenty thousand Alemanni with their German allies have already crossed the Rhine, and there are an uncountable number still coming behind."

The centurion to Ulrich's right whistled appreciatively. There was a murmur in the crowd that Julian did not attempt to suppress. He stood placidly, wearing his scholarly toga, trimmed beard giving him a visage uncannily like the marble bust of Sophocles that stood in Cologne. Ulrich would never grow accustomed to the incongruous sight of the scholar amid a sea of armored soldiers.

"Shall we retreat?" Julian asked into the quietude, his voice neutral.

There was a long silence. Severus stared at the ground, saying nothing. Eogan shifted his weight nervously. Clodovicus, standing across the circle from Ulrich, cleared his throat and opened his mouth. He looked as though he were about to speak, but then he shut his mouth again, shaking his head. None were comfortable with the thought of retreating.

Finally, Ima stood. She had dressed in mail and wore a white and red Roman tunic bearing an Imperial Eagle. Her long sword was strapped across her back, and her voice was clear and level.

"If we were to retreat, where would we go?" she asked. The question was rhetorical, and she continued without a pause. "We may be safe if we hide in our fortresses. But then the Alemanni would rule the countryside just as they did this winter. Only, this time, harvest season approaches. They would have our crops and our fields and our livestock. They could starve us out. They could starve all of Gaul."

"Are you suggesting that we fight them now?" Severus asked. "The odds would be three, or perhaps even four, to one. Even Barbatio, with a force much larger than ours, could not stand against them."

"Do we have any choice?" Ima asked. There was pride in her voice, and the council responded to it.

Clodovicus spoke up. "Ima is right. Retreating before this barbarian horde would solve nothing. But now our enemy gathers before us. We have a priceless chance to finish them off once and for all."

Severus nodded thoughtfully. "Initiating battle now does have some strategic advantages. With the Rhine at their rear, they will have a difficult time retreating. A victory here could significantly reduce their capability to wage further war with Rome."

There were grins starting on the faces of the gathered commanders. Julian looked around the crowd. Severus met his eye and nodded his assent. Eogan's eyes sparkled with delight. Hesitation had fled. Fear was gone. His soldiers wanted war.

Julian nodded. "Then we fight. Get your men ready; we leave at dawn tomorrow. Provide double rations for all the men and carry double grain for the horses. It's a long march to the Rhine."

CHAPTER THIRTY-EIGHT

U lrich spent the rest of that last day of peace working the forge. His long-trained muscles were comfortable swinging the blacksmith's hammer, and he took great satisfaction in the steel that shaped itself elegantly on the anvil. Before the sun set he inspected his equipment carefully. He was proud of his steel armor, which was now faced in the bright yellow and blue symbols of the Petulantes. The Roman helmet was light and strong, and he made sure the leather-stitched interior was clean and tight. His tall oval shield was sturdy, and he found no loose rivets on the metal rim or heavy steel boss. His two pila javelins were stacked neatly against the wall, and their points were honed to a razor's edge. The five plumbata darts fit smoothly in their customized sheath. The long spatha sword was sharp, oiled, and slid easily in its bronze-fastened scabbard. Satisfied, he fell into bed and slept a deep, dreamless sleep.

Meanwhile, Sigmund hardly slept at all. He spent the evening deep in debate with the general. Julian mused on Alexander the Great, and the two of them talked enthusiastically about the Persian expedition of old. They discussed the strategy of the Battle of Issus until well past midnight. Finally, Sigmund dragged himself away from the enthusiastic young scholar to flop down on a nearby couch and grab a few hours of shut-eye before the morning's march.

Tau went to Ima that night. The anticipation of the next day's battle made their love desperate. It was a hot night, but they clung to each other, holding tight despite the sheen of sweat that formed between their naked bodies. Tau lay awake, blissful and relaxed, for some time after Ima's breathing had gone deep and even with sleep. His last memory before drifting off was kissing the tangled hair piled messily on her head. He dreamt of this golden woman, hand clasped tight to his, as they walked together in a city of golden spires.

In the morning, Ulrich, Tau, and Sigmund gathered with the Petulantes. The army mustered in the fields outside Saverne an hour before dawn, and the moment the sun broke the horizon, the march began. Their unit marched at the head of the column, a fact for which Ulrich was grateful as the thousands of boots pounding on the road threw up a thick cloud of dust, a cloud which smothered the following ranks. They moved fast, trotting along at double speed, and all the while, were flanked by the light Auxilia cavalry that rode beyond the causeway on both sides, fording streams and cantering up hillsides to get a look at the country all around.

The first leg of the journey was a steep climb into a beautiful land of high-sided hills and rocky drops. Soon though, the road, straight as an arrow, leveled off as they reached the top of a high plateau. A curious fox, unafraid of the jangling, clanking mass of armored men, loped along beside the column. Sigmund, free at the right-hand side of the line, jogged out of formation to reach down at the orange creature. The fox shyly danced out of reach, and Sigmund straightened to smile down at the furry little beast, still jogging to keep pace with his unit. Clodovicus, seeing this, whistled. He produced a strip of smoked pork which he tossed to Sigmund. Sigmund tossed the piece of meat to the creature and watched as the fox caught it deftly out of the air. The animal held the offering in his mouth for a moment, still loping along, before diving into a dense bush to devour the salty present. Sigmund rejoined the company.

A typical day's march for a Roman regiment was ten miles, and Ulrich counted mile markers as they went by. They came quick at this fast pace, and Ulrich counted to ten before midmorning. The army showed no sign of slowing. He wondered how far they would go. A flight of starlings, surprised by the sudden appearance of the jogging men, burst out of the undergrowth. The flock of small birds zoomed low over the paved road's dusty surface before rising high into the air, a flowing murmuration high in the cloudless mid-morning sky. Other flocks joined until thousands of starlings wheeled and dived, rose and spun together in a mesmerizing dance in the air. Ulrich had seen the phenomenon hundreds of times before, but this time he felt as though his senses were sharpened. The morning air was pregnant with anticipation, and the energy of the regiment was palpable.

Despite the long march, Ulrich felt suffused with vitality. His heart thumped strong in his chest, and he fought an urge to sprint ahead, stretching his legs to race along the road on this glorious day under this brilliant blue sky.

By mile fifteen, Ulrich started to feel tired. He asked Clodovicus how far they would go, but the centurion answered honestly that he did not know. Clodovicus said that it was twenty-five miles from Saverne to the Rhine along this road, but he thought that for sure they would not cover all that distance in a single day. Tau looked comfortable, stretching his long legs to take three steps to each of Ulrich's four. Sigmund was suffering. The heavy man's sandaled feet plodded, but his jaw was set, and he refused to complain. They jogged on.

By mile twenty it was nearing noon. Hunger pangs were now added to the soreness of Ulrich's muscles and were beginning to dampen his mood. He was sweating profusely and had nearly finished the water in his wooden canteen. He had eaten the smoked meat he had brought in his pouch and was now craving some dark Roman bread and olive oil.

A scout, horse lathered with sweat, topped a crest in front of them. The man sped down the road toward them, rushed past, and disappeared into the dust behind. Minutes later, Severus appeared. He galloped to the front of the column and ordered the march to halt. At mile twenty-one the army finally stopped. The soldiers relaxed gratefully.

Ulrich stretched his sore muscles. He bent double, straightened, squatted a few times, and extended his stiff joints. He yawned and took a last swing, emptying his canteen. His feet were sore, his back hurt, and there was chafing across his shoulders where the straps for the heavy armor rested. Quartermasters and their assistants appeared with carts, and bread was passed out to the Legion and Auxilia. They ate hungrily while they waited for orders.

Presently, Julian himself appeared, riding to the front of the column. On this day he was dressed in the full panoply of war. He had traded his scholarly robes for an ancient, decorated muscle cuirass which covered his torso and mimicked the look of human muscles. A long spatha was buckled about his waist, and his bearded head was bare. Once he was in the center of the road he stopped and cleared his throat.

"Men," Julian said. The army was quiet as their commander spoke. Runners stood attentively, ready to pass his message to the sections of the army that lay out of earshot, farther down the road.

"We have found the enemy," Julian continued. Julian was speaking in Latin, but Clodovicus quietly translated the words into German for his nearby Auxilia soldiers to hear.

"The Alemanni gather on the banks of the Rhine just ahead. They know of our coming, and they hold the high ground." As Julian spoke, cavalry trotted in from the surrounding fields to hear him better.

"I know that you have marched long and hard today," Julian continued. "It is only noon, but if you are tired, perhaps it would be wisest to rest now. We could construct our marching fort, rest tonight, and meet the enemy fresh in the morning." Severus was on his horse sitting placidly nearby. The army waited under the gaze of the two commanders.

A long moment passed in which no one spoke.

"Or would you rather fight today?" Julian asked.

At these words a murmur started in the ranks. The murmur rose and rose and rose until it sounded like a thousand men speaking at once. Out of this noise came a cheer which turned into a chant.

"PUGNA!" the army yelled, voices rising in unison. The word was Latin, but Ulrich knew what it meant, and he joined in. It was an order that was given at the end of a long chain of other orders. It was given after the order to raise shields and after the order to unsheathe swords. It was the order given for the killing stroke, the order to drive into the enemy and slaughter them. It was the order to fight.

"PUG-NA! PUG-NA! PUG-NA!" came the brassy baritone chant. Two hard syllables, emanating from thousands of throats. A stamp started, and thousands of boots struck the turf, creating a rhythm that synchronized with the martial chorus. It sounded like a giant's heartbeat, a massive percussion drum that played the song of war, the song of victory, the song of death. It was intoxicating, and Ulrich felt the adrenaline surge within him.

Julian looked serene. He merely nodded, turned his horse around, and trotted up the road. The army followed, their organized chant devolving into a cheer as the army marched to battle.

CHAPTER THIRTY-NINE

T he last few miles of road fell away under their feet then they turned into the woods. Following the advance scouts, the army moved through a thicket of trees and out onto a field of tall wheat. The field sloped gently upward, and at its crest was the enemy. They were perhaps half a mile away and already deployed, filling the whole skyline. Ulrich could not count them at a glance, but he could already tell that the Roman army, as impressive as it was, was outnumbered. His unit, the first one out of the woods, went forward toward the foot of the slope as the rest of the Romans streamed out behind. Directly facing them, at the top of the long hill was an enormous mass of Alemanni infantry, drawn up into a shield wall that covered the entire visible ridge from side to side. To the right was the enemy cavalry, herded into a loose mass, and to the left was a dense wood that descended the slope from the Alemanni horde to border the flank of the Roman army, gathering at its base.

Ulrich's unit was ordered into formation. The Roman army shook down into three lines. In the center of the front line, four full-strength Legions, one thousand men in each, stood shield to shield. They formed an aegis of heavily armored infantry five ranks deep and eight hundred files across. Two regiments of Auxilia, five-hundred light infantry in each, defended each flank of this armored core—the Petulantes and the Heruli were arrayed on the left, while the Cornuti and Brachiati were on the right. Ulrich found himself in the front rank, on the far left of the battlefield, standing alongside Tau, Sigmund, and Clodovicus. Eogan walked before the line making sure his regiment, five ranks deep and one-hundred files across, was razor-straight. On the Petulantes' right, the Heruli's formation mirrored their own. There was nothing to the Petulantes' left except tall wheat and dense woods.

In the second line of battle stood the archers, one thousand of them. They were Auxilia, wearing their light chainmail and deployed in a loose formation to allow space to wield their weapons. They looked cheerful with their finely crafted short bows and colorful helmets. The bowmen waited a few paces away, ready to launch their missiles over the heads of the men in the shield wall. The third and final line, some twenty paces away, was the reserves. Julian held in reserve one full Legion and four regiments of Auxilia to reinforce any weak points that might appear. Julian was on horseback, riding alongside Severus and followed by an escort of aides and messengers. He rode toward where the cavalry was forming up.

Separate from the main battle line, the Roman cavalry deployed into six massive wedges of five hundred men each. The Roman cavalry force was truly impressive. Every type of modern Imperial cavalry unit was in attendance. Two units of Auxilia cavalry, with their long straight swords and oval shields, formed neat triangles on the field. There was a unit of cavalry with short bows that could fire from horseback and a unit of cavalry with long javelins that they could throw to harass the enemy. Finally, the heavy shining cataphracts formed the vanguard. There were two squadrons of these tremendous weapons—one thousand great horses weighed down in their tonnage of heavy armor. Sunlight reflected from the thousands upon thousands of polished steel scales that hung from horse and rider alike. Their riders bore massive, heavy lances. With their impervious armor of gleaming steel, they looked invincible, the absolute pinnacle of modern military technology.

Once the bustle of organizing the lines of battle was completed, Ulrich had time again to gaze up the field and gauge the enemy. They still waited at the crest of the slope. It looked like the Alemanni outnumbered the Romans about three to one, and if Julian led thirteen thousand men, then Chnodomar must lead thirty-five or forty thousand warriors. It was difficult to get an exact count because they were not in ordered formations like the Romans. In fact, it was hard to tell how much organization they had at all.

Flags of all shapes and sizes flew above the enemy army, and the dress code varied as wildly as the banners. Front and center were Chnodomar's picked men. This force wore the familiar white tunics, mimicking the Roman style, and they were well equipped in chainmail. They had matching shields and bore fine swords and long spears. They made up about a quarter of the enemy army, some ten thousand warriors, but the remainder of the horde was not so well equipped. Among the masses flanking the Alemanni elite were men bearing mostly spears and simple axes. Body armor beyond leather and fur was rare, and only half the men had shields. Still it was a numerous and imposing horde, and what they lacked in equipment they made up for with a fierce energy. The noise of their war calls began to permeate the intervening air.

The Alemanni cavalry looked weak. After seeing them appear in overwhelming numbers east of Bremen, Ulrich was surprised to see so few horsemen. Perhaps they had difficulty getting all their mounts across the fast-flowing Rhine. The enemy horsemen only numbered perhaps a thousand mounted men. They stood in irregular clumps, clustered in the tall grain to the right of the enemy horde. They looked poorly equipped and poorly led.

Normally, the minutes before a fight were filled with fear. The mind raced, and the heart thumped in terrified anticipation, but on this day there was only calm. The Romans considered their enemy with a detached tranquility, as though it was just another day on the training field. The experience was surreal for Ulrich. He shifted his weight and found that the ground was dry and firm beneath his feet. His heavy cuirass was snug about his waist. The tall Roman shield, thinner and lighter than the thick, primitive, Saxon boards, rested easily on his arm. Tau, on his right, looked relaxed and expectant. Sigmund, on his left, saw Ulrich glance at him and grinned back reassuringly.

Julian rode onto the field and stopped in front of his army. Severus, riding just behind him, raised an arm to command attention but the gesture was unnecessary. The silent Roman Army of the West patiently watched their commander beneath the noonday sun.

"Comrades! The time for fighting has come," Julian called. "This is the moment for which we have been waiting. These savages have attacked Rome. They have tarnished our honor. They have made fools of us, and they think they can do it again. Today we wash away the stains and restore the honor of Rome. Their own madness will bring them to ruin as they are doomed to fall before us on this field. Give no ground."

He paused, letting the anticipation build. He drew his sword slowly, holding it high in the air.

"For Rome," he called.

Thirteen thousand voices shouted back in unison. "For Rome!" the army bellowed, then was silent again.

Chnodomar likewise rode before his men. He was conspicuous in his shining, conical helmet with its long, red, horsehair plume. A hundred warriors rode with him. A chorus of voices were rising from the Alemanni line, and Ulrich strained to hear what they were saying. A light breeze was rustling the wheat, and the soft noise was just enough to distort the enemy words.

"They sound angry," Sigmund said, frowning.

"They're calling to Chnodomar," Tau said. "I can hear them shouting his name."

The words became a chant, and Ulrich listened attentively, curious.

"They're telling him to get off his horse!" Sigmund exclaimed. With angry voices the Alemanni army was demanding that Chnodomar dismount and fight alongside them.

"They must be worried he is going to run away if things go poorly," Tau mused.

Centurion Clodovicus, immediately to Tau's right, guffawed. "That doesn't bode well for them at all," he said grinning. "You hear that men?" Clodovicus shouted, "They're worried their leader is going to turn tail and run. They already know they're going to lose!" A desultory cheer met the centurion's words. The soldier behind Ulrich chuckled.

"Quiet in the ranks," Commander Eogan said patiently, and the regiment was silent again.

Chnodomar dismounted. His horse was led away, and he, with his bodyguard, joined the front rank of his army. An order was shouted, and the massive Alemanni horde started forward.

At this, Legate Severus gave the order to march, and the Roman army advanced. They entered the tall wheat and marched stolidly uphill, crushing the long stalks beneath their measured pace. The difference between them and the barbarian army became ever more apparent. When the Alemanni moved, their lines immediately lost cohesion. The front ranks became ragged, the rear trailed behind, and the flanks lagged. But when the Romans marched, it was in precise order; not a single man was out of place in the close rank and file. They were a solid, unbroken wall of shoulder-to-shoulder shields, units keeping perfect geometric right angles as they moved.

The Alemanni began working themselves into a frenzy. A hundred different war cries resounded. The noise was chaotic and frenetic. Men beat their weapons on shields, stamped their feet, and shouted insults as they came to battle. Meanwhile, the Romans marched in silence. The only noise from the Roman line was the crushing of grain underfoot and the soft jangle of metal equipment in leather holsters. There was something ominous in their steady silent march as they closed the distance. It was more intimidating, in its own implacable way, than the bluff and bluster of the enemy.

Suddenly Julian unleashed his ultimate weapon. He sent all his cavalry into the attack at once. Three thousand precisely ordered Roman horsemen raced uphill. They were aimed at the mounted enemy who still clustered loosely on the enemy's left. The Alemanni cavalry looked frozen and indecisive. They had stopped moving and merely milled about, disorganized and leaderless. The heavy cataphracts led the Roman charge. They were a tight wedge of hardened steel, ready to tear a bloody path through the inferior enemy.

Julian saw his horses speed into the gallop and knew that the battle was won. He was already planning his next moves. Soon, the enemy cavalry would be destroyed, and the initiative would be his. His superior horsemen could then wheel left and plunge into the vulnerable flank of the enemy line. Only a very well-organized group of infantry could fend off a determined cavalry charge, and the flanks of the enemy line were anything but organized. On the Alemanni sides and rear were the weakest of the German warriors, the reluctant and cowardly who shirked from battle. Once they were cut down, panic would spread among the Alemanni line, and the enemy's greater numbers would mean nothing. Broken, the enemy would be ridden down and defeated, slaughtered where they stood, trapped on the wrong side of the Rhine as the infantry advanced. Julian imagined it all so clearly.

But he was wrong. The cavalry did not bring victory, but disaster.

CHAPTER FORTY

The tip of the shining cataphract wedge pierced the flank of the enemy cavalry herd, but something strange happened. The enemy was not falling; Julian's cataphracts were. The steel-clad heavy horsemen tumbled off their horses. They dropped into the grain in droves, horses collapsing in bloody ruin, and Julian finally saw the hidden threat. Thousands of spears rose out of the tall wheat. The enemy had foreseen this attack and had laid a trap. Infantry had been hidden among the enemy horsemen, crouching low and unseen amid the dense stalks of grain. They were everywhere, rising within the ranks of the charging Roman cavalry, unseating riders and driving their long spears up into the armored horses' unprotected bellies. The ranks of cavalry behind, carried on by their own momentum, could not turn away, and they went down too. All order among the Roman cavalry dissolved. Their careful formations were shattered by the unexpected threat as entire squadrons fell, and others turned away in disorganized panic. Then the Alemanni horsemen led a counter-charge, and they did terrible carnage, slicing their axes and spears into confused men who were attacked from both above and below.

Julian swore. His gambit had failed, and it now looked as though his shattered cavalry would rout. He gathered his reins and prepared to ride to rally them, but he called Severus to him first.

"We still need to turn their flank," Julian told the officer hurriedly. He pointed to the dense forest to the left of the battlefield. "Take half of the reserves and move into the woods. Climb the hill unseen and attack the enemy from the left just as they engage our main force. As outnumbered as we are and fighting uphill with our men tired from a long march, a flanking maneuver gives us our best chance at winning this battle."

Legate Severus nodded. "Yes, General," he said dutifully and galloped away. Julian rode the other direction to try to avert the disaster mounting among his horsemen.

Meanwhile, the Roman infantry had continued marching, but it would still be some time until they met the enemy. The reserves were following close behind, keeping their even spacing from the main force, and Severus rode to them. He selected three fast-moving Auxilia regiments, together with their attached archer cohort, and led them toward the woods.

Seconds later, as Julian had feared, the Roman cavalry broke entirely. They routed. Every man who could flee fled from the victorious Alemanni spears. Julian galloped out in front of them, shouting at his men to stop as they raced downhill, but it was too late. Panic had infected the men. A whole troop of cataphracts, horses spooked and out of control, careened wildly toward the Auxilia regiments on the far right of the Roman line. Two elite units held the Roman right flank there, the Cornuti and Brachiati, standing under their pagan standards of horned serpents. Seeing them come, the Auxilia paused their march and braced themselves.

They had no time to form a proper testudo, but at a word from their officers, they tightened their formations and raised their shields. The front rank crouched to receive the blow, the second rank bolstered the first with their weight. The panicked mass of horses and men slammed into the Auxilia shields and rebounded. The tide of cavalry hit the obstacle, found it unyielding, and flowed around it. In another moment, the flailing hooves and thrashing manes were gone, fleeing down the field, and the infantry stood. Bruised, but unbroken, they rejoined the marching line.

Ulrich could sense that tensions were starting to mount among the men. The infantry had seen the failure of the Roman cavalry, and minds began to wonder what other surprises the Alemanni might have in store for them. The initial exhilaration had worn off, and the infantry was feeling the effect of their twenty-five-mile march. Feet were sore, and bodies were chafed. Muscles ached, and hunger pangs returned. The summer day was hot, and the handle of Ulrich's shield was slick with sweat.

They were less than a hundred paces from the Alemanni army, and the overwhelming size of the enemy force had become vividly apparent. The huge mass of German warriors overlapped their line on both sides and was three or four times as deep as their own. Moreover, the size of individual enemy warriors could be fully appreciated. Every visible German warrior was bigger and taller than the Roman soldiers they faced. Many were well over six feet tall, and they were muscled, tanned, and hardened from a lifetime beyond the wild frontier. The Romans, in comparison, were more than a head shorter throughout. Even in their sturdy armor and with their tall helmets they were dwarfed by the big swarthy warriors who roared and bellowed as they closed the distance.

"Pila," Clodovicus ordered, and the Petulantes unlimbered the javelins strapped to their backs. The enemy was now fifty paces away. Ulrich's palm was sweaty on the rough wooden shaft. They did not stop marching.

"Iace." Clodovicus ordered, and with a lunge the front row launched their missiles. Precision aim was not necessary. At this short range and throwing into the dense mass of enemy, it was impossible to miss. Screams and blood spurted from the Alemanni line where the sharpened steel javelin points found flesh. Ulrich's own javelin fell somewhere in the second rank of the enemy, but Ulrich could not see what damage it caused. Tau's missile was well thrown, catching a big, bare-chested man in the belly and flinging him into the men behind. A flight of arrows from the Roman archers soared over Ulrich's head and slammed into the front ranks of the enemy. Enemy warriors fell in droves, and the barbarian line stalled as warriors stumbled over their dead and wounded companions. The Romans marched on.

"Spatha stringe," Clodovicus shouted, and from all along the Roman line came the ominous hiss of thousands of swords sliding in unison from thousands of scabbards.

"Barritus!" Clodovicus ordered.

Ulrich frowned. This was not an order he had heard in training. He glanced at his companions when something strange began to happen. The Roman lines, silent thus far, began to hum. It was a low noise, and men leaned close to their shields, using the wood to amplify the sound. It grew and grew and grew, slowly sounding out the long syllables of a strange word.

"BAAAAARRRRIITUUUUUUSSS!" the Roman army growled with sinister deliberation. By the time they reached the final syllable, the sound had risen to a deafening roar. This was the war cry of a victorious empire, and on its final note the army struck home. They slammed into the Alemanni horde with a measured stride, and the killing began. Shields smashed into faces; desperately swung German axes were deflected harmlessly off Roman shield bosses, and the Roman swords stabbed forward. The numerical superiority of the enemy meant nothing in this densely packed kill zone, and hundreds of Alemanni warriors and their German allies went down, disemboweled by the sharpened steel of the implacable Roman swords.

All this time, the Roman arrows flew. The archers fired as fast as they could, each one able to keep several arrows in the air at once. The missiles arced over the Romans and fell in a constant rain within the enemy horde. The Alemanni elite at the center, with their modern shields and heavier armor, could withstand the deluge, but the leather-clad warriors on the flanks suffered horribly. The arrows were killing even faster than the hungry Roman swords.

When the cheer had started, Ulrich had felt his heart thrill. It took all his self-control to maintain an even pace with his companions when he wanted to sprint forward and leap upon the enemy. When the armies met, a big German swung a massive axe at him, and Ulrich crouched behind his raised shield. The well-made Roman shield deflected the blow, and Ulrich stabbed his sword forward. The point ripped into the man's groin, and Ulrich twisted the blade, pulling it back as the man fell. The line continued its advance, and Ulrich repeated the motions: block, stab, twist, and look for the next target. It was all so easy.

Sigmund, never much of a swordsman, swung his weapon awkwardly at a lithe man who danced back out of range, but it did not matter; the whole line advanced again, and there was nowhere for the enemy to go. The nimble young man who had dodged Sigmund's swing stumbled on the feet of the man behind him and died on a Roman blade.

A flight of enemy arrows rose from up the field, and the shields in the second and third ranks of the Roman line snapped up in response. These shields covered the heads of Ulrich and his companions, and the German missiles bounced harmlessly off the protective roof. The battle had only been joined for the briefest of moments, and already there were hundreds of barbarian dead and dying littering the field. As far as Ulrich could see, not a single Roman soldier had yet been wounded.

"Consiste," Clodovicus commanded. Ulrich knew that this word meant stop, and the line halted. There was no longer any reason to continue driving into the German lines. The enemy was coming downhill at them. Those in front were driven forward by the pressure of those behind. The Romans held their ground and kept on killing.

Meanwhile, Julian had managed to rally only a handful of his fleeing horsemen. To his consternation, most of his cavalry, their leaders killed or missing, had scattered far from the battlefield. He despaired of them returning before the battle was over. He gathered what few he could and reformed them into ad-hoc squadrons, preparing to send them back into the fight. It was with satisfaction that he saw his infantry holding firm. In no point of contact had the overwhelming mass of Germans managed to break the Roman lines. The Legion, flanked by their staunch Auxilia, stood their ground, fighting uphill against odds of three to one. Pride filled him at the sight.

To the left of the line, however, Severus had stalled. Instead of advancing into the woods as ordered, he, with his three regiments of Auxilia, had stopped short. His force was not engaged with any enemy. They merely stood at parade rest, javelins held upright and resting on the turf. Julian frowned. That force represented fifteen hundred men, over a tenth of his entire army, that was doing nothing. They were too far left of center to act as reinforcements to the front line, and they were nowhere near a position to outflank the enemy line as he had hoped. Frustration seethed within him, but he had no time to worry about that problem. His remaining cavalry looked to him for guidance, and he needed to redeploy them fast. The Alemanni cavalry, having won the earlier skirmish, was forming up for a charge on his right flank, and they represented the most immediate threat to his men. He called to his lieutenants.

CHAPTER FORTY-ONE

Where Ulrich was fighting, the pressure was lessening. The most energetic of the barbarian warriors had been in the front ranks of the enemy line, so they were, for the most part, dead at his feet. The rest of the enemy, packed together in a thick mob, were keeping their distance. Far to Ulrich's right, where Roman Legion met Alemanni elite at the center of the battle line, the fighting still raged fiercely, but out at the wings, the German warriors were now contenting themselves with missile fire and the occasional brave spear jab. Ulrich missed his axe. Six months of training with the sword did not replace a lifetime of muscle memory with the battle axe, and he was convinced that he would have been twice as effective had he been allowed to field the heavy weapon. Still, his side was winning, and the Alemanni were losing. Ulrich was content.

Eogan had taken position in the third rank of his regiment. He stood in the middle of the chaos holding his shield over his head to defend against the occasional desultory barbarian missile. He gauged the enemy

"This is the boring part, gents," Eogan yelled cheerfully to his men. "They are learning to fear us. Nobody fall asleep. I promise we will get to run them down soon enough."

The soldiers chuckled, and Eogan laughed aloud. In all the world, there was no place he would rather be than right here, fighting with his beloved regiment.

Far off, in the center of the Alemanni line, Chnodomar's huge voice bellowed an order, and the whole German horde suddenly withdrew. They walked backward, shields held up until they were out of arrow range. Then the enemy formation changed. Warriors streamed to the center, depleting the wings. The middle was being reinforced until the mass was several hundred-warriors deep. The Roman line, only five soldiers deep, looked fragile and paper-thin in comparison.

"'I've seen this before,'" Clodovicus said softly, addressing Ulrich and his companions. "They call this attack the 'swine head.' They mean to smash the center and split the line in two. If they succeed, our flanks will be exposed and we will be overrun."

The centurion sheathed his sword and drew his last javelin, Ulrich did the same. Despite the hundreds and hundreds of enemy that had fallen, that was only a small fraction next to the tens of thousands that remained. The enemy was endless, and they shepherded their strength for a terrible blow.

Chnodomar led the charge. The huge man bore a massive double-bladed axe, and he raised it high as he roared down the slope. The globus of his army followed and slammed at full tilt into the center of the Roman line. To Ulrich's horror the Roman line buckled. The most disciplined veteran Legion in the world could not stand firm against that tremendous force. It was no longer a matter of skill or courage, it was a phenomenon of mass and inertia. For each Roman soldier standing firm, the momentum of a hundred angry warriors hit him at a sprint. Where Ulrich stood on the flanks, no enemy faced him, so he could only stand and watch.

The soldiers in the center, the storied Legion regiments Herculiani and Joviani, were thrown back. Most were able to keep their footing and either walked slowly or slid backward before the pressing tide of Alemanni, fighting all the while, but many lost their balance and fell before the sudden onslaught. Those who stumbled, died—cut into by a dozen swords and stomped into the dirt by a hundred heavy boots.

An enormous cheer erupted from the enemy ranks when they realized they had broken through. If the Roman line was split, each separate section could be flanked, surrounded, and overwhelmed. Now the immense numerical superiority of the Alemanni army would dominate the battlefield as cut-off Roman units were attacked from all sides. The cheer was feverish and exultant, and the Germanic warriors fought like demons, hacking frantically at the desperately defending Roman Legion. Victory was within their grasp.

But Julian had seen the globus coming and prepared his counterstroke in advance. The instant the Alemanni had broken through the center, they faced, not a broken flank of desperate men, but the ordered shields of the Primani Legion—Julian's elite honor guard—marching to fill the gap. Julian had committed his reserves. They were joined by the final Auxilia regiment, and together they faced the horde and stopped the Alemanni in their tracks. Rather than outflanking the Roman line, the Alemanni instead found themselves attacked on three sides as the Roman wings turned in on them. Unable to advance, but too stubborn to retreat, the Alemanni fought on in the summer heat. The day's bloodshed was far from over.

All this time, Severus with his three reserve Auxilia regiments had stayed put. The minutes ticked by as the Legion fought. Even as the swine's head struck, he had remained impassive. When the Alemanni army had nearly broken through, he did not go to reinforce the line; he stayed where he was. His soldiers fidgeted as they leaned on their javelins, staring at the empty tree line to the Roman left.

Severus kept his men where they stood because he knew something that the rest of the army did not. He had disobeyed a direct order from his commanding officer because he had seen something important. There were enemy hiding in those woods— thousands of them, and to march under the eaves would be walking into a trap. Patience was one of Severus's great personal strengths, and he knew with complete certainty that the hidden enemy would grow restless long before he would.

Finally, his gambit paid off, and the unsettled enemy broke from cover. They were led by Chnodomar's nephew, the slender Serapio, with his white-coated elite and, like elsewhere on this day's battlefield, they outnumbered Severus's small force three to one. They burst from the trees and howled across the gap toward the waiting regiments. Severus grinned in triumph, for this was exactly what he wanted. His men went into action. He wanted this fight over quickly, so he had deployed his archers in front of his line, just within range of the woods. As soon as the enemy cleared the trees, arrows were already streaking into them. The Roman bowmen fired fast, walking backward in skirmish order as the enemy closed. Their shield wall parted for them, and they ran through it, taking up positions behind the rear ranks, continuing to fire over the heads of the waiting shield wall.

Severus ordered the plumbata launched next. Every man who had line-of-sight with the enemy threw their five darts in quick succession, and the effect was impressive. The small missiles were only nominally lethal, but they wounded wherever they struck. The darts were painful, cutting muscles and tendons and sticking into flesh with their barbed heads. All across the enemy swarm they stopped men in their tracks. Once those munitions were expended, both javelins were thrown, and enemy died by the score. By the time the attackers reached Severus's line, perhaps a third of them were already down, either dead or bleeding. He ordered the full charge, and his men, long swords drawn, slammed into the weakened enemy.

Nowhere across the battlefield was the speed of slaughter greater than here. His three picked regiments were crack, veteran Auxilia, at least as good as if not better than, any heavy Legion of the Empire. He did not stop the charge until the enemy was annihilated. His men moved forward at double speed as they slashed into the Alemanni. Serapio was killed, and the enemy was broken, fleeing frantically back into the woods.

Severus joked to his junior officer that the survivors would not stop running until they got back to the Black Forest. He halted his force, wheeled the three regiments around, went to join the main Roman line.

Ulrich's unit advanced with the rest of the left wing, moving to hem in the globus of Alemanni who had failed the breach the Roman center. The Petulantes advanced across a field of dead and wounded Germans. Ulrich had cut the throats of a half dozen dying men who, in pain, had begged him for the quick release of death. They reached the enemy to find them scared and surrounded, backing into each other, and trying to stay out of sword's reach of the encroaching Romans.

A frightened young warrior, tall, but only barely old enough to fight in the shield wall, swung gingerly at Ulrich with a long axe. The blade scraped harmlessly against Ulrich's shield. Ulrich did not bother to counterattack. He lowered his sword.

"Go home," Ulrich yelled. "Just give up and go home." The enemy seemed to quiver under the weight of his words. They hesitated, looking at each other indecisively.

The call was taken up by Ulrich's regiment.

"Go home," the Auxilia cried. "Go back home." Ulrich was not the only one feeling sorry for their battered and defeated foe. He

227

even heard Eogan encouraging the enemy's surrender.

"You've done enough," Eogan called in German. "We have shed enough of your blood." The Auxilia commander sounded tired after this hot, dusty day.

The Alemanni responded to the shouts. They were hurt and exhausted. They knew they were defeated. Everywhere men edged away. Shields were dropped. Axes fell to the ground. At the rear of the Alemanni mass, Ulrich could see a scattering of men retreating, turning their backs to run away up the slope.

Suddenly, Ulrich saw Chnodomar. The big man was fleeing. His red-plumed helmet was visible deep within the crowd, pushing its way uphill and away from the Roman lines. Ulrich felt a sudden fury fill him. He would still avenge Rag. He would avenge Wiglaf. All this death and pain was that bastard's doing. Ulrich would not let him escape.

"Eogan, fill my place," Ulrich called. He broke formation.

CHAPTER FORTY-TWO

Ulrich stepped one pace forward then ran to the left. He held his shield in front of him as he pushed his way through the tenuous space between the Roman and Alemanni lines, but the Alemanni were breaking, and no enemy swung at him. He finally made it to the end of the line and burst out of the dense crowd. He found himself on a patch of open ground on the far left side of the battlefield. There he found what he had hoped for: A riderless horse cropped the grass calmly. It must have belonged to an unfortunate Alemanni horseman because it bore a rough leather saddle, and a big German battle axe was strapped to the beast's right side. Ulrich sheathed his sword, dropped his shield, and mounted the animal.

As Ulrich feared, Chnodomar had found a horse too. A boy ran from the crest leading a tall white stallion. Chnodomar leapt into the saddle and savagely kicked it into a gallop, leaping uphill and away from the battlefield, running toward the banks of the Rhine to the east.

Ulrich gave chase. The great battle was over, and the Alemanni army was retreating in panic. The fleeing enemy streamed north and east, away from the victorious Romans, and Chnodomar was riding just ahead of this flood. Ulrich was forced to curve wide to avoid the dense mass of people, and Chnodomar gained distance on him as he did so. By the time Ulrich reached clear ground, Chnodomar had reached the crest and vanished out of sight.

Cursing, grinding his teeth, Ulrich was consumed by frustration and rage. His horse was already at a full gallop, and he could only hope that some miracle would allow him to catch up. He pounded up the slope and beheld the vista beyond.

In front of him was the Rhine, the great boundary that separated wild Germania from civilized Gaul. The blue river wound languorously through rolling hills and lush green countryside. The sight was breathtaking, but Ulrich had no eyes for anything but his prey. Chnodomar was a hundred paces ahead and had angled to the right, aiming for a shallow ford across the river. The crossing was already clogged with fleeing Alemanni women, children, and baggage carts. A troop of Alemanni warriors was there, acting as rearguard. They were in a semicircle aimed outward, bearing long spears to defend the only route home. Chnodomar, thinking himself safe, straightened and relaxed, allowing his stallion to fall to a trot. Then he glanced behind and saw Ulrich coming for him. Chnodomar leaned forward over the horse's neck, kicking his mount again and again, encouraging it to speed as he resumed his headlong flight.

It was still a long chase. More than a mile of gentle slope remained before the safety of the ford, and the two men rode as though bound in a frozen tableau, pursuer unable to close the distance, and prey unable to break free. The ground was getting softer as they neared the river, and Chnodomar's horse slowed suddenly as it struck a marshy patch of ground. Ulrich was exultant as the distance closed fast, and he drew his Roman longsword. The triumph was short-lived though, as Ulrich, following close behind, struck the same patch of wet turf and slowed as well. Again, the horses seemed bound together, each moving at an awkward canter as they picked their way through the cloying mud.

They were fifty feet apart when Chnodomar's horse found dry ground and began to pick up speed. The gap was widening fast, and Ulrich snarled in frustration. He dropped his sword, heedless of where it fell in the mud, and pulled up the big German axe from where it was strapped to the saddle. He cocked his arm back and threw the weapon at Chnodomar with all his strength.

The axe spun, curving in a high arc through the air. Dropping out of the cloudless summer sky, it fell toward the fleeing Alemanni leader. The throw was inches too far, and it landed in front of the horse, bouncing in the turf. Ulrich cursed, because he had missed, but then the beast tripped. Its front legs tangled in the axe's long wooden shaft, and Chnodomar tumbled onto the dirt. The horse rolled over, found its footing and stood. It tossed its mane, looking offended, and cantered away, leaving Chnodomar stunned and supine on the ground.

Ulrich rode toward the fallen leader and dropped off his horse. He grabbed the axe from where it lay in the grass and stalked toward his foe. Chnodomar had risen to his hands and knees and was trying to stand but his right leg had been broken by the fall. He glared fiercely at Ulrich and tried to put his weight on the limb but grunted from the pain and slumped as the leg buckled underneath him.

Ulrich stood over his enemy. He hefted the axe and tried to decide just where to plant its blade in the big man's skull. He saw that Chnodomar's hands were bleeding and torn from wielding his own axe. Chnodomar's face was bruised and blue from where he had taken blunt hits in battle, and his expression was a mask of pain and anger. He tried again to stand and stumbled forward yet again. He had no weapon. Chnodomar roared in frustration. Suddenly his eyes were full of tears. His bare hands gripped the dirt beneath him. He had lost.

"Ulrich," Chnodomar said, his voice strained with pain. "I remember you. You fought bravely." Ulrich's axe hand tightened in an involuntary spasm on the handle, but he did not move. Chnodomar closed his eyes. "Please, before you kill me, put a weapon in my hand, I cannot appear before my ancestors without a blade."

Ulrich said nothing. He looked up. The Alemanni guards at the ford had not moved. They were focused on protecting the fleeing crowd that swarmed across the river. Nearer by, a troop of Roman cavalry crested the hill and approached at a trot. Ulrich's vengeance was here, but no amount of bloodshed would bring back his family. He took a deep breath and let it out slowly. Chnodomar should not die on the battlefield. He should not die a hero. He should have to face his ancestors bearing the shame of his defeat. The blood rage left Ulrich, and he lowered his axe. He was tired.

"Take him," Ulrich said to the Roman cavalry when they arrived, and Chnodomar wept.

The battle was over.

CHAPTER FORTY-THREE

The Romans tallied the dead. Julian's lieutenants had, so far, counted over six thousand enemy corpses on the field, and many more had likely drowned in the river. In their haste to flee, Julian had seen panicked men, women, children, and beasts swept downstream when they tried to swarm over the narrow river crossing. The count of his own dead? Only two hundred and forty-three Roman soldiers and four officers, mostly from the routed cavalry. Although there had been loss of life, it had been a great victory. They had won this day against impossible odds. Chnodomar was in chains, and Julian knew that the world would be safe from the Alemanni threat, at least for a time.

Julian rode the battlefield. Alemanni corpses were being burned in a great pile, and his soldiers were resting, eating, and tending to their wounds. The sun burned red and low in the western horizon. He rode alone.

He was looking for someone, and finally, he found him.

He saw Ulrich sitting on the ground with a great battle axe thrust into the dirt beside him. Sigmund and Tau sat nearby, talking softly and sharing a flask of wine. Julian dismounted and walked to the small circle of friends. Ulrich and Tau watched him come but did not rise; Sigmund smiled up at his friend as he approached.

The Caesar of the West of the Empire of Rome, dressed in the full royal panoply of war, sat on the dusty ground with three barbarians.

"We won," Julian said simply. Ulrich frowned, and Julian measured his face.

"Are you thinking that you should have killed him?" Julian asked.

"Yes," Ulrich admitted.

Julian shook his head. "Chnodomar is worth much more as a living symbol of our victory than as a corpse. He will be paraded in Rome and humiliated in front of an entire empire."

"That is a pleasing image," Tau said with a grin. Ulrich gave a wan smile.

"I want you to join me again," General Julian said. "And not as soldiers in the Auxilia but as members of my own personal retinue." He paused, and his eyes grew distant. "The Alemanni were a minor threat compared to the foe I face next. I need the very strongest men by my side."

There was a long silence. Wind rustled through the trees. A laugh rose from nearby where a troop of Auxilia broke a loaf of bread.

Ulrich shook his head finally. "No. I am not a soldier. My destiny lies elsewhere." He looked deep into Julian's brown eyes. "You are a wise man, Julian, and a good leader, but I am no Roman."

Julian gave an understanding nod. "If that is how you feel, Ulrich, then you are excused from any further obligation to Rome. You have served us well."

Sigmund was looking at the ground. "I think I am a Roman," he said. He looked at Ulrich, and Sigmund's eyes were sad. "I am sorry, friend, but I want to stay."

Ulrich's expression softened. "I understand Sigmund." He smiled suddenly. "You were never much of a barbarian anyway," he said. Sigmund grinned back.

"I will join you, Julian." Sigmund said to the general. "I want to see where this campaign takes us next." Julian smiled back at him then looked at Tau questioningly.

Tau shook his head. "I go with Ulrich. My debt to him is not yet paid. Thank you for the generous offer, General."

"Alright then," Julian said and stood. "There is much to attend to and many plans to be made. Sigmund, please meet me in my quarters at dawn. The army will move out tomorrow." He bowed low to the three men. "Thank you for your service to Rome," he said.

The general turned, mounted his horse, and rode away.

Ulrich, Tau, and Sigmund looked at each other. "Right," Ulrich said, energy returning. "Let us first get some food and then go find Johanne and the kids."

"And Ima too," Tau interjected.

The three friends stood, brushed the dust off their clothes, and went into the twilight. That would be the last night they all were together for a very long time to come.

EPILOGUE

A month had passed since the Alemanni's crushing defeat at the Rhine, and three companions stood their horses on a ridge in far northern Germany. The wind tossed Ulrich's unruly mane of brown hair. His face was brooding and dark as he considered the land before him. Tau was there, with his two long elegant swords strapped about his waist. Ima sat nearby, comfortable in her saddle and looking thoughtful, as though her mind was elsewhere even as her body was gracefully still.

They looked on ruin. Only ash and rubble remained of what had once been the great fortress town of Hamburg. This had been Ulrich's birthplace. Ulrich's birthright. Ulrich's lost kingdom. All Ulrich's youth, he had thought that his destiny would be to reclaim his father's castle. That was the task that Wiglaf had trained him for, and the quest that had driven him until the Alemanni had interrupted it. Now there was nothing left. There was no kingdom, there was no castle, there was not even a treacherous uncle to defeat so as to avenge his father. He was now a man without destiny.

"I have sworn to follow you wherever you go," Tau said loyally.

Ulrich sighed.

"I don't know where to go, Tau, and I am tired of leading," he said. He looked at his friend. "Is there anywhere that you would like to go?"

There was a long moment of silence. The wind swept noisily over the dry German hills.

Tau was thinking of Ghana, a city of gold, and of a throne that should be his. He finally spoke.

"I think I would like to go home," Tau said.

HISTORICAL NOTE

Since the crisis of the third century, a matter that is beyond the scope of this book, Rome was in danger. The undisputed world domination and lofty heights of Imperial rule was a thing of the past. Corruption from inside, a weakening military, and ever-strengthening barbarian incursions threatened all corners of the Empire. The Alemanni were one such tribe of barbarians, although they were, more accurately, a confederation of tribes, led by the Suebi and likely fleeing other conflict erupting from the Eurasian steppe. They represented a part of the great barbarian migrations of the fourth and fifth centuries.

Beyond their need to cross the Rhine for their own survival, the Alemanni also had a grudge with the Romans. The relationships between them and several Roman emperors, including Constantius and the earlier Caracalla, left them bitter and vengeful, and the proud Chnodomar was likely to advocate these wrongs as his casus belli. Enmity ran deep, and the battles between this alliance and Rome were fierce. That brings us to the Battle of Argentoratum, 357 A.D.

Our best record of the military career and short rule of Emperor Julian, "the Apostate," comes from a contemporary historian, Ammianus Marcellinus, in his Res Gestae. Published in 390 A.D., the surviving text covers the deeds of Rome and its emperors from the years 353 to 378. Ammianus's admiration for Julian colors books 16 through 18 of the work, where he declares,

"The great deeds that he [Julian] had the
courage and good fortune to perform in Gaul

surpass many valiant achievements of the
ancients...to the dust of battle, he vanquished
Germany, subdued the meanders of the freezing
Rhine, here shed the blood of kings, breathing
cruel threats, and there loaded their arms with
chains."

Ammianus's words could perhaps lead the modern reader to believe that in Julian we have a great warrior, a hardened expert in battle in the style of Rome's classical heroes. The truth is actually far more nuanced and much more interesting. We have only to consider the raw facts to draw our own conclusions. Julian was born in the year 331 or 332 A.D. (accounts differ as to the exact date) in the Roman city of Constantinople. His half-brother, Emperor Constantius II, fearing challenge to his claim to the throne, had Julian's family massacred when the boy was only five or six years old. Constantius spared Julian, but kept him sequestered, far from power, and allowed him to become a scholar, spending his life studying in Athens and Cappadocia (modern day Turkey), where he became a minor official with the Christian church. It was only from desperation that Constantius, after the mutiny of one of his senior commanders, and perhaps with some remorse over the massacre of 337, appointed Julian his representative in Gaul in the year 355. Young Julian's mission there was to win back Colonia Agrippina (Cologne) from the Franks, and with General Barbatio's help, to coordinate the destruction of the growing power of the Alemanni across the Rhine.

Therefore, by the year 357, Julian was only 25 or 26 years old. He was a peaceful scholar who loved to debate philosophy but who had little battle experience. He was leading an army of 13,000 Roman legionaries and auxiliaries and was abandoned by the larger Roman army of 25,000 men under General Barbatio's command. After a long day of marching, he and his small army faced odds of three to one, fighting uphill against the hardened warriors of the Alemanni on a battlefield of the enemy's choosing. They won a decisive victory, and Julian's first great battle was his crowning achievement. This accomplishment created jealousy and conflict with the Emperor, leading to an open challenge of his half-brother Constantius II and ultimately winning Julian the throne of Rome. The Battle of Argentoratum became one of the Empire's last great triumphs in its fading years.

But our story is not yet over. Tau, Ima, Sigmund, and Ulrich have further adventures to ride and destinies to fulfill. They will be back.

Made in the USA
Columbia, SC
16 February 2019